"It is not a lack of love, but a lack of friendship
that makes unhappy marriages."

- Friedrich Nietzsche

Also by Christopher L. Malone

Hangdog

Harold
In The Name
of
Love

by

Christopher L. Malone

Silver Bow Publishing
720 – 6th Street, Box # 5
New Westminster, BC
V3C 3C5   CANADA

Title: Harold in the Name of Love
Author: Christopher L. Malone
Front Cover Photo: Wuttichai Nanchaikan
Back Cover Photo: Ann Gonzalez
Cover Design: Marcie Z. Bartlett
Editor: Candice James

ISBN 978-1-77403-019-6 (softcover)
ISBN 978-1-77403-024-0 (e book)

Library and Archives Canada Cataloguing in Publication

Title: Harold in the name of love / Christopher L. Malone.
Names: Malone, Christopher L., 1984- author.
Identifiers: Canadiana (print) 20190082895 | Canadiana (ebook) 20190082925 | ISBN 9781774030196
(softcover) | ISBN 9781774030240 (HTML)
Classification: LCC PS3613.A35377 H37 2019 | DDC 813/.6—dc23

info@silverbowpublishing.com
www.silverbowpublishing.com

Dedicated to my brother, Nicholas

Acknowledgments:

A lot goes into the process of putting together a novel, as an author relies on a collection of voices for guidance along the way.

Special thanks goes out to the following voices:

Nick Malone – For asking about Harold and encouraging his story to be told

Anna Malone – For defending Nancy

Nick Johnson and Sean Causley – For anchoring the writing process

Danielle Rice – For enthusiastically reading the first draft

Chasi and Cameron Malone – For being my constant companions and allowing me the space and time to be a writer

Chapter One

Harold's Fourth Attempt (A Story About Now)

Harold took a long, deep drag from the cigarette pinched between his lips and almost immediately began coughing. A plume of smoke burst out from his mouth and the cigarette was spat forward with the cherry touching face down on the freshly shampooed carpet. When Harold finished his coughing fit, he looked down at his feet where the cigarette landed, and his red, watery eyes rolled toward the back of his head, looking up to the rafters above him.

"Well, doesn't that just figure," he muttered to himself, and he picked up the pencil and notepad sitting on the table in front of him and began to read over his list once again:

I don't know how to live
I don't know how to die

It was a scant list, but he knew it wouldn't stay that way for long. Harold could always add new things if he thought hard enough, and a moment later he was hunched over with the notepad pressed against his knee, scribbling on the next fresh line:

I don't know how to smoke cigarettes
As an afterthought, he also added:
I don't know how to keep my carpets clean

This was List Making 101, according to Harold, and he preached this often to the clients he'd been able to secure for his fledgling business: *Don't lie to the list. You'd only be lying to yourself if you did.*

These were words that echoed inside Harold's thoughts, and the more the weird moments started to pile up on each other, the more Harold needed to do something that would satisfy his Type A desire for control and order. He'd tried killing himself before, and after every unsuccessful attempt, he felt even more lost, like he was losing focus. He had to remember *why* he was doing it, and moreover, what he was leaving behind. Harold thought these were all important things to consider whenever he tried to take his own life. Like any other decision, major or minor, responsibility demanded that he weigh the pros and cons of the situation.

Harold looked at his list and felt himself growing bolder the more he thought about things, and it was the coughing fit that seemed to sell him on his next course of action. Honestly, who would want to live the type of life where smoking cigarettes seems blatantly uncool and painfully impossible? Smoking cigarettes was supposed to be chic and sexy. Instead, Harold couldn't handle the cloud of fog resting in his lungs for even a second, and now he'd managed to ruin his upholstery. In fact, he'd even come close to burning his own foot; and hadn't he been the one to tell his clients that while being dangerous might be sexy, being a danger to yourself is not? He looked down at his notepad and scribbled some more:

I don't know how to be appropriately dangerous

Now the list was starting to take some shape, and at that moment it struck Harold that it seemed like all he ever did anymore was write lists and plot his own demise. Creating lists helped compartmentalize what would otherwise be chaos, and it was a coping mechanism he successfully pushed onto his most famous client, Damon Alton, who desperately needed help taking control of his life and future so that he could finally figure out exactly what he wanted to pursue.

Harold didn't have that problem. He knew exactly what he wanted but was very bad at achieving it. After all, he was preparing to make attempt number four! Most people had it figured out by two at the latest, and those that didn't were probably just crying out for help.

That wasn't Harold, though, and every time he prepared to take another stab at killing himself, he became more methodical about the process. When one method didn't work, he moved on to another, because he couldn't stand to repeat failures. As Nancy had always said, "I never chew my food *twice*," so after Harold's first attempt failed, he created a list of ways he'd kill himself. It had looked something like this:

- ~~Jumping off the balcony~~
- Cutting wrists with the shaving kit
- Toaster in the bathtub
- Hanging in the living room
- Head in the oven
- Inhaling car exhaust

Now there were lines running through "cutting wrists" and "toaster in the tub", both of which ended up being puzzling experiences, to say the least. Worse than those failures, though, was the fact that he couldn't talk to anyone about his frustrations; it would only sound like a cry for help, and he knew these attempts weren't cries for help at all. Harold didn't need *that* kind of help. He knew exactly what he was doing, and that meant he had to contemplate his failures alone. Those failures, though, both great and small, were starting to pile, including the cigarette that he had yet to pick up, still burning a hole in the carpet by his feet.

He placed the paper and pencil back on the table top and gingerly picked the cigarette up off of the carpet. He held it between his forefinger and thumb like it was a spider that was about to be let outside, and he crushed the lit end into the bottom of the brand-new black ashtray he'd picked up at the store with all of the other purchases he'd made earlier. Almost immediately, Harold regretted doing this for two reasons:

1) he felt he should have at least made one more attempt at smoking the cigarette, if not for anything else than to cross something off of the new *"I don't…"* list, and

2) it was a brand-new ashtray, which like the carpet, had been pristine before the cigarette left its own ugly gray char mark. It was off-center in the round ashtray, too, and it slightly upset him that one of the last things he'd see before dying was an off-kilter eyesore that he created. He could just imagine it, too, swinging from the rafters, being choked to death by the rope around his neck, and all the while his eyes would only be able to dart back and forth between the cigarette burn in the carpet and the ugly off-center ash mark in an otherwise very nice ashtray. Maybe he was more OCD than he cared to admit. He thought about it, then picked up his pencil and notepad again, and scribbled once more:

I am more OCD than I care to admit

And now his list was up to six points.

He wished he could just kill himself and be done with it, like when he tried the first time around. The trouble with surviving the first attempt though was that it gave him time to think about things in depth, things he hadn't fully considered the first time through. In fact, on that first time around, Harold was just trying to work up the nerve to actually go through with his big jump. Ignoring how awfully that experience had ended, just getting to the point where he felt like he could jump was a chore in and of itself.

Now, he had time to think, and there were so many things he had to consider in doing something like this. For starters, there was the matter of the condition of his living space. Once he died, someone was going to have to take over his home; it was a small world, after all. Harold thought his apartment was a fine place to live, and it probably wouldn't be the easiest thing to rent out after he died inside of it. When attempt number two didn't work out, he'd had time to think about how he'd do things differently the next time around. He figured, in the future, the least he could do was to make sure his place was as clean as possible, ensuring there wouldn't be too much to take care of after the cops and the EMTs completed their job.

The thought crossed his mind that other people (people who had found success with this sort of thing) also had the same idea: to make sure they died in clean surroundings, but not necessarily out of courtesy to their landlord or the medical professionals stuck with taking care of their bodies once all was said and done.

Harold imagined suicidal people probably spent several hours cleaning up their places just to make sure no one found any racy journal entries or scandalous movie collections; not to mention whatever terrifying internet browsing history they accrued during their worst moments of loneliness or boredom. Everyone fears the legacy they'll leave behind and no one wants to be remembered as a closet pervert, but in cases of suicide, you were *sure* to be remembered as the closet pervert who inexplicably took their own life, without any chance for rebuttal, unless you left behind a note that read, "Don't judge. We're all horny, and we all die alone."

By now, Harold had written three suicide notes, and each one was as unique as the method with which Harold tried to kill himself. He wrote them as though they were one of his final acts, like he had to be sure he was capturing every single one of his thoughts, right up until the last minutes where he had to stop writing in order to die. Harold did his research, read a lot of good and bad letters made public, and developed his own philosophy on how they should be written. It went like this; a *good* suicide note was usually short and sweet, to-the-point, and emphatically placed the blame solely on the person pulling the trigger, or whatever method they chose to use. A *bad* suicide note was trite, overly poetic and cliché, and usually blamed a lover, parent, society, or the world-at-large.

Harold felt like his first attempt at writing was a mixture of both. It was poetic and cliché, but it was also short and sweet, and didn't blame any outside party for his death; not anyone that was still alive and could be eaten up by their own guilt, anyway. Really, Harold's first note only had this to say: *For better or for worse, in sickness and in health, until death do we part.*

Harold imagined that a coroner would read that and understand completely what was going on. "This wasn't a guy who felt slighted by the rest of the world or wanted to send society a message," the coroner or detective investigating Harold's death would say, and then they'd read that first note once more and declare, "This is just a man who missed his wife!" Harold hoped that's what they'd say, anyway. It wasn't until he was sitting on his bed, drying off from his first failed attempt, that he realized his suicide note wasn't very good, and could probably be improved upon.

The second note he wrote, although shorter, did a much better job of explaining the circumstances surrounding his would-be death. It read:

I really just miss my wife.

Initially, that sounded to Harold like everything he thought his suicide note should read. The subtext was obvious: *This isn't anyone's fault*, the note would really say, *and there's nothing anyone could've done. It's just a thing I decided to do.* Hours after his second botched attempt though, he thought long and hard about his one-sentence note while he rubbed his forearms down with aloe-vera and first-aid ointment and came to a new conclusion: One sentence definitely couldn't convey all of the things he initially thought it could.

For his third attempt, he thought he'd have to write a full professional letter to explain *exactly* what was going on. He'd even reference the first two attempts just to show people that his death shouldn't be a total surprise, considering that he'd tried dying on multiple occasions. With that in mind, he crafted for the third time what he thought was the perfect note; shortly before what was surely going to be his final attempt. He should've known better.

But what was so wrong with that last suicide note? Couldn't he just recycle his third letter for his fourth attempt? Harold had poured over the letter several times, and not just because he was forced to read by candlelight, due to the massive power surge that knocked out the electricity right as he was going for attempt number three. Sitting on the couch in his bathrobe, surrounded by candles and looking uncommonly romantic for a man who was a suicidal widower, Harold read the letter over and over again, and when it finally hit him, he ripped the letter into tiny pieces, dumped them into the kitchen sink, and used one of the candles to set them on fire, thereby expunging this letter from the history of his demise.

Maybe it was *because* he was forced to read the letter over and over again in the candle light that he realized the problem. When you combined his words with the lights and shadows dancing on the wall, it occurred to him that he was being entirely too heartfelt, and someone was bound to take it the wrong way. The letter had gone like this:

Dear Nancy,

You're probably wondering why I'm doing this, sweetheart. You may even be wondering why this is my third time trying, and why I don't feel blessed to have been spared the pain of death twice now. The truth is this: A life without you is a life that can never hope to be blessed, and I'd much rather be spared from the pain of living than the pain of dying, especially if death means finding you once more in the hereafter.

Life has not been worth living since you've been gone, and I will always feel like I failed you that night when you died in my arms. What a powerless feeling that was; watching you slip away from me. I know that I promised "until death do we part," but I'm simply not ready to part from you, and furthermore, I don't think I'll ever be! I really just miss my wife.

And so, I have decided to take the power back. This is no one's fault, especially not yours. I'm a man acting on free will, but more importantly, I am acting on my principles of love and devotion. I cannot wait for nature to run its course; I refuse to. I will be with you again, my love. Very soon, indeed.

Love always,
Your Harold

Harold had put hours of thought into that letter, and in the end he had decided it best to destroy it. Someone would most certainly take it out of context, and even in death, Harold would never be able to live with himself if he knew that his suicide had inspired someone else to take their life in the name of love. He wasn't trying to *romanticize* suicide, after all; not in the way that William Shakespeare had done with Romeo and Juliet. Harold's situation was special; unique. Who knows what would've happened if he had completed his task? The local news could've covered the story, and their website would have flashed the headline for easy clickbait:

"HAROLD DANCY KILLS SELF IN THE NAME OF LOVE: Victim Leaves Behind World's Most Eloquent Suicide Note – Scroll for More"

Harold could never accept being a role-model for a mass of confused suicidal lovers who only *thought* they were as much in love with each other as Harold *knew* he was with his wife. And so, the letter was destroyed, and weeks later Harold was brought to his current situation: An overabundance of concern towards lists, letters, the evolution of suicide rituals, and the proper way to tie a noose.

He peered over his current list, then rubbed his eyes. The house was mostly clean, except for the carpet burn, and he'd tried something he'd never done before - smoking. Now, he'd fully regain his determination. No more being self-diagnosed with OCD, or being bad at appearing dangerous in the sexy way, or even being unclean. No more being unable to smoke, or being bad at living, and by God, no more being bad at dying.

Resolved, he got up from his chair by the table and went into his office, removed a blank sheet of paper from his desk and grabbed the pen that Nancy had once given him for Christmas. And for what he hoped would be the last time, he put pen to paper and scribbled down his final words. He'd just have to be blunt with everyone and tell it to them straight:

To Whom It May Concern:

This should not be a surprise to any of you. The only thing that is surprising about this situation is that it's taken four tries to get it done. As the old adage goes, "If at first you don't succeed..."

My reasons for doing this are my own, but since you must know, it's because I miss my wife very much, and I am determined to be with her again. You can disagree with my choice, but that's your business, and what's yours is yours and what's mine is mine.

Please tell my landlord that I'm sorry for the cigarette burn in the carpet and I understand if she takes it out of my security deposit. I clearly had no intentions of hoping for its return.

> *Sincerely,*
> *Harold Dancy*

It was colder and more formal than the previous letters, but it would have to do. Harold placed it next to the ashtray, then thought better of it, and placed the ashtray on top of the note, just in case a phantom breeze picked up and blew the note away under a piece of furniture, never to be discovered. Strange things had been happening around him for months, and he couldn't rule out the chance that they wouldn't continue up to his final moments. Satisfied, he reached underneath his chair, which he had chosen for its straight back and sturdiness, and grabbed the length of rope he had meticulously prepared.

At one end of the rope there was a noose, which he had tied and retied three times before finally being satisfied with the result. On the other end was a simple loop tied off with a double overhand knot. Harold had taken the time to measure the distance from the floor to the rafters overhead, then his own height, and the height of his chosen wooden chair, allowing him the perfect measurement for what his rope should be. Death by hanging was a tricky thing, and Harold was alarmed at the number of ways people could hang themselves: the pole method, the standard drop, the short drop, the long drop, and then the preferred method for suicidal folks everywhere, plain old suspension.

Harold read a lot about the subject, and the things that could happen with spinal cords and blood vessels and airways. The thing that bothered him most was the possibility of experiencing a *priapism*, or what's more commonly referred to as a "death-erection". The research was very specific, and conclusive. Due to the restriction of various blood vessels or stress on a certain part of the brain, a small population of hanged people could achieve quite the long-lasting hard-on, and that was the only thought that gave Harold the slightest sense of hesitation. He could just imagine what a scene that would be to walk in on: a cigarette burn on the carpet, a dirty ashtray on the table, and Harold's dead body dangling just above with his penis near ready to burst out of his pants. Who needs a suicide note when you can draw conclusions based on that imagery alone? It was almost enough to make him want to scrap his plans altogether, but Harold had the rope in his hands, and persisted.

He threw one end of the rope over the rafter directly above him, and standing on the chair, was able to reach up and bring the end down so that he could slip the noose through the double-overhand loop. From there, he pulled down on the top of the noose, until the overhand loop was tight against the rafter, and then he tugged on the line two more times to make sure the knot would hold, and it did. Then he let go of the rope and let the noose dangle in front of him, watching it frame his face perfectly. His measurements had been accurate. He looked up one more time to convince himself that everything was in proper position. He was satisfied with what he saw.

"Okay, Harold," he now said to himself out loud, listening to his voice disturb what was otherwise a very quiet apartment. "Nothing's going wrong this time. No freak landings, no bad batches of razors, and no weird power failures at the last minute. It's a static rope, weight-tested and certified. There is no way you're not dying today."

He stood there for a minute with the noose patiently waiting in front of him, so he could give his apartment one final look over before slipping off into permanent darkness. The apartment had become a lot more barren since Nancy's death one year prior. In the early months, before he committed himself to dying in the name of love, Harold had attempted to move on and find closure by shipping some of Nancy's things down to her mother in Florida. Offering them up as keepsakes of the daughter she'd moved so far away from after her husband, Nancy's father, had passed away.

At first, he'd only meant to send off a few things, and just the ones that he couldn't stand to look at for the pain of it all; the sports memorabilia and pictures from the past. With each one of those items gone, however, new ones cropped up to offer the same potent memories. Harold kept sending things until he received an email from Nancy's mother thanking him for all of the wonderful gifts but asking him to stop since she was running out of space to put things. After that, he rented out a storage facility and had the rest of her things moved there, determined that it would make the grieving process more manageable, but it didn't. Instead, the absence of Nancy's things left Harold in a nearly barren apartment; everything, all the items, had belonged to her. It wasn't until they were gone that Harold realized just how big a part of his life she was. The apartment that he looked at now, with the noose dangling in front of his face, was symbolic of the life he felt he was leaving behind. Without Nancy, it was just an empty space.

In that moment, resolution found him, and Harold grabbed the noose, pulled it over his head, and fit it around his neck. This was it; the moment he'd spent the better part of his weekend preparing for. All of the affairs he cared about were in order, and with his client's new-found success, Harold doubted his services were of any real value to him anymore. All parties could be ready to move on.

An icy chill went up his spine, and it was a familiar feeling. He felt it every time he was on the precipice of his final moment; jumping out the window, pressing the razor to his skin, releasing the toaster from his grasp... It was almost as if his body had become accustomed to his suicidal intentions, and this feeling of momentary coldness was a product of that. It meant it was time to end things.

Harold took a deep breath, shut his eyes, clenched his fists, and made to step forward. When he tried to move, however, he only managed to wedge his toes tightly into the front of his shoe; the soles of his feet were stuck to the chair. He opened his eyes and looked down, unsure of what to expect, but saw nothing out of the ordinary. His hands relaxed and his arms spread out as if to better balance himself, and rather than try to step forward, Harold simply tried to raise his right foot off the chair. He could feel it shifting slightly inside of his shoe, but the shoe would not move. He tried his left foot and achieved a similar result.

"It's happening again," Harold said aloud. "I don't understand why this keeps happening?"

He thrust his right knee forward in a vigorous attempt to dislodge his foot from his shoe, when things turned even stranger than they already were; he actually felt his shoe laces *tightening* against his struggle. He looked at his left shoe and repeated the same attempt he'd made with his right, and he *swore* he could see the laces tightening before his eyes. Panic made his heart start to pound in his chest. His other failures, even the second attempt, could be explained away plausibly enough; this was a whole new experience.

He immediately took his head out of the noose and went to untie his shoes when a slight wobble in the chair made him rethink his course of action.   He had chosen this chair specifically for its sturdiness. Now there was a sense that maybe it wasn't as structurally sound as Harold thought it was. His eyes swept the apartment again, except this time he was expecting to catch someone or something in the act of sabotaging him. The room was still empty though, and Harold became more unnerved than he thought he would if he'd actually found someone.

"This isn't a deal-breaker," Harold said to the room, looking around at the empty air, feeling compelled to talk loudly. "I can get through this. I *will* die today. Whatever this is, you're not going to stop me."

He slowly lowered himself into a squatting position, letting his backside rest on the back of the chair while his hands reached down tentatively to grasp at his shoe laces. He'd untie them, slip his feet out of his dress shoes, and then he'd be back on track. When he tugged on the laces, though, their knots wouldn't budge. Further perplexed by this, Harold stared down at the tops of his shoes. He had tied his laces the way he'd always tied them, with a single knot. Doubled knots always looked bulbous and unattractive, and really only worked for sneakers anyway. Harold never wore sneakers and had never tied a single knot that couldn't easily be undone with the slightest tug. Now he pulled on the lace hard, and the knot only had the slightest flex; it would not come undone.

"What the *hell*?" Harold said, his frustration mounting. The universe was calling out to Harold, and the message was very plain: *Don't do it.* Harold was tenacious, though, and he refused that universal call steadfastly.

He stood straight up and put the noose back around his neck. For the sake of trying, he once again attempted to step forward, but his shoes stayed stuck to the seat of the wooden chair. In his desperation, his determination to die, he squatted to his lowest point, hoping that would be enough to strangle him. It was not: once again, his backside was rubbing up against the back of the chair before he could achieve full tension in the rope. It should've been cause for confusion, since Harold had measured everything so carefully, but Harold was beyond confusion at this point. He was locked in an obstinate battle of wills. He knew what he wanted.

Death. Now.

Still squatting, an idea came to him, and Harold wrapped his arms around his knees and hugged them to his chest. Success! Inexplicably, the chair stayed glued to his feet, but it was no matter. By bringing his knees to his chest, he was able to hang. The chair hovered less than an inch from the ground, and Harold hugged his knees hard, dangling slightly in a mock canon ball position, as if he were jumping into a pool of water. The rope was tight around his neck. He felt immense pressure behind his eyes and he could not breathe. It was his ultimate goal and was now problematic by the nature of his position. Dangling for twenty seconds, cut off from oxygen, Harold's arms became very weak; beyond that, it was almost as if there was a force he was up against, pulling at his precarious grip.

His arms sprung forward, the chair dropped with a heavy creak underneath him, and a rush of air entered Harold's lungs, completely automatic and against his will.

He stood there for a moment, hands on knees, breathing heavily, exhausted by what he had just attempted. All was not lost, though. He'd heard the way the chair groaned when it landed, and it felt much more fragile than it had initially, which gave him an idea.

"I can still do this!" Harold said, wide-eyed and panting. He straightened up once more, and looked around the room, the noose still snug around his neck. "Shoes glued to the chair? Fine! Laces too tight to untie? Fine! Can't hold a pose long enough to die? That's fine, too! We'll see how well I survive when I break the chair!"

Harold squatted slightly, arms back, and thrust his feet downward while throwing his hands up into the air. He jumped straight up, and the chair came with him. When he came back down, the chair gave out a splitting sound. Harold felt a rush of adrenaline. This would work. He jumped up again, landed, and an even louder split was heard. He jumped up a third time, landed, and the chair exploded underneath him, splintering into large chunks. Finally, the rope achieved full tension, and Harold was snatched up violently by the neck. It was an unexpected rush of pain; he'd never had this much success before, and it scared him that he might actually succeed now. His feet dangled, his hands automatically went to the rope, and the primal urge to stay alive kicked in as his fingers tried to desperately dig underneath the rope to provide some air. The blood was rushing to his cheeks, and he gurgled and spat as his body convulsed.

And just as everything was going dark, and Harold could feel Death's grip closing around him, he felt a tugging sensation from directly above him. Finding the wherewithal to look upward while the rest of his body focused on survival, Harold watched in wonder, looking at a spectral image floating above him. A feminine figure composed of glowing green light, the specter's ghostly hands gripped the rope, and pulled down as if she was pulling taffy. The fibers of the rope collectively flexed, stretched, snapped, and then popped; the top end whipped upward toward the rafter, while the bottom end fluttered toward the ground.

Instantaneously, Harold crashed to the ground, falling on top of the coffee table in front of him, which shattered into pieces under the force of his fall. His neck was on fire, his eyes burned, his head pounded, and his lungs gasped for air. He rolled over onto his back and felt the ashtray that had been left on the table dig into his spine. He looked up, just in time to see the ghostly image of the woman hovering above him dissolve into nothing, and the words escaped his lips before he could even think of what he was saying.

"Nancy?" he wheezed, and a sudden force of exhaustion swept over him. For the fourth time, Harold had failed to kill himself. Instead of dying, he passed out face up, rope still around his neck with the splinters of the broken chair and table lying underneath him.

Chapter Two

Whatever Happened to Nancy? (A Story About Then)

The sun peeked over the top of the building, and the sky turned pink as the color of night slowly faded into the coming dawn. It would've been a beautiful sight to behold, the kind of sight that made you stop in awe of how gorgeous nature could be, making you think how glorious a day it was to be alive. You'd look at that sight and want to smile and wave at the person nearest you, and even be inclined to ask them about their weekend plans. You'd look at that sunrise and feel graced by a powerful optimism that today was going to be a good day. The morning light told you that you were going to be successful.

Nancy never looked at the sunrise. She kept her sunglasses on and waited inside her idling car, sipping black coffee alone so that she could enjoy the only few moments of her day when she didn't have to talk to anyone. She hated her job, hated people, hated getting to work before dawn, and had really grown to hate everything. An overall bitterness had been slowly consuming her over the course of the last two years, and now it had come to this: sitting in solitude with the windows up and the radio blaring a talk show she only pretended to listen to so anyone walking by her car wouldn't feel the need to knock and ask if she was okay.

She brought the travel mug to her lips, finished the last swallow of coffee and then placed it back in the cup holder beside her. As she turned the car off and opened the door to get out, a thought crept into her mind, the same thought that she'd been having for a while now: *"What the hell happened to me?"*

It wasn't always like this for Nancy, being so wrapped up in self-loathing. It had grown slowly over time, ever since the death of her father. Before that, *he* was the only man she truly hated, and she lived happily, spitefully, reveling in the dismay she caused him with each life decision she'd ever made, rueful victories against a timeless adversary. Once he passed though, she had no concrete figure to concentrate her hatred toward, so she projected it freely to everyone else in her life, and at work, the statute of limitations on patience with the bereaved had long since run out.

There was only so much understanding her employees could give her. Before long, Nancy developed a reputation for being a shrewish manager: nit-picky, overbearing, and easily angered. They griped about her in the break room, told funny stories about being lucky enough to catch her in one of her rare moments of ineptitude, and commiserated over how tense things were ever since she'd come back from bereavement leave. In fact, the only thing they stopped short of was calling her a *bitch*, though it wasn't out of some inherent nobility. Why call Nancy a bitch when you could just call her by her name?

Nancy Dancy!

It was so sing-song, so patently ridiculous for a woman who demanded their utmost respect - to be named Nancy Dancy. Everyone knew it, and that's how they always referred to her:

"Hey guys, did you get your end of year statements done? Nancy Dancy wants them on her desk, pronto."

"Don't forget to turn out the lights when you lock up, guys! Nancy Dancy doesn't like a lot of things, and wasting light is one of them."

"Heads up, everyone! A big client's coming in today. Nancy Dancy's dressed real fancy..."

The last straw was when she'd walked into the break room one day to grab a coffee filter. Duke Franklin was entertaining the guys on break by marching back and forth with his shoulders bunched up, his fists curled tight, and an angry scowl on his face, chanting, "Do the Nance Dance, ugh ugh, it's the Nance Dance, ugh ugh, do the Nance Dance..." The guys were getting a real kick out of it, too, until Nancy walked in the room and killed the mood. The laughter cut off immediately, and Duke turned on his heel to face his boss, red-faced with embarrassment.

"Jake? Clayton?" she asked, looking through Duke to the two sitting at the table, both sipping on cans of soft drink.

"Yes, ma'am?" Clayton answered, speaking up for the both of them.

"Break time's over," she said, curtly. "We've got a packed lot out there and I think we're sitting heavy because all of our cars look like shit. Get them washed so we can get them rented."

Jake and Clayton got up quickly and shuffled out of the room quietly, nearly cringing as they walked pass their boss. Nancy didn't acknowledge them, though. She kept her eyes trained on Duke, who tried to follow his two friends out to the main room.

"Mr. Franklin?" Nancy asked, and Duke stopped short, eyes cast downward.

"Yeah, boss?"

"You've got two options," she said, and there was an unnerving calm in her voice. "You can stay employed, and I'll be sure to make your life a living hell for the next six months, which is about how long it will take me to forget about what I just saw, or you can do the Nance Dance out to your car and wait for us to send you your last paycheck. Lady's choice."

"Sorry, boss," Duke said, softly. "I need this job. It won't happen again."

"Good," Nancy replied. "Grab a bottle of wax and get out to the lots. Every vehicle out there gets the new-car shine."

"Yes, ma'am," Duke answered, and he walked out of the room as quickly as he could before breaking into a full trot to get outside. When he was gone, and the room was empty, Nancy allowed herself a moment to shudder at her own behavior. She'd actually used the phrase *lady's choice*. That was her father's go-to when he wanted to finish an ultimatum with some heft. Nancy was even talking like him now, and worse than that, she was *thinking* like him, too. In that moment, it all came to her at once, like a great epiphany:

"Oh my god," she'd thought to herself, "he was right."

He was right about her name.
He was right about Harold.
He was right about everything.

It had always been in her nature, though, to defy her father, ever since the first time she'd done it and had found such great success. It was so intoxicating that she just kept walking down that same road of rebellion, wearing it to a tread until it became worn down and dusty. It kicked up giant clouds of confusion that obscured a father and daughter's view of each other until finally one of them died, allowing the dust to subside, revealing the other to be lost, heartbroken, and alone. Who was she now if not her father's obstinate daughter? She didn't know. She only knew what she'd been.

∗∗∗

The first time Nancy felt the taste of independence, her streak of rebellion come to life, was when she was thirteen years old, standing with her friends on a softball diamond. Her father had dropped her off and was unpacking her ball bag when he came across her new mitt.

"Nancy, hon?" he beckoned, and she broke away from her friends to see her father holding up the glove.

"Yeah, Dad?" she asked him, unaware that anything was wrong.

"Where'd you get this?" he asked, and she was picking up the sense that this wasn't light-hearted curiosity, but heavy-handed concern.

"It's the mitt Mom got me when we went shopping last week. You said to go pick up a used one while we were out, and we found this one for a great deal."

"But it's a *catcher's* mitt," he said, still holding it up, looking at it sideways as if it was somehow defective.

"Yeah, I know," Nancy said, confidently. "It's already broken in and everything. I talked to the guy at the counter and he said that was the lucky thing about buying used, was that stuff was already broken in. I mean, it's still in good condition, right?"

"No, the glove is fine, sweetheart," her father said, turning his attention to her. "It's just that you're an outfielder. You're not a catcher."

"I know I wasn't a catcher *last* year," Nancy said slowly, with a greater sense of what her father was angling toward, "but I think I could have a decent shot at it this year."

"Eh," her father muttered dismissively, "I'll tell you what, honey. Why don't I look in the trunk of the car for one of your older mitts, and you and I can work on catching stuff in the backyard sometime. That way you don't have to embarrass yourself."

A switch flicked on inside of her at the sound of the word *embarrass*, igniting a fire that had always been dormant before this moment, before the influx of hormones coursing through her body transitioned her from an innocent child to a prepubescent girl knocking on the door to something bigger than what she was already. Soon she would be a woman, and soon she would roar. At that moment on the ball field with her father, though, she was just learning to growl.

"Well," she said, and her eyes bored into her father's with a refusal to cower or be intimidated by the suggestion of failure, "it's a good thing *you're* not the coach! I'd rather let him be the judge of whether or not I'm an embarrassment!" She snatched the glove out of his hand, stuffed her left hand into it for dramatic effect, and marched back to her friends still socializing on the pitcher's mound.

To her father's credit, he'd taken his daughter's words in stride, and if he felt publicly disrespected, he did not show it. That's not how Charles Edward Allister operated. Rather than take Nancy to task for brazenly talking back to him, he just smiled when his daughter grabbed the catcher's mitt and ruefully walked away, knowing that she was dying to prove something to him.

When he saw her quietly rejoin her friends, standing on the outskirts of their conversation with her arms folded over her chest, fuming silently, he walked over to the wooden bleachers near the left side batter's box, and pulled out the folded over paperback he kept in his back pocket for just such a time. Charles liked to read a book while he waited, and in this instance, he kept a book in front of his face while he waited for the inevitable.

When Nancy's coach arrived, he announced he'd start filling positions quickly. There wouldn't be much time for the girls to prove themselves, because the season opener would be upon them sooner than they'd realize. The girls sat on the bench in the dugout while the coach stood in front of them, glowering. He was a towering man and had the appearance of a once-spry athlete that had let fatherhood settle him down some. He had three daughters of his own, and one of them sat next to Nancy, nervous under her father's gaze.

The coach's hands were planted firmly on his hips, and in spite of his protruding belly, he stood before them in a broad position of authority, gazing over them on down the row like he was making a mental checklist of who'd be best suited for outfield and infield, who'd have speed and who'd have power, and who might pitch and who might catch. Some of the girls flinched when their eyes met his, and some looked away.

Nancy looked back at him coolly, though, ready to prove herself worthy, thereby proving her father wrong, and it was no surprise to the coach that when he asked for pitchers and catchers to get out to the field and warm-up separately, Nancy was one of the first to jump off the bench.

While those girls got their gear on and stretched their arms, the rest of the team went to the outfield and did a lap from foul line to foul line to get their legs warm. When they returned from their short jog, they put on helmets and lined up at first base.

"This activity is three-fold, ladies," the coach barked. "I want to see pitchers throw speed and hit the strike zone. I want my runners to get a good jump on the ball, steal second, and get dirty while they do it! That's right girls, we're sliding this year, and if you can't do it, I'll send you into the outfield to practice in the grass until you're ready to show me what you can do in the dirt!" He was looking at his daughter when he said this, and she appeared near ready to cry, but Nancy was exhilarated by it all. This coach was tough on his own daughter! When he made Nancy the starting catcher, it would really show her father a thing or two about being embarrassed.

"Finally," the coach continued, breaking eye contact with his girl to look at the three standing off to the side in their catching gear, "I want to see catchers that can actually catch the ball and make the throw to second. Bonus points if you can get the ball to my glove in time for the tag. I hate it when someone steals on me.

"I'll have an assistant in the outfield to collect overthrows, an assistant on first to coach the runner, and like I said before, I'm on second to call strikes and field the throw down. Any questions?"

The girls were all silent, and the coach nodded approvingly. "Get to your positions," he said. "Smith is on the mound first, and Clifford's behind the plate. I'm not giving too many pitches to any one of you, so be prepared to get off the field and in line to run." Charlotte Smith walked over to the mound with a softball in hand, while Denise Clifford jogged over to her position, and the rest of the pitchers and catchers went back to the dug out to wait.

Smith's pitches could be a little wild, but Clifford had done a good job of framing them like strikes. Unfortunately, when she made the throw down, it fell just over the mound, dribbled forward, and rolled to a stop before it could get to the glove. The coach only tolerated that twice before he barked, "Get me a new catcher! Allister!"

Nancy jumped up and nearly sprinted to the plate. Denise Clifford's failure only made her more confident, and when she squatted into position, she cast a glance over to her father. He didn't acknowledge her though, and instead only kept his nose planted in the worn paperback, too bored to notice what his daughter was doing. That was fine for Nancy, though. He'd be looking up from his pages soon enough.

Sharon Hodges was on first base, waiting to take off running. Charlotte Smith got into her windup and wind-milled a screamer right down the middle. Sharon's reaction time was just a second off, and Nancy caught the pitch cleanly. Sharon could be thrown out no problem, and Nancy pulled back to throw, only to put way too much arm into it. Coach tried to jump up to save it, but the ball flew over his glove and into center field, skipping once before hitting the assistant coach's glove. Sharon slid in cleanly and jogged to the back of the line. Nancy's cheeks burned with disappointment.

"Sorry, coach!" she said, feeling the need to explain it away. "I got excited and lost control. I'll get it this time."

"Nothing wrong with a little excitement, Allister," the coach said, a little softer in tone than he had been. "The footwork was good. Let me see some control."

They set up again, this time with Lizzie Gibson on the bag. It was the same situation, however. A good throw, a late jump, and still Nancy overthrew second. Her anger increased, and she glanced over at her dad, who now wore a small grin as he read his paperback. Nancy couldn't help but think it had nothing to do with the story.

"Brush that off," the coach barked. "Let's try a new pitcher."

Annie Dawes took the mound now, and Nancy stayed behind the plate. Another one of the girls, this time the coach's daughter, stepped onto first base, anxiously awaiting the pitch.

"It would *really* mean a lot to me if you'd get the ball into my glove this time," the coach said to Nancy, and the coach's daughter kicked a little cloud of dirt toward him, ready to take off running.

Annie came in with the pitch, the coach's daughter got the perfect jump on the ball, and Nancy let it rip as soon as she felt it hit her glove. It was no good, though. For the third time, the ball sailed over the coach's head and into center field. The coach's daughter was safe on second, and the coach looked up at Nancy. "Strike three," he said simply, "Get outta there, Allister."

Nancy gave one more look her father's way and saw that his smile had grown larger. While Lucie Arepat took over catching, Nancy ripped off her gear and got over to first base as quickly as she could, cutting in front of all the other girls so that she could run next. The coach took notice.

"You got something to prove?" he asked Nancy, but the fire in her eyes said everything she needed to say. She wasn't going to pout, and she certainly wasn't going to throw a temper tantrum and give her father the satisfaction. She internalized all of it, instead, and was ready to explode with an energy to be the best.

Annie Dawes got into her windup and made the pitch. It was a swift one in for a strike, but Nancy's reaction time couldn't have been better. Even though Lucie Arepat's throw wasn't terrible, Nancy was still able to beat it cleanly. "That's the best throw down we've had so far," the coach conceded to Nancy when she got up from sliding into second, "but that's also the cleanest steal I've seen today. We'll have a spot for you in the outfield for now, and we'll see if you can track a fly ball. If you figure out your control issue sometime, let me know and we'll give you another look behind the plate. I liked the footwork, I just didn't like the rainbows you were throwing after you made your step. Get it together, then come back and see me."

For anyone else, those words would've been encouraging, but for Nancy, they inflamed her sense of being. On the car ride home, she didn't say anything to her father, and Charles Allister let the silence pervade. He'd been right, and he thought Nancy had learned something in that moment. Little did he know that he'd created the start of a rift that would exist between them until his death seventeen years later. In fact, it was only when he tried to offer Nancy one of her older gloves for a catch in the backyard that he realized there was something still off between them.

"Here," he said, approaching her as she was working on some math homework. "Why don't you take a break and I'll throw you some pop-ups. We can work on tracking the ball."

"No thank you," Nancy said curtly. "Mom's going to work with me on my throw down."

Nancy's mother, Emily, looked up from her laptop in surprise. She was a sales associate representing a small catering business, and she managed its clients and their contracts; she did not manage sports. That's why Charles was there.

"Oh, I don't know," her mother began, but Nancy interrupted her before she could dispute anything.

"Mom, I'm tired of only having guys coach me in this sport. It's a team full of girls and I want to learn how to throw to a girl."

"But Nancy," she replied, "I don't even have a glove, and I've never been good with catching things..."

"Here," Nancy said, and she yanked the glove out of her father's hands and tossed it to her mother. "Come out to the backyard with me. Dad can catch anything I throw at him. I'd rather work with you. If I can get the ball to you okay, I can get the ball to anyone."

And just like that, Nancy shut her father out of that aspect of her life.

Much like his daughter, Charles internalized what he was feeling, but didn't explode. He steadfastly refused to be excluded, and the three of them went out together, with daughter throwing, mother catching, and father critiquing technique. Soon it became a regular part of their life, and by the season's end, Nancy had won the starting job at catcher. It was a small victory but did nothing to soothe the relationship between Charles and his daughter. Instead, a new chemistry had formed between them.

Nancy would typically do whatever her father thought she couldn't, and in response he would always find something to say about it, refusing to be ignored or overruled. In the case of catching, this worked quite well. Nancy developed into one of the best in the state, leading her high school's team to two state championships, where she was dubbed Nancy "All Star" Allister by the local papers covering her team's dominate game play.

In the case of everything else though, Charles did more damage to his daughter than being the greatest catcher in the state could ever make up for. As high school was nearing its end, Nancy was relying upon making life decisions primarily out of spite for her father, regardless of whether or not he'd ever lost sight of what was going to be best for her future. It would explain a lot of the choices she'd made since being a thirteen-year-old with a used catcher's mitt that her father thought she shouldn't have. It certainly explained her relationship with Harold.

* * *

Harold and Nancy had gone to school together for several years, and although Harold was well aware of who Nancy was (especially as she gained prominence in the local sports scene), Nancy had no idea that Harold existed, and for good reason. Harold was the guy who sat three or four chairs away

35

from you and was likeable enough when you needed to copy notes or borrow a pencil, but since he did nothing to participate in the culture of his own generation, he was otherwise invisible. He moved in a different circle from everyone else, and it was a circle of four friends who were very intelligent and thrilled by life on the fringe. The circle that Nancy and her friends existed in was much larger and more mainstream, and their two groups rarely overlapped.

When it came to television, for example, Nancy and her friends loved the angst-ridden teen soap-operas, and they'd have small but fierce arguments in the locker room over whether Joey should end up with Pacey or Dawson. Harold and his crew, on the other hand, watched old British comedies on public television, and they were more apt to debate things like whom the funniest member of Monty Python was, or who might've been the best iteration of Doctor Who.

The same could be said for each group's taste in music as well. Harold's gang played in the marching band and jazz ensemble, which led them to studying guys like Miles Davis and Buddy Rich, or Harold's favorite clarinet player, Pete Fountain. Nancy and her teammates, for the most part liked hip hop for their warm up music but jammed to the modern alt-rock groups of the time like The Common Miscreants, whose front man Damon Alton was a mess of sex appeal and bad decisions, singing songs about intense, passionate longing and how he'd be better if he just had the right girl standing by his side.

Even Nancy, as head strong as she was independent, could not make herself immutable to the charming quality of a Damon Alton character. He may have been a clichéd bad boy, but he was really good at it, and that was the type of boy Nancy fantasized over, when she fantasized at all. Damon Alton was the opposite of Harold Dancy, so much so that Harold didn't even register as a romantic option for Nancy. There was nothing storybook about how the two came to be, in that sense. Instead, Harold had asked her out on a whim, and Nancy agreed, though it was mainly out of spite for her father and a dearth of other options.

That dearth of options, and the lack of suitable beaus just lining up for the opportunity to knock on Nancy's door, wasn't really her fault, but an issue with how she was perceived. Sure she was beautiful, but she was more than that, and that was the problem. Nancy was strong, opinionated, and brash, like her father. In sum, she was intimidating. The guys around her didn't see a normal teenage girl, but a local celebrity and fantastic athlete. They assumed things: she was too stuck up for them; too good for them; too pretty for them; or what was more likely than any of those other things, already spoken for. How could someone of such high social standing ever worry about being alone on a Saturday night?

That was Nancy, though: too popular to be asked out and too proud to ask anyone out herself. Only Harold Dancy, who was unique in his own right and in his approach to other people, figured out Nancy's situation, and only on the last day that tickets were available for their Senior Homecoming Dance.

Jack Edwards, a member of Harold's tight circle of friends and the six-string strummer to Harold's clarinet in the jazz ensemble, was the class secretary, and therefore in charge of selling tickets. Harold sat next to him in the cafeteria, and for every pair of tickets bought, Jack took care of the accounting while Harold highlighted the seats sold. Eventually a master list of table placements was created, and the two friends examined their map, charting out what cliques were sitting where.

"Drama kids are all over here," Jack had said, pointing to the upper left corner.

"Honors kids in the bottom right," Harold motioned.

"Aw, and there are all the band geeks!" Jack exclaimed, pointing to the area right above the honors kids.

"Hey now!" Harold protested. "The kids in the band aren't geeks. Look how close they're sitting to the jocks." And as the two leaned over their seating chart, examining who sat where, Harold noticed the famous name that was missing.

"Where's Nancy sitting?"

"Nancy?" Jack asked, looking closer at the chart, perplexed.

"Nancy Allister," Harold answered. "Isn't she in the running for Homecoming Queen?"

"If she is, she hasn't bought her ticket yet," Jack said.

"Why would she buy her own ticket?" Harold asked innocently. "Doesn't her boyfriend have some big plan or something?"

"Boyfriend?" Jack replied, but his tone was sarcastic. "Since when have you ever seen Nancy Allister walk the halls with anyone?"

"Really?" Harold said, stunned. "Now that I think about it..."

"Yeah," Jack continued, "Too busy being the All Star. You don't get to be the top athlete in your state if you're distracted by a boyfriend."

"But everyone deserves to go to the Homecoming Dance during their Senior year," Harold said, frowning at the thought of Nancy not going. "Especially if you have a real shot at being the Queen..."

Jack looked at his buddy and laughed. "You're one to talk," he said. "I don't see your name on the seating chart."

It was true, Harold hadn't purchased a ticket. His parents were going to be away the weekend of the dance, and he was supposed to watch their two bulldogs, Tank and Bailey. Although he'd wanted to go to the dance, he was worried about the mess he'd have to clean up from the dogs being left alone for too long. Hearing that Nancy was without a date left him at a crossroads, and Harold, ever the optimist, made a bold and fortuitous decision. He saw on the chart that there was one empty chair at a table of band geeks, and directly behind it, an empty chair at a table full of jocks. Harold got out his wallet and gave Jack the cash for two tickets, indicating which seats they were to purchase.

"Are you serious?" Jack asked but accepted the money all the same.

"What's the worst that could happen?" Harold said, smiling brightly. "If she says she doesn't want to go, I can always sell the tickets back to my best friend who will totally refund me the money, regardless of school policy." Jack glared at his presumption but did not disagree with him.

Harold made his move as Nancy was leaving her last class for the day and heading to her car to go to Herlihy's Batting Cages. Two seasons prior, she had worked out a deal with the local owner, Ray, which gave her creative use of his pitching machines. Instead of going into the cage with her bat, she could go in with her glove, so long as Ray was supervising, where she could catch softballs instead of swing on them to practice her footwork and famous throw down.

It was something she'd been doing twice a week in the off seasons of the past two years and was a credit to her competitive edge. Ironically, on the days she didn't catch, she went elsewhere to get her practice swings, usually over at Charlotte Smith's house, who had developed into quite the pitcher since their younger days. When the manager asked why she didn't just do it all at his batting cages, Nancy told him a pitching machine can't replicate the movement of a lady's fast-pitch windmill, and besides that, she only had so many quarters to spend in a week. Still, softball training never really stopped for Nancy, and she cherished her trips to the cages; it was a routine she looked forward to. What was *not* routine, however, was having someone waiting for her by her car after school, especially when that someone was Harold Dancy.

"Can I help you?" she said as she approached him, and although her tone was fairly cold, Harold was unfazed. He smiled at her, reached into his pocket, and produced two Homecoming tickets.

"Nancy Allister," he said, with a bit of bravado in his voice, "Would you like to go to the dance?"

"With you?" Nancy asked with a tone that had shifted to mild disgust. Harold remained unaffected, though.

"In a roundabout way," he answered, and before Nancy could counter with something snarky, Harold pled his case in the plainest terms possible.

"They're single seats," he continued. "Our backs would be to each other and you'd be seated at a table with a bunch of people you hang out with, just like I'd be at a table with a bunch of people I hang out with. We could go together if you want, and I'll pick you up in my dad's car with a corsage and everything. If you want to go stag, that's fine, too. The point is, you've got a ticket if you want it."

"So you're just giving me a ticket, then? It's not a date?" she asked, unable to hide the confusion in her voice. Harold's confident smile didn't falter.

"Not unless you want it to be," he answered, self-assured.

Nancy thought about it for a moment, then walked around him, got into her car, started it, and drove off to the batting cages, with Harold still standing where he'd been, two tickets in hand, watching her go.

She barely knew Harold Dancy, never thought about him, and hardly knew what to think of him if she did think about him. It was the boldest move she'd ever encountered from a guy she went to school with, and a creative one to boot. Sure there were guys that dropped lines on her and pathetic come-ons, but they were easily dismissed. Harold, even after the non-answer and driving away from him, was not as easy to ignore. She got so caught up in thinking about his asking her out that she missed three softballs inside the cage an hour later, including one that painfully glanced off of her left shoulder, much to her mother's concern.

"Nancy, honey!" Emily said to her daughter when she saw her walk in the house, nursing her shoulder. "What happened?"

"It's stupid, mom," Nancy answered, dropping her gear off in the hallway and making her way to the kitchen freezer for a bag of frozen vegetables. She tucked the bag underneath the strap of her sports bra and slumped into an empty chair at the kitchen table. Emily sat down next to her, took her daughter's hand, and looked at her meaningfully.

"Did something happen at school today?" she asked, preparing to hear the worst, though she had no idea what that might be.

"Yeah," Nancy replied, examining the chipped nails on her free hand, ignoring her mom's penetrating look. "A boy asked me out to the Homecoming Dance today... kind of..."

"Oh, that's wonderful, sweetheart!" Emily replied, squeezing her daughter's hand. It was the opposite of what she expected, and a nice surprise. It was the first time her daughter had ever come home with the news of anyone asking her out, which Emily thought was long overdue, though her husband, Charles, sometimes disagreed when they talked about such things privately.

"Is it?" Nancy asked with a sudden flash of anger, scaring her mother into letting go of her hand, like she'd just done something wrong in trying to comfort her daughter.

"I don't understand," Emily began, with a note of maternal concern, and Nancy interjected with an immediate explanation, as though she were dying to unload the formulating thoughts from her catching practice that were so distracting and damaging.

"To begin with," she said, "it's the first time anyone's asked me to a dance that wasn't a part of a big group of girlfriends!"

"Oh, I always liked that you went to dances with your teammates," Emily replied wistfully, thinking back on the last few years of dances, dresses, and living room pictures. It only made her daughter even more upset, though.

"They've all got boyfriends now, Mom!" Nancy exploded, "Except for Heather, but she came out two years ago, and even she has a girlfriend!"

"Heather's got a girlfriend now?" Emily asked.

"Yes!" Nancy lamented. "Her name is Ann and they've been together for six months. They're very happy, and meanwhile I can't get but one person to ask me out!"

Emily didn't know how to respond to that, so she just sat there quietly while her daughter fumed, hoping Nancy's father, who was reading a paperback in the living room, would come in and add his own thoughts. Navigating the varied emotions of their teenage daughter was always best when it was done as a pair, as it could be scary when done alone and without support. Charles stayed in the living room, however, either listening in quietly or ignoring it altogether.

"He didn't even ask me as a date," Nancy continued after her pause, softer now. "He made it optional, like we could go as friends or something, but we're not even friends. I hardly even know the guy."

"Well what's his name, honey?" Emily asked, and she took her daughter's hand again, feeling it safe to do so. Nancy leaned in to put her head on her mother's shoulder, though it meant having the bottom of her cheek press up against the frozen bag of vegetables still cooling the bruise on her shoulder.

"Harold Dancy," Nancy replied, and that was the moment her father appeared in the doorway of the kitchen, tucking his paperback book into the back of his blue jeans.

"Did you say Harold Dancy?" Charles asked, and Nancy glared at him out of habit.

"Yes," she said firmly, "Why?"

"I know that family," he replied. "I was doing contract work down at town hall, and I saw the whole family in there bitching about their water bill. It was an overcharge that amounted to something stupid like 67 cents or something, but there they were, making a big stink about it."

"So what?" Nancy asked, and the tone in her voice was accusatory.

"So that whole family is a bunch of peckerheads," Charles said bluntly. "You don't want to go to the dance with a peckerhead, Nance."

Nancy didn't say anything to this, but only glared at her father. Charles rolled his eyes in response, as that was on par for the way his daughter interacted with him. In truth, he'd admired the type of young woman she'd become, and even liked the attitude. It was a *champion's* attitude. No boys meant no distractions, and it was a relief that Nancy hadn't been seriously asked out by anyone up until now. What's more, if even half of what Charles thought about the Dancy family was true, the kid (whatever his name was) wouldn't stand a chance with his girl. Little did he realize, however, just how strong the antagonistic relationship was between father and daughter.

Nancy kissed her mother on the cheek, brushed past her father without regarding him, and went straight into her bedroom, shutting the door behind her. She got on her phone, called three or four different friends to ask around, and finally came up with Harold's number. When she called him, the conversation was short:

"Be at my house by 6:30," she told him. "You can leave your car parked at my place. My dad will drive us to the school." She hung the phone up after that, not waiting to hear what Harold had to say. If he was serious about taking her to the dance, she'd let him prove it by showing up on time. To Harold's credit, he was a master at taking instruction.

***

When Charles Allister saw Harold Dancy knock on his door, he felt the slightest twinge of anger from deep within his chest. Nancy being contrary for the sake of being contrary was something he'd grown accustomed to, but it never occurred to him just how far it would go. He had deemed the whole Dancy family a bunch of peckerheads, and certainly enough, Harold was on his front doorstep dressed like one, wearing a second-hand tuxedo that hadn't been fashionable since the early 80s, complete with an obnoxiously large cummerbund and the wrong colored shoes. The kid held a slightly wilted corsage and

43

looked up expectantly at Charles, as though he was waiting for an invitation to come inside.

"Can I help you?" Charles asked, and a look of confusion came over Harold. Just as he was about to answer, Nancy's mother wedged herself in between Charles and the front door and beamed positively at her daughter's date to the Homecoming Dance.

"You must be Harold!" Emily cried, and Harold smiled at the warm reception. "Please don't mind my husband," she continued. "Nancy's never had a boyfriend come to the house before!"

"MOM!" Nancy cried from somewhere inside the house, and Emily looked over her shoulder in response.

"A FRIEND WHO IS A BOY!" she shouted back at her daughter, and then turned her attention to Harold again. "My goodness!" she said, "I certainly hope she isn't as temperamental with you, young man."

Anyone else would've been bewildered by the sight of Charles and Emily Allister poking out halfway through their front door, but Harold was never one to blush in the face of awkward moments, and only politely asked, "Should I wait outside by the car, or would you like me to come in for pictures?"

"Wait outside by the car?!" Charles protested, but Emily's smile grew wider and she elbowed her husband gently before fully opening the front door to their house.

"He's only kidding with you, Harold," Emily explained. "It's a 'dad' thing, I think. Come right in! We'll get your pictures by the mantle place, and then Nancy's dad will drive you to over to the dance."

Charles glowered at his wife, but it was only momentary, and Harold did not notice it. The look that Emily gave him in return made him shore up his behavior, and things went smoothly after that. The young couple took awkward pictures together in the living room as Harold placed the corsage on Nancy's wrist, and when they got into the car, Charles quietly drove them the ten minutes to school, allowing an uncomfortable silence to pervade. When they got to the dance,

Nancy got out first, and Charles held Harold captive for a brief two-minute lecture on all the different bones in the human hand that could be broken, capping it off with the moral of the story, which was to keep one's hands to one's self. Harold accepted the information quietly, with a smile that never wavered. If he was scared, he didn't show it, and he thanked Charles for the advice before getting out of the car.

"Ready to go inside?" Harold asked as he approached his date. Nancy looked warily at her father's car as it slowly pulled away from the school.

"What was that all about?" she asked him, and Harold chose Nancy's mother's words to explain it away.

"I think it was a 'dad' thing," he said. "Be respectful, in a manner of speaking."

"Ugh, whatever," Nancy protested, thinking about what her father may have said. "Let's just go inside and get this over with."

Harold should've been disheartened by Nancy's reaction, and maybe even a bit hurt, but he only laughed instead. He was fascinated by Nancy's attitude, and wondered how long she would be determined to have a bad time. As it turned out, Nancy was fairly determined in everything that she did. True to the seating arrangement, they sat with their backs to each other. Nancy declined all of Harold's offers to dance, and they did not share a word. When the Homecoming Queen was announced, it was *not* Nancy's name that was called, but her teammate and friend, Denise Clifford, who danced with Manny Stevens, the football team's starting center and crowned Homecoming King. While everyone else was gathered to watch the pageantry, Nancy stayed seated, and Harold stayed near her.

"Do you want to get out of here?" Harold asked, and they were the first meaningful words he'd been able to say to Nancy all night, who was in an impenetrable mood.

"Sure," Nancy said, apathetically. "Do you want me to call my dad to come and pick us up?"

"Would you mind if we just walked back to your house?" Harold answered, and Nancy looked at him suspiciously.

"Why?" she asked, and Harold answered her very plainly.

"I'll be absolutely honest with you, Nancy," he said, "This has not been the most ideal date, and I'm okay with that. I know we're not actually an item, so I figure I've got nothing to lose when I say that your father is kind of a jerk. He threatened to break the bones in my hand when it was just the two of us in the car, and I'd rather walk than have to catch another ride with him."

It was not a romantic sentiment, but Nancy had never heard words more sweet. It opened up an avenue she hadn't expected in a relationship with a boy, and Harold had unwittingly stumbled upon the key to her heart. They walked back to her house, and Nancy talked more than she had ever talked before about her father and how everything was between them. Harold was a great listener and didn't add in his own opinions or try to make the conversation about him, and it was exactly what she needed. When she had exhausted everything she wanted to say, Harold filled the silence with his bits of idle chit chat, specifically talking about how strange his own parents could be, what it was like to care for the world's most rambunctious bulldogs, and what he sometimes did for fun when he wasn't busy with school or jazz ensemble.

By the time they got to Nancy's front porch, Harold had made himself much more amenable than he had been at the start of everything. He was a perfect gentleman, had carried her shoes along the walk so she could be more comfortable in bare feet, and more importantly, had not made anything weird by coming at her with unwanted advances. She didn't necessarily feel anything special for him, but certainly wasn't averse to his being there, either. Still, what had happened next was a bit of a shock to both of them, and it had happened just as Charles opened the door to see his daughter and Harold standing there.

Nancy saw her father out of the corner of her eye, acutely aware of his presence and the light pouring out of the house into the darkness of night. Without hesitation, she leaned into Harold, and their noses pressed together as she jammed her lips onto his. Harold's eyes went wide, and he actually stumbled backwards when she released him from the kiss. Without a word, Nancy snatched her heels from Harold's grasp, and walked past her father into the house, leaving the two to regard each other. Charles' face was menacing, but Harold's dopey grin could not be subdued. He waved casually to his date's father as he strolled back to his car, lighter in step than he'd been the moment prior. When Charles walked back into the house, he did not mince his words.

"Nancy, you knock this off right now!" He didn't necessarily raise his voice when he said this, but he spoke firmly, as though he'd finally acknowledged that their father/daughter dynamic had gone far enough.

"Knock *what* off?" she smarted back to him, and Charles clenched his teeth.

"I'm not going to let you do this," he said. "You have no interest in a boy like Harold Dancy. You're just dating him to piss me off!"

"Charles!" Emily said, coming out of the kitchen and into the living room where her husband and daughter stood, looking like two fighters ready to come to blows. "That is a terrible thing to say your daughter!"

"I'm done tolerating this ridiculous behavior, Emily!" he answered, and it was plain to see that Charles was having a truly cathartic moment, his voice rising with every syllable. "I don't know what the hell I did for her to act the way she does, but it's high time we get to the bottom of it. Everything she does, she does to spite me! If I say walk, she runs. If I say speed up, she slows down. Left goes right, up becomes down, and now she's going out of the house with a goddamn peckerhead, making out with the boy right in front of me, and all just to get underneath of my goddamned skin!"

Emily gave her husband a sharp look and rebuked him immediately. "You watch your tongue in front of our daughter," she said. "Stop it right now, before you say something you regret!"

Charles didn't listen to his wife, though. Instead, he paused briefly, collected his words, and then gave them to his daughter with all of the gravity he had within him. He held her eyes in his own, striving to break through to some sense of reasoning with her.

"Nancy," he began, "I've never understood what I could've done for you to be this way toward me, when all I have ever wanted for you was what was in your best interest. I am telling you right now, picking a boyfriend for the sole purpose of pissing off your father is a terrible way to make a decision, and it doesn't speak volumes about the intelligence I know you possess. If you want to be contrary with the little things in life, that's fine, but you ought to be more considerate of whom you go about dating. You can be a young woman with high standards and find someone who is an actual match for you, or you can date the goddamn Harold Dancys of the world just to get a rise out of your old man. Lady's choice, Nance, but I'm willing to bet you could do a lot better in the decision-making department than you have been."

Nancy heard everything her father had said, and at the same time, she hadn't heard a single thing. It was a terrifying use of reverse-psychology, and absolutely unintended. Their spat in the living room ended with Nancy tearfully storming off to her bedroom while looking at her mother, saying, "Harold was right. Dad really is a jerk."

For the rest of the school year, Nancy and Harold were an item. Unlikely as it was, they carried their relationship into college. Harold was such an affable guy with no serious flaws, and therefore he never gave Nancy any good concrete reasons to end things. As they got older, they established their own form of intimacy, and while it worked for them, and they satisfied each other's needs, it was in no way what anyone else would call *passionate*. They were sufficient partners, compatible without being compatible, and ultimately unaware of the love that they lacked. They were each other's only lover and all they'd ever known, and Nancy had yet to stray to find out what sex could be otherwise. She was too busy defying her father at every opportunity.

When Charles suggested she take the athletic prowess and goodwill she developed in high school and use it toward some form of athletic studies, Nancy went the other way. Although she still played ball in college, she ignored any academic pursuit of the physical science she'd dedicated herself to for the whole of her formative years, and threw herself into a business management program, instead. Years later, after the wedding and settling into their apartment, Nancy was venting to her mother about Harold's grand idea to use her degree to help him start his own life-coaching company. Charles made the mistake of scoffing at the plan, which caused Nancy to throw all of her energies into helping her husband get it off the ground. Later still, when wrestling with the topic of whether or not to take on a management position at a car rental place to help make ends meet while Harold searched for clients, Charles once again made the mistake of letting slip his notion that a car rental agency was beneath the dignity of his daughter. Sure enough, Nancy accepted the position after the first interview.

Nancy's life fuel was spite, and if Harold ever suspected that this was the foundation of their union, it was an understanding that he kept buried deep within, consciously or not. He viewed the world as all hopeless optimists do, and he chose to see Nancy as a loving and supportive partner in life, nothing less. When his father-in-law passed away of heart disease, he knew it would take its toll on Nancy, but remained blissfully unaware of the impact it had on his marriage.

And now Nancy felt stuck.

She was stuck in a job that she hated, where in the mornings, she hid inside of her idling car for as long as she could before she absolutely had to get out to open the branch; stuck in a marriage that was loveless, where at night she'd taken to pretending to be asleep so that she wouldn't have to have sex with her husband; and worse than everything else, stuck with the realization that as much as she hated her father, he was right about the one most important thing. Deciding out of spite is no way to decide at all, and the realization of that came over her with such a powerful force that she knew as soon as the branch was up and running, she was going to schedule herself a half day and let that no account Duke Franklin run things in her absence.

It was time to start making better decisions with her life.

Lady's choice.

It was time for her to leave her husband.

Chapter Three

Harold's Auto-Erotic Excuse (A Story About Now)

Damon Alton had seen a lot of things in his younger years with *The Common Miscreants*, and there wasn't much that surprised him. He was only 16 when he and his cousin, Jenna, originally created their pop-punk power trio. In the ten years that the band was active, he'd gone around the world and back again, collecting a multitude of experiences along the way.

In those early years it was all just for fun, and they paid homage to all of the trios he and Jenna liked to listen to, including newer acts like Sleater-Kinney, and older groups like The Violent Femmes. When they formed *The Common Miscreants*, they only covered songs played by other power trios, giving them a unique catalogue that was different from a lot of the other local bands in the scene. Jenna thrashed around on the guitar and sang songs that fit her voice, while Damon wore his bass so low that it knocked against his shins while he aggressively plucked its strings and sang the songs that Jenna wouldn't. They harmonized when they could, and Jenna's friend, Erin, was recruited from her school's marching band to sit in as their drummer, following in the footsteps of great drummers like Gina Schock and Sandy West, whose sound they wished to capture. The novelty of a female lead guitarist and drummer got them in the door of a lot of the smaller clubs: a *girl group* that just happened to have a guy on bass. The ambiguity of their band's name also kept them from being completely pigeon-holed, and they eventually developed a tiny following in the Baltimore alt-rock scene.

By Damon and Jenna's senior year of high school, their band had developed a sleek sound and they saved every cent from their local gigs to purchase time in a recording studio. Their first EP, *Half and Half*, consisted of two songs sung by Jenna, and two sung by Damon. They financed a small run of CDs they sold out of the trunk of their car, and after one fateful show, they unknowingly sold a copy to the scout of a hot shot record label looking for new bands to sign. The EP caught his ear, and the scout quickly booked them for the opening spot at a gig in a prominent New York club to see if they were the real deal.   Before they knew it, while other kids their age enjoyed Senior Week at the local Maryland and Delaware beaches, The Common Miscreants played a show that cast them into the firmament of rock stars.

They'd been set up with an invitation to open for an Electric Records showcase at *The Bitter End* on Bleeker Street in Greenwich Village. Although they'd all thought the Baltimore clubs where they cut their teeth gave them a certain pedigree, they were overwhelmed by the sheer scope of the audience. This was not like playing at The Brass Monkey in Fells Point, where there were holes in the ceiling above the stage from other punk acts throwing their guitars in the air and misjudging the distance, or where the unwashed floors and cash-only bar gave it a certain grungy credibility. The Bitter End was a place where legends began and often revisited with new material to tune up before going on tour. Dylan had touched this stage, as did Carly Simon and Joni Mitchell. You didn't beg your friends to come see you at a place like this. The Bitter End already had an established crowd.

Electric had a five-piece act they thought was ready to blow, and a last minute slot to warm up the crowd had become available for three unknowns from Maryland who were booked solely on the strength of an EP sold out of the trunk of their car. They'd get a twenty-minute set to make sure the levels were just right for when the *real* musicians came on, and they were supposed be happy with whatever attention they received afterward at the merch table set up for them off to the side. During their pre-show huddle, however, Jenna had other ideas.

They found a darkened corner just outside the green room and hugged each other closely. Erin kept her long brown hair tucked behind her ears, and she whispered a mantra to herself, repeating, "Not too fast, not too soft. Feel the beat, not the adrenaline..."

Jenna hugged Damon closely to her shoulder and said, "You remember the story about Jerry Lee?"

Damon, still young at that point, and pale faced at the prospect of such a daunting crowd, feebly replied, "Yeah, I remember..."

"What did Jerry Lee do?"

"Set the room on fire just to piss off Johnny Cash..."

"That's right," Jenna replied. "We don't open, do we?"

"No," Damon answered, and his nerves began to settle, harnessed into something ready to be unleashed on the audience.

"What do we do?" Jenna asked, and now Erin broke out of her mantra and answered for them all.

"We close!" she roared, and the three of them broke their huddle like they were athletes ready to take the field, but instead went directly onto the stage and plugged in for the most raucous twenty minutes of the night. They didn't just play the four songs from their EP; they *performed* them. The way in which they attacked each note created a frenzy that made people stop their conversations and take note. Erin did her best to not let her own nerves take over and was able to keep a steady rhythm that sounded closer to what they recorded, instead of the usual frenetic energy that caused them to play faster than what their songs called for. Jenna glowered at the audience and had all the makings of her future rock goddess stature, a short, dark-haired young woman that towered over everyone when she had a microphone and a guitar. Damon, feeling the twinge of what was to come for him, soaked up all the adulation from the audience, and almost magnetically knew when any female in the crowd was checking him out. With three minutes left of their set time, and having already played their four originals, Damon spontaneously called out to Erin, "Next to You!" and Erin immediately pounded out the opening beat on the toms. Jenna flew into the first chords of The Police's song, and Damon finished their set by channeling the energy of Sting, growling his vocals into the microphone while making eye-contact with every woman standing before him who'd made it onto his radar. In the end, it was the birth of the rock and roll monster he was to become.

The Electric reps quickly forgot about the act they were supposed to see, and instead zeroed in on Jenna, Erin, and Damon. There were stars in their eyes, and they saw all of the marketing possibilities in a band like The Common Miscreants. Soon, the three bandmates were caught up in the tidal wave of fame. While Jenna and Erin were able to deftly ride it out and onto better things, Damon got sucked into an undertow of groupies, yes-men, teen-idol magazines, and delusions of his own grandeur. Jenna and Erin tried to save him, but he was quickly devoured, and the stories of his erratic behavior eclipsed anything positive The Common Miscreants were producing.

It didn't help that Electric had selected all of Damon's songs to act as the band's singles, just like it didn't help that all of the magazine covers insisted on having Damon front and center while Jenna and Erin bookended him in matching outfits. When it was just the first album where this had happened, the three of them had laughed it off. When it happened again for the second album, Erin was the first to voice some displeasure, and rebelled by only wearing tuxedos whenever she was behind the drum kit, carving a unique identity all for her own. By the third album, Jenna could see the situation for what it was, and family or no, Damon was not someone she could be in a band with. He was a shadow of the cousin she grew up with, who could say the most hurtful things to people when he didn't get his way and didn't understand that he was being used for his image just as badly as he was using the women who would flock to him after the shows. On top of everything else, he stopped making decisions that would benefit the band, and started making decisions that would mainly benefit Damon Alton. Nearly eight years of his antics had worn her down, and even though he was only 26 at the time, she convinced herself that Damon was too old to change his ways. Jenna and Erin left the band to form a new group called "Women and Children", and the duo found a home on the progressive indie rock circuit, where they sang feminist-inspired lyrics and the absence of a bass player became symbolic of their belief that Damon Alton represented everything wrong with toxic masculinity.

Damon's fame quickly eroded, and as the money disappeared, so too did all of the yes-men and the groupies and the magazine covers. In time, he himself disappeared, hiding away for the better part of a decade, until a small label convinced him that it was time to return. Their hopes were for a solid nostalgia act that could generate some record sales, but Damon had bigger plans. He didn't want to play old songs and prance around on stage for the same groupies that had fawned over him years ago. He wanted to play new material, make his comeback, and transition into an elder statesman of rock, with the ultimate goal of reconciling things with Jenna and Erin. The Common Miscreants could then make one more go of it, with Jenna, not him, front and center.

Of course, he hadn't known that he'd wanted all of these things; not until he met Harold, and not even then at first. Harold had started out as an enemy, someone to be hated, a hired crony for the label, a babysitter. Then they clicked, Harold and he, in the most unlikely of ways, and after everything with Nancy... Damon had long wanted to say something to Harold about it all, so that the two of them could go forward in earnest, but it all gets so complicated when a wife dies.

He'd gone to Harold's to dig into the topic of Nancy and how he was concerned over the way Harold was still handling her death a little over a year later, but such a conversation was not to happen. When he opened Harold's door, he was shocked by the familiar sight of a rock star's bedlam that lay before him. The acts of sexual congress and the hard partying that came with it during his Miscreant years made him well-prepared for what to expect when walking into such a scene, but he marveled at the scope of destruction that could come from Harold Dancy, of all people.

"Well done, Harold," Damon exclaimed, exasperated by the sheer disorder of it all. "Who knew you had it in you?"

Harold was the Type-A sort, someone who was unabashedly neat and lived that way as a rule. This scene went against everything he'd been preaching to Damon for the past year and a half. Furniture was askew, dust hung in the air, and the split end of a rope dangled from the rafter in the living room, just ahead of the couch.

Damon stepped forward cautiously and called out, "Harold? Buddy? Are you still with us?" He was hoping for some reply, but only heard the silence of the room. Harold's behavior had been worrying him for some time now, and Damon feared that Nancy's death had caused him to come unhinged, as he knew all too well what that kind of erratic behavior looked like. That third-story cannonball into the pool Harold had performed a few months back, for instance, could've been suicide if he'd missed the landing, but he'd pulled it off like it was a wild stunt, popping up from the deep end with an *I'm all right!* and a gasp for air. Was this going to be another one of those scenes? Would Harold pop up from the middle of the room to say he was all right, and would they have a laugh about it later? Damon stepped forward again and called out for his friend once more.

"Harold?" Still there was only silence. He walked further into the room, closer to the dangling rope, and just over the horizon of the couch, the entire scene came into view. Shattered furniture and bits of splintered wood littered the ground, and there beside the dilapidated coffee table was Harold Dancy, unconscious with a noose around his neck, and what looked to be a massive erection protruding from the crotch of his pants. Damon examined the evidence, connected the dots, and made his assertion.

"Good lord," he whispered, "Harold's nearly killed himself trying to masturbate."

After ten years of experience with the rock and roll touring circuit, Damon was well practiced in what to do next and picked up his phone, having made two calls of a similar nature before - once for a friend, and once for himself. He did his due diligence, eschewed dialing 911, and instead got hold of a private ambulance that he knew to be very discreet.

"Please come quick," he said over the phone, calmly standing near the entrance to the apartment. "I think my friend Harold's just had a bit of a bad experience with auto-erotic asphyxiation, and he's nearly taken off his own head... No, the big one... Yes, the one on his shoulders..." Minutes later, paramedics were on the scene, and Harold was placed onto a backboard, neck stabilized, ready to be carted off to the local hospital, while Damon followed behind in his own car, ready to be there for his friend in need.

***

When Harold came to, he was groggy, and had trouble discerning where he was. It felt as though he was floating through air, while an array of lights glided over him, one by one. He stared at them intently through the fog of his vision, hoping to catch a glimpse of Nancy, but as his vision cleared, the lights became less ethereal and more fluorescent. Likewise, he no longer felt as though he was floating, but instead felt like he was being carted along, firmly strapped to a bed enclosed with metal railings. The familiar smells of the sick and the dying, masked by the pungent aroma of disinfectant, wafted over him. As he became more aware of his surroundings, his ears flooded with the sounds of beeping machines, squeaking wheels, hushed children, and quiet conversations.

"This is not Heaven..." he said, but the words themselves were whispers, unable to be more than that as fire shot through his throat with every word that passed over his vocal cords. Slow tears streamed down the sides of his face, and when he found he could not move his head from side to side, his breath hitched inside his chest with the force of an oncoming panic attack.

"Relax, Mr. Dancy," a voice said from the head of his bed, and it was calm and soothing in tone. "You're still being restrained out of an abundance of caution, until your CT scan comes back. In the meantime, the doctor thinks you're in remarkable shape, considering the circumstances."

"Circumstances," Harold echoed, trying to figure out just what that meant, and immediately cringed in pain when the word left his mouth.

"Try not to speak," the voice said. "Your throat won't feel right for quite some time. It's best to get some vocal rest while you wait for your results. In fact, you should probably get some rest overall, Mr. Dancy. You look exhausted."

Harold tried to check his surroundings, but he could see nothing beyond the fluorescent ceiling lights gliding above him, one after the other, until they became hypnotic, lulling him back to sleep.

When he woke again, he was in a grey room. His bed was elevated so, and there was a small television mounted to the wall. A weather report was on, and Harold could see by the view from the window that the forecast was accurate: cold and overcast, with a chance of rain, and no hope of sunlight for the rest of the day.

"There's my guy!"

Harold heard the familiar sound of Damon Alton's voice, and he looked over to the doorway. Damon was there, filling the frame with his tall, lanky build. He was bundled up in a long wool overcoat, and stringy wisps of jet-black hair spilled out of the knit cap he wore on top of his head, falling down to the length of his chin. Harold smiled at the sight of him and was caught off-guard by just how happy he was to see a visitor.

"You look like a mess," Harold rasped, and he winced as he did so, his voice still somewhat tender.

"Yeah, well I just came from outside," Damon replied. "It's mercilessly cold and the wind isn't doing anyone's looks any favors. And besides," he added, "at least I'm not the one laid up in a hospital bed after a good wank gone bad."

"What?" Harold asked, and though he cringed in pain, it was not enough to hide his bewilderment at what Damon had just suggested.

"Don't worry," Damon said, reassuringly. He approached the bed like he was sneaking into a room that was off-limits, and he looked around the area to check for eavesdroppers, before continuing on in a low voice. "They tried to write this up like it's a suicide attempt, but I did my best to set them straight. I told them, 'Harold Dancy's my professional *life coach*, for God's sake. What kind of life coach thinks to commit suicide?'"

"So then what do they think happened?" Harold asked, urgently in his hoarse voice.

"Relax, Harold," his friend reassured him. "You've nothing to feel ashamed of, man. When I came in... sorry, *walked* in, you were still pitching a tent. Look, I get it, and I'm the last person that gets to judge. You've got needs, and there's nothing wrong with experimenting with your comfort zone when you hit your thirties."

"But what do they think happened?" Harold repeated as emphatically and loudly as his voice could handle.

Damon couldn't help but laugh at his friend's anxiety. "Don't be a prude, Harold! It's just me! So you tried to choke yourself during a handy? Big deal. Just be glad you didn't pull a David Carradine."

"A David Carradine?" Harold asked, still put off by the conversation as a whole. Only a former rock star could treat something so patently ridiculous with a degree of normalcy.

"Oh, come off it," Damon replied, slightly offended. "You know who David Carradine is! He was the star of *Kill Bill* and the man that blessed us with the TV show *Kung Fu*. My father used to watch that show religiously, and it was one of the few things he and I could do together without it ending in a fight. How's that for irony? Anyhow, it's common knowledge that David Carradine died of auto-erotic asphyxiation."

"Auto-erotic..." Harold echoed, confused.

"Asphyxiation, yeah," Damon confirmed, "and I told the doctors that that's what this was, but they still have to ask you a few psych questions before they can let you go."

Harold stared at Damon for a moment, really considering what he could say, but instead reached a hand out to his friend and whispered hoarsely, "Thank you."

Damon took Harold's hand and squeezed it gently. Without warning, he felt a small hitch in his own throat and gave his friend a meaningful look. "Listen, Harold, all this wild stuff that you've been doing since Nancy... look, there's a story there, man, and it's got to be told, but I can't set out to achieve my goals, *our* goals... not without you, anyway. I won't even be able to get out of my own way if you're not around, yeah?"

Harold saw him sniff back something inside, like he was fighting off a teardrop, and he squeezed his friend's hand in return. "Yeah," he replied. "I hear you."

"So just maybe talk to somebody, okay?" Damon continued.

Just then, there was a knock on the door, and Harold's nurse, an attractive black woman who looked to be around his age, walked backward into the room, pulling a small cart of food along with her.

"Is Mr. Dancy awake," the nurse asked, keeping her eyes toward the ground as she looked for a spot to park the lunch cart. "If so, I've got a lovely selection of milk shakes or smoothies that he could choose from, and all the applesauce he can handle." When she looked up to see her patient in bed, she caught sight of Damon Alton in full view and froze. Damon recognized the look, and in spite of all his new-found maturity and the personal growth he'd experienced in his dormant years, a boyish grin came over his face and he felt a flirtatious urge come over him. It was always that way when he met a fan.

"Has anyone ever told you that you look like..." she began to ask, and Damon was ready to pounce on the opportunity before him, but then he caught sight of Harold, lying in his bed, and they were still holding hands. In that instant, he realized that maybe some of the maturity he felt within him was legitimate, and he strayed from his usual tact.

"You think I look like the guy from that one band?" he asked her, and she raised her eyebrows in delight.

"The Common Miscreants!" she exclaimed, "Oh my goodness, yes. I had their poster up on my bedroom wall. You look just like Damon Alton would, except maybe a little older."

Damon's excitement faded somewhat at the remark, and Harold laughed audibly at this, before immediately grunting in pain. Damon smiled at his friend and squeezed his hand playfully before letting it go, trying hard to not let any embarrassment show on his face. "Yes, well," he said, collecting himself, "time has its way with all of us. Ten years ago, I was a dead ringer for the guy."

"Mmhmm," the nurse laughed jovially, "and I'll bet you used that to your advantage, too, didn't you?"

"Guilty," Damon replied, "but I'm actually Harold's business partner."

"Well, it's nice to meet you," the nurse replied. "All of my patients and their guests call me Nurse Shawnee," she said, and she smiled at Damon and Harold both.

"Lovely to meet you, Nurse Shawnee," Damon said, then asked, "So what's the situation with Harold? Any updates?"

"Last I checked," Nurse Shawnee answered, stepping away from the cart and picking up a chart from the foot of Harold's bed, "Doctor Pruss just needs to check in with Harold before he's cleared to leave. She'll ask him a few questions, and if he's good to be discharged, I'll come in and explain what he should do with food and medication for the next few days."

"Wonderful!" Damon exclaimed, and looked over to his friend. "You'll be out of here in no time, Harold." He then turned his attention back to the nurse. "Would there happen to be a chaplain about, miss?"

"We have a chapel just on the other end of the hall, if you need it," Nurse Shawnee replied. "Our clergy tends to rotate on a volunteer basis though. We have a Catholic priest in this afternoon, Father Ackley. Is that okay?"

"If he knows how to listen, then he'll do just fine," Damon answered, and Nurse Shawnee smiled back at him.

"Father Ackley is a wonderful listener," she told him, and Damon excused himself from the room to go to the chapel. When they were alone, the nurse pulled up a small table next to Harold and asked him if he wanted a milkshake or smoothie. Harold smiled at her, but shook his head no, and Nurse Shawnee placed a cup of applesauce, a small bottle of apple juice, and a Styrofoam cup of ice water next to him instead.

"That's smart of you to not use that voice, Mr. Dancy," she told him as she began to wheel her cart out of the room. "Save your strength and let it heal. I'm sure the doctor will be in to see you shortly."

When the room was empty, Harold opened up the applesauce and took in a few spoonfuls, but he found it hard to swallow. It wasn't because it hurt too much to eat, but the increasing awareness of his situation. If he wanted to get out of here, he supposed he could play along with Damon's supposition of the events that put him there in the first place. What bothered him, the more he thought about it, was the thought that he *saw* Nancy, if only for a second. It felt so real, and not at all like an aberration; it called into doubt everything he believed regarding his rotten luck with suicide.

As he started to get deeper into the thought of it, he heard a soft knock on the door, and looked over to see an older man dressed in black, with a white cloth collar around his neck. He had salt and pepper hair, and his cheeks were littered with the ancient cragged scars of childhood acne, but he had gentle eyes and a kind smile, and when he approached the bed, Harold felt no apprehension.

"Would you mind if I had a seat, sir?" the priest asked. Harold shrugged his shoulders in response, and that was permission enough. The priest pulled up a stool, sat down, and extended a hand in greeting. "I'm Father Ackley," he said. "How do you do?"

Harold reached out for his hand and grasped it firmly, shaking it twice before letting go. "I'm Harold," he rasped.

"If you don't wish to talk," the priest replied, but Harold found a voice to protest.

"No, Father, I'll be okay," he said. "I want you to stay. I've got some questions I want to ask."

"Your friend indicated that you might have something to say," the priest replied. His voice was warm and inviting, and Harold seized on the opportunity to speak.

"Will what we talk about stay between you and me?"

"Well, that depends," the priest said. "Is this a conversation, or is this a confession?"

"It's a confession, Father," Harold rasped. The priest nodded in understanding, left his chair and went to the door, where he put a tag on the handle requesting privacy, before shutting it entirely and returning to his seat.

"And now we have the sacred seal of confession," the priest replied. "You may proceed."

Harold paused for a moment, collecting his thoughts. It had been well on since his wedding day that he'd entered a church, and confession was not something he did regularly, as he never really felt the urge. He was Catholic though and he knew the rules, so he started from the rote memory of how these things began.

"Forgive me Father, for I have sinned," he wheezed. "It's been a very long time since my last confession."

"Then let us remedy that, my son," the priest told him.

Harold stared up at the ceiling, searching for words. The priest sat beside him, patiently waiting. A small brown wrist watch ticked away against his wrist, but the priest never made to check it. He allowed Harold all of the time he needed, and when Harold next spoke, the priest leaned over intently, so that the words were only as loud as they needed to be.

"Father," Harold began, "Do you think I'm bulletproof?"

The priest chuckled at the thought of it, and gently patted Harold's wrist. "I have to admit no one has ever started a confession with a question like that! And what an odd question, too! Why do you ask such a thing?"

"Well, I'm guessing my friend may have made a suggestion as to why I'm here," Harold said, and he paused to grab a drink of his water. It truly hurt to speak, and he relished the feeling of the cold water passing over the strained muscles inside his throat. The priest allowed him a moment before responding in kind.

"He made a suggestion, but I certainly wouldn't be surprised if there was more to the story than what he alleges happened."

Harold smiled. "Damon has a habit of seeing what he wants to see. Really, this was the fourth time I tried to kill myself."

"I see," the priest said, and a grave quality took over in the tone of his voice. "The fourth time, really?"

"Do you believe in ghosts, Father?" Harold asked.

"I believe in the Holy Spirit," the priest replied. "But beyond that, horror movies have been kept to a guilty pleasure, if that's what you're implying."

Harold waited a few seconds before he could find the strength to speak again. He had so many things he wanted to say, but he could only handle so many words. Finally, he found it within him to mutter aloud, "Father, I think I'm being haunted."

He waited for the priest to become insulted and leave, but this man, Father Ackley, had an aura about him that suggested Harold could say anything, and he'd take it seriously. When Harold realized that this priest might be the only person who'd give his story enough respect to hear it all the way through, he reached out to the priest's forearm, partly for comfort, but mainly to keep him there by his bedside, until he finished what he wanted to say.

"My wife died," Harold said, fighting to put the story in its simplest terms. "We were on the highway. I was driving... something jumped out... she grabbed the wheel..." He took a breath, and then another swallow from his cup of ice water. "She took her seatbelt off, so she could reach me. We hit a lamp post. She got thrown..." Harold's voice began to break, and the tears started to form at the bottom of his eyes. "She didn't make it."

The priest let his free hand fall on top of Harold's, the one gripping his forearm, and he patted it for comfort. "I'm sorry for your loss, my son. Please, go on."

"I put on a happy face," Harold continued. "Smile. Nod. I'm all alone at home, though. First try, I go to jump out a window. Not thinking. Should be a stain on the sidewalk. I go to jump, though, and Father, I feel this force, this *push*, and I swear to God I fly off the balcony. Land in the pool. People go nuts. Damon thinks I turned into a party animal."

"But that wasn't your intention," the priest interjected, and allowed Harold a chance to stop talking and get another drink. Harold took a sip from the Styrofoam cup and shook his head in response. Then he gathered up his strength and went on.

"Made a list of ways after that. Less public. Inconspicuous. No guns. Too loud."

"I see," the priest said, still patient, fully confident the confession would lead back to the question of ghosts. "What ways, then?"

"Second try was razors. Fresh pack. All dull. Grinded them into my arms like a hacksaw. Nothing. Just red skin. Burned like hell."

"For your third attempt?" the priest asked him.

"Grabbed the toaster. My parents bought it for us as a wedding gift. Makes breakfast sandwiches."

"Do they know anything of what's been going?" the priest interjected again.

Harold shook his head. "They found work on a base in Germany, teaching army kids. Otherwise, I guess they'd be around. Couldn't even make it to Nancy's funeral. I'm not mad about it. They sent a card..."

The priest shook his head in disbelief, feeling like this was a larger part of the story than Harold was letting on, but Harold continued with his confession before anything could be said.

"Next... filled up the bathtub. Got in. Power surge, I swear, just as the toaster hits the water. Blackout. Thing fell right into my crotch. Swollen down there for a week. No shock."

"And so then you tried to hang yourself?"

"Couldn't do it."

"Second thoughts?"

"Feet stuck to the chair. Couldn't step off. Could jump, though. Jumped a few times. Chair broke. I'm swinging, dying..."

"And then what happened?" the priest asked, more enraptured with the story than he realized. He leaned in closer, as Harold's voice was growing weaker.

"I saw her."

"You saw who?"

"I saw my wife. Nancy."

"I see," the priest said, and he leaned back on his stool, thinking about what was said to him. "So you believe that you experienced a miraculous event?"

"Four of them," Harold replied, quieter now at the weight of his confession. "I think Nancy's been keeping me from dying..."

"If that's the case," the priest said, "can I ask why you've been so persistent?"

"I really just miss my wife," Harold whimpered, as the thought of it caused him to cry. The priest did what he could to comfort Harold, holding his hand and rocking ever so slightly on his own stool to produce whatever lulling effect he could create.

"Why is she trying to stop me?" Harold pleaded, and even with the harsh quality of his voice, it held the sour notes of despondence.

The priest thought of what he might say in response. He cycled through all of the scripture he had in his memory, but inspiration took hold of him, and the internal forces that guided his wisdom led him to quote a guilty pleasure instead: his favorite musical, *Sweeney Todd*.

"Life is for the alive, my son. Perhaps Nancy wants you to keep living?"

"You think so?" Harold asked, looking up at the priest with complete sincerity.

"I must," he concluded. "And you must, too. I strongly recommend counseling, and this is a point I must be very insistent on. When Doctor Pruss comes in to release you, she's going to ask you a few questions. I urge you to be as honest in your responses as you were in this confession. Do you think you can do that?"

Harold looked away at the thought of telling someone else such a bizarre story, and in his mind, he flashed through all the possible outcomes that might come with telling the truth. When he looked back at Father Ackley, he nodded weakly. It was a lie, but maybe he could be forgiven for that, as well.

Father Ackley looked at him sternly for a moment, as if he had some insight into Harold's mind, but then let out a sigh and clasped his hands together. "For now," he continued, "we can start by ending this confession with an Act of Contrition. For penance, I'm suggesting one of the Corporal Works of Mercy."

"No Hail Marys?" Harold asked wryly, and the priest smiled at his humor.

"Praying always helps," he replied, "but it sounds like you need to get out and interact with the world. The love of one person is a beautiful, Godly thing, but the loss of that love cannot negate love for the world. Now let us pray."

They prayed together, and when the priest left, Harold shut his eyes, and fell asleep.

***

Two hours later, Harold woke up to the sound of the doctor entering into the room.

"Mr. Dancy," she replied. "I'm Dr. Pruss. Before we discharge you, I'd like to ask you a few questions. I know your throat is sore, so I'll try my best to keep them to 'yes' or 'no' questions, okay?"

Harold nodded his head in response, and the doctor continued.

"The gentleman who brought you here did his best to explain the situation, and I hate to cause you any emotional discomfort, but you are aware that he explained this was a case of auto-erotic asphyxiation?"

Harold nodded his head in confirmation. He'd said what he'd needed to say to the priest, and although Father Ackley urged honesty, he didn't think he could afford it, especially if it meant a long stay at the nearest psych ward, Sheppard Pratt. Damon's theory of how the events occurred would have to work if he wanted a means of leaving the hospital without being institutionalized.

"*Was* that the case?" the doctor asked.

Slowly, Harold nodded his head in confirmation. The doctor gave him a studious look, evaluating the veracity of his nod, and made a note inside the folder she carried under her arm.

"Mr. Dancy, have you ever thought about attempting to kill yourself?"

Harold shook his head, no.

"Have you ever told someone that you were going to commit suicide, or that you might do it?"

Again, Harold shook his head, no.

"On a scale of one to ten, with ten being highly likely, and one being highly *un*likely, how likely is it that you will attempt suicide someday?"

Harold raised up a single finger. The doctor regarded it, scribbled another note in her folder, and then extended a small business card to him.

"This is the number of a therapist that I'd like to recommend to you," she told him. "He specializes in the type of behavior that put you here. It is very dangerous, what you did, and you need to be more considerate in the future."

Harold took the card and examined the print without actually reading it. He then looked up at the doctor and smiled at her in silence. Unnerved, the doctor scribbled another note down, and then placed the folder back underneath her arm.

"Nurse Shawnee will get your discharge papers together. Make sure you schedule a follow up appointment with your primary care physician in the next two weeks to have your neck examined."

"Thank you, doctor," Harold rasped, and the doctor politely nodded at him before leaving.

A few moments later, Nurse Shawnee came in, and her presence was much warmer than the doctor's. She explained what Harold should and shouldn't do, and then gave him the final paperwork that would allow him to leave. Just as she was finishing up her instructions, Damon reentered the room with a set of car keys in hand.

"The chariot awaits, Harold," he said, and the nurse smiled at him.

"Your cover's blown, by the way," she told Damon, playfully tapping him on the arm. "One of the other nurses on shift is an even bigger fan of your work than I am, and I recognized you immediately. It's not often we get rock stars on our floor, but I can see why you'd want to keep a low profile."

Damon smiled at her, happy for the attention. "I try to be just like anyone else," he told her, which elicited a short laugh from Harold, followed by another painful grunt. The nurse looked over at Harold and shook her head.

"You're lucky you've got someone like Damon Alton in your corner, Mr. Dancy," she said to him. "I'm sure he's a good friend to you."

"Oh, we're more than just good friends," Damon told the nurse, smiling broadly. "Harold and I are best friends."

Chapter Four

Damon and Harold Are Not Best Friends (A Story About Then)

Harold never even had a chance. In spite of whatever redeeming qualities he thought he possessed, he was doomed the minute Damon Alton found out his name, what he did, and voiced his opinion freely on the ride over to Harold's office.

"A *life coach*?" Damon shouted at his new manager, Brian Squires, absolutely incredulous that such a thing could exist. "What in the hell is a life coach supposed to do for me!?"

"A lot of things," Brian replied, doing little to hide the disdain for his client. He'd thought it a mistake to sign Damon Alton on to their fledgling line-up and told the owner of Charm City Sounds as much. He explained his feelings on the subject in detail, including his assertion that if the great and all-resourceful Electric Records couldn't reel in Damon's behavior, then he wouldn't be worth the headache for their little upstart, even if it had been a decade since the man's last known performance. People don't change, he explained, and Damon Alton's current attitude was proof of that. It was like the last ten years of obscurity didn't count for anything. Damon was as obnoxious today as all the stories suggested he was back then.

"*A lot of things*," Damon mocked, rolling his eyes.

"Yeah," Brian shot back, "like helping you find some originality." Damon's face went slack with anger, but Brian wasn't having any of it. "You listen to me, Alton," he said, really winding up for the same heart-to-heart he'd had with a number of musicians who'd tasted fame before falling from its graces. "Don't go getting confused about what you are, and what *this* is..."

"Sorry, but what's this guy's name again?" Damon asked, cutting Brian off mid-sentence, before the lecture could really get going. He could smell a speech whenever it was starting to percolate and had long ago lost his taste for them. It was better to just change the subject.

Dismayed at being stopped short, Brian gripped his steering wheel tightly and cast a glance into his rear-view mirror, hoping the menacing glare would catch Damon's eye, but it did not. Damon was too busy to notice anything, lounging in the backseat, his feet propped up on the upholstery, seatbelt undone, and staring out the window.

Brian grunted, readjusted his mirror so that he wouldn't have to look at Damon, and answered sullenly, "His name is Harold Dancy."

"Harold Dancy," Damon said, dismissively. "Does he go by Harold, or is he a *Harry?* God help me if he's a *Hank.*"

"I don't know him personally," Brian replied, "but I think he goes by Harold."

"Ugh," Damon spat, "and with a name like *Dancy* to follow it. The man sounds ridiculous. Ridiculous name and a ridiculous job. Why in the hell is any of this necessary?"

"Insurance purposes, Damon. We needed to make assurances that that bloated reputation of yours is a thing of the past, so much so that we literally had to hire a *life coach* to keep you in line. Not only does this guy's credentials qualify, but he's also the most affordable."

Silence followed Brian's explanation for the briefest of moments, as if Damon were contemplating what was said, and then he muttered a curse under his breath.

"What was that?" Brian asked.

"I called you a cheap bastard," Damon said, and he made sure to articulate the last two words emphatically. Brian only laughed.

"I might be a cheap bastard, but I'm not the one footing the bill for this guy. *You* are. His cost will come directly out of what you gross in performances, so unless you wanted us to go with the most expensive guy on the market, I'd suggest you say, 'thank you' and moan about it privately."

Damon chose not to say anything for the rest of the car ride, and Brian was thankful for that, enjoying the last fifteen minutes of serenity before they made it to Harold's apartment. When they got there, however, Damon resumed talking, with a bit more venom too.

"This guy must be the bottom of the barrel, Brian. He can't even afford professional office space."

"It's a down economy," Brian replied. "Lots of people are doing what they need to do to make things work. At least he's held a job for the last ten years."

Damon could've stormed off in that instance. Brian Squires was a little man, and it was annoying that Brian didn't understand that about himself. Damon had dealt with so many like him, the Brians of the industry, always wanting to bark and wrangle you into a state of compliance, mainly because they themselves never had what it takes to make it to the stage. They simply didn't have talent or charisma. The best they could hope for was to stand next to somebody that did, if only to mooch off of their existence, and while they did so, they'd try to deify themselves for having to "put up" with someone else's talent. Damon knew show business was disgusting like that, but it beat having to book his own shows, make his own posters, and beg people to buy tickets like he had to back when it was just Jenna and Erin and him...

Jenna and Erin. He'd show them he was worth keeping in a band. He'd rise to prominence and blast their little girl power project out of the water. All he needed was the right bit of promotion, and some new material to go with it. He didn't need partnership. He just needed a creative break and for everyone else to kiss off.

They took the elevator up to the third floor of Harold's building and walked to the end of the hall, stopping at number thirty-six. Damon stood in front of the door sullenly with his hands stuffed in his front pockets and his shoulders slumped, feeling the weight of the burden that was this visit. Dread began to set in. He'd have to deal with Harold on a regular basis, if not a daily one, and God only knew what this *life coach* would ask of him. The only upside to any of this was that he'd see less of Brian in the process, and that was at least something. Harold was an unknown variable. Brian was a prick.

Before anyone could knock, the door opened wide, and Harold Dancy stood in the doorway, unknowingly making his very first impression on his client. Damon examined Harold quickly from top to bottom and took in all of the details at face value: Harold's medium height, his thin, almost sickly build, the way the red stubble on his cheeks stood out in contrast to his pale skin, and how the left part in his hair indicated a receding hairline. He'd dressed himself in pleated khakis and a plaid shirt, tucked in behind a brown belt that didn't exactly match the rest of his outfit, and he had on sandals instead of shoes, paired with white socks.

Harold Dancy was decisively below average, and that was not good news. If show business was a series of at least average men seeking to prop themselves up on the shoulders of greater beings, then it stood to reason that Harold was going to be one hell of a burden. Damon's mood darkened. When he was invited inside, he walked right past Harold without acknowledging him, immediately located the living room couch, and placed himself on the middle cushion with his knees spread out to make it clear he was not inviting anyone to sit near him.

"My apologies, Mr. Dancy," Brian said, loudly enough for Damon to hear, "but Mr. Alton seems to be suffering from delusions of grandeur today. I'd ask him to get off his high horse, but I think he's afraid of heights..."

Harold laughed and patted Brian on the shoulder affably as he guided him toward the living room. "Nonsense, Mr. Squires," he said brightly, making his way to the middle of the room so he could be in Damon's line of view. "I don't believe in hostility. Everyone's entitled to a moment or two, especially when they have to wrestle with their own creative temperament. Isn't that right, Mr. Alton?"

Damon regarded Harold with a smug grin. He could certainly sell an opening line, but Damon wasn't anyone's rube, and he knew better than to fall for the nice guy routine. Instead, he grunted dismissively in Harold's direction, then replied, "If that's your experience, sure, but then again, what kind of experience do you have?"

Harold's smile didn't fade, and he mistook the remark for an invitation to discuss his credentials. He pulled up a chair close to the couch, rather enthusiastically, and settled down close enough to Damon to suggest familiarity, but just far enough to respect his space.

"I'm so glad you asked," Harold said, hunching over with his elbows on his knees, like they were really going to get to the heart of something. "Establishing credentials is an important aspect to starting any working relationship. In terms of experience, I've had a wide-range of clients, and I practice a form of life coaching that I learned from studying at Georgetown. I'm a member of the Maryland chapter of the International Coach Federation, through which many of my clients have found me. Most are of limited means, and I've spent a lot of time helping individuals reenter the workforce, like those who are coming out of retirement, or others who've just been released from incarceration. I've helped a few clients who are working to go back to school a little late in life, and occasionally I've given support to some who are fresh out of college. You've caught me in one of my occasional lulls in clientele, however, so I'm happy to say that not only are you my first client from the entertainment industry, but you're also one of the few currently soliciting my services! That means I'll be readily available to help you with whatever it is that you might need, whenever you need it."

"And what do you think I'll need from you?" Damon asked, and although the tone of the question was not lost on Brian (who gave Damon yet another one of his menacing looks), Harold himself was unaffected. He either didn't catch Damon's meaning, or he refused to let it get to him. Instead, he answered very plainly.

"Honestly," Harold said, "I can't tell you what you need. That's part of the process. It's your thing, man. We can goal set, for which I've come up with a few ways we might do that, at least until you realize your own personal vision for yourself. Likewise, I'm a pretty big fan of list-making, so we'll probably start from there, but once you understand where you're at in life, and more importantly, where you *want* to be, it'll be my job to provide whatever resources I can to get you there. I try to work simply, and I like to work at your pace. We can meet as often as you'd like, or as little. It's completely up to you."

"He'll meet with you as often as the label says he needs to, Mr. Dancy," Brian said, asserting himself into the conversation with a forceful tone. Harold turned to Brian and gave him the same smile that he'd given Damon, as if nothing in the world could bother him.

"Why don't we talk about a schedule in my office privately, Mr. Squires?" Harold asked, and then turned to Damon. "You look comfortable on the couch. You don't mind waiting out here, do you?"

Damon sneered at him and said, "Run along with Brian and plot out our playdates."

In spite of the fact that Damon was intentionally being condescending, Harold never flinched nor even addressed it. He simply got up and politely invited Brian to his office, closing the door behind him.

"That makes him a doormat," Damon thought out loud from his position on the couch and began to examine the walls around him. For whatever Harold lacked in fashion sense, he made up for in décor. It was a smart looking living space and very modern, with elegantly framed art prints that suggested a cultured mind, and a few ceramic pieces that accentuated taste. A few photographs stood out on one wall, and Damon got up to look more closely at them. One of them featured a group of students in graduation robes, though he could not spot Harold in the crowd. A second featured an attractive and fit young woman in a softball uniform, with her hair done up in a high ponytail that made Damon arch one eyebrow in thought. The third picture, however, made him smile, and it was a devious smile.

"So he's a *married* doormat!"

If Harold Dancy wanted to be the new wrangler in his rock music career, Damon Alton could always try some wrangling of his own.

***

As Nancy drove out of the parking lot, her head was in a rush of varying thoughts. Within the static and white noise sounding off in her brain, one phrase kept cutting through the cacophony, over and over again:

Lady's choice.

Duke Franklin still shook up from being dressed down, readily welcomed Nancy's half-day with the measure of relief that can only come from a pissed-off boss leaving for the rest of the afternoon. The fact that Duke thought it had anything to do with him was fine by Nancy, as it meant he'd be doubly careful not to make any mistakes in her absence. Besides, they'd had a run on rentals just the day before. There were only a few cars left from their fleet that were still available, and therefore not much to manage or screw up. It was an ideal time for Nancy to take off and get her head straight.

Straight, however, was not the path that she found herself on. It was crooked and corkscrewed with varying degrees of doubt and hesitation, and as she left work to make her way toward home, she found herself losing certainty with every passing mile. Her initial thought was to leave Harold, but now she didn't know. What did she *really* want, and what was she prepared to do to get it? Was there a difference between comfort and happiness? She found that as she meditated on the subject more and more, she wavered on her feelings toward Harold. He wasn't a bad person, or even a bad husband. Was he a bad lover? She didn't know. She'd only been with him, and he'd only been with her, which was a fact that made her feel pathetic when she concentrated on it.

She used to be Nancy "All Star" Allister! She was beautiful, wasn't she? She was still fit and athletic, right? It's not as though she'd lost a step. It was ridiculous to think that she hadn't experienced a whole variety of lovers. She could've had anybody, but a youthful anger toward men in general and their cowardice when faced with a confident woman had caused her to prematurely settle. She was convinced of that. Harold, who on dumb luck had asked her out and said the right thing at the right time, probably had no idea that was the reality of his situation and their marriage. He might be happy with how things were going, but she wasn't. Like some stunning revelation, she'd only just become keenly aware that she no longer felt like herself. It was as if she was coming out of some great fog, and she needed to find her footing. She needed to prove that she hadn't really lost a step. Without any more thought, she rerouted herself and doubled-back toward the local mall, near the rental agency, but not to head back to work. Instead, Nancy stopped by Playtime Sports, and started browsing.

A small bright bell rang when she walked in, summoning an enthusiastic young woman who came to assist her. After a few brief questions and forty-five minutes of browsing, Nancy heard the same bell sound again as she exited with an armful of athletic apparel, a new set of sneakers, and a large barrel softball bat that she would've killed for in high school. She didn't bother putting anything in the trunk of her car, and instead loaded everything into the front passenger seat. From there, she headed over to a staple of her youth that she had not visited in some time.

Herlihy's Batting Cages still looked like it had when Nancy was a senior in high school, but its owner had aged notably in the passing years. Still, when Nancy walked through the door, Ray Herlihy lit up with joy, and in spite of the crow's feet that had settled around his eyes and the fact that his telltale shoulder length hair had gone grey in her long absence, his smile was still as youthful as it had been well over a decade ago.

"And what to my wandering eye should appear, but the door full of Nancy in softball gear!" Ray belted from behind his counter, just as he always had when she'd appear in the winter months, his play on the holiday classic.

"It's not even Christmas, Ray," Nancy protested, unable to conceal her own smile. She felt a spark of happiness as she stepped inside, as well as a sense of the old control she'd once felt. When she approached the counter, she was surprised by the way she now perceived Ray, who long ago was just the friendly batting cage manager she dealt with. Now, he was more like an old pal she was getting to reunite with.

"But it must be Christmas if you're swinging by," Ray said with an unfaltering smile. "How else would you explain a gift like this? It's not even my birthday!"

"Stop," Nancy said, blushing lightly at the bubbly way he was presenting himself. "You probably say that to all of the has-beens that walk through here."

"Oh, please!" Ray protested. "Nancy Allister a has-been? I doubt that very much. Once a state champion, always a state champion, and for you, that's *two* state championships! Just to think that this old business might've helped to get you there..." He looked around wistfully at his own little sports complex, a shrine to the games of Baseball and Softball. Technology had advanced in the years since Nancy graduated, and even the register that Ray now used was connected to the internet, able to process any type of credit card, gift card, or banking card that was out there. The cages, however, were exactly the same. The pitching machines were well-oiled, fine-tuned, and still throwing at the speed advertised. From their elementary years and up until the moments before college, kids still showed up to the cages to get in their swings. No one else ever *caught* inside them, however. Nancy was the only one he'd ever allowed to do that.

Nancy was also feeling somewhat wistful, though not at the thought of the cages themselves, but at the way Ray addressed her. It was the first time in a very long time that someone had called her by her maiden name, and that initial spark of happiness she was feeling inside grew a bit larger at the sound of it. It had such a nice ring to it... Nancy Allister. She remembered the musical quality of it, and how close *Allister* was to being *All Star*.

"So what brings you back my way?" Ray asked. "You've got a bat in your hands! That's not a sight I'm used to seeing from you."

"Well, Charlotte Smith isn't around anymore to throw to me," Nancy replied, "and it's been over a decade since I've swung a bat. I just got an itch and felt like I wanted to see if I had any of the old timing."

"I guess you're at the age now," Ray mused. "I've seen it a few times now that I'm getting a little long in the tooth."

"What do you mean?" Nancy asked, and Ray laughed at the change in her expression.

"Don't look so worried!" he said. "I just mean that the really serious athletes I've seen come through here at one time or another, much like yourself, make their way back later in life, wondering if they've still got it."

"Is that what you think this is?" Nancy asked.

Ray shrugged his shoulders at her. "If it's a social call, I'm always up for some socializing," he answered. "Though not much has changed since you've been gone, if you were looking for updates. Your old high school has made it to the playoffs a few times, but no one in the county has seen a title run since the last time you girls won a second championship. Do you still keep up with any of your old teammates?"

Nancy frowned at the thought of it and answered soberly, "No, not really. Nothing beyond seeing updates online, anyway." It was true that she still had some connection to her old high school teammates, but in a way that was personally impersonal. She saw the wedding pictures and baby photos that they'd sometimes post, and she'd read their online musings on the state of politics or entertainment, but she was never one to react or reply, though she didn't know why. It just felt like she was no longer part of their lives anymore, but a relic that belonged to their team's former glory. No one bothered organizing reunions - not for the team and not even for their graduating class. Thanks to social media, everyone already knew what had become of everyone else, or at least the people they cared to keep tabs on. The internet effectively killed the ten-year reunion.

"That's typically the way things go," Ray mused. "People grow up, get married, have kids, and start the next chapter. Nobody ever means to drift apart, but it happens anyway. It's just a fact of life. That doesn't mean it has to stay that way, though. Look at you now, giving ol' Ray a visit!"

"That's true," Nancy said, and Ray's words sunk in to a greater degree than he probably realized. It wasn't so much that she'd gone to visit the batting cage, but that she took the first step toward something different, even if it was toward the familiar. Things didn't have to stay the same way. She could change the nature of things. She could change things with Harold.

"Do you have a cage open?" Nancy asked suddenly, gripping her new bat with a firm, confident grasp.

Ray's smile broadened. "For you? I'll give you an hour on the house. We'll see if you can still swing a bat after that, old-timer."

Nancy laughed a small, high laugh, but was good-natured about the exchange. She'd never been called an old-timer before, and coming from Ray Herlihy, it was quite funny. When she got into the cage, however, she gradually understood what he meant. Her timing was off, and for the first fifteen minutes, she missed nearly every ball. The ones that she did hit came off the bat poorly and sent a shockwave into her hands that stung her palms. Still, she kept on, until finally catching a pitch just right. The old follow through came out, and she felt the power in her legs and the torque of her turning hips come through the barrel of her bat, catching the meat of the ball just as it was crossing the plate. Feeling the satisfying pop that sent the ball in a high arc toward what would've been center field sent a thrill through her body, and she felt something like her old self. Gradually, she found her rhythm, and by the end of an hour, she found Ray wasn't wrong at all. Sweat poured down her body and her arms were close to dead, but she could sense a confidence from her youth that had been missing from her for some time. She thanked Ray for the free hour and told him the next time she came to take swings, she'd insist on paying full price.

There was no dread inside her on the ride home, and she felt nothing like when she'd initially taken off. She was confident and sure of herself. She'd go home, sit down with Harold, and they'd have an honest conversation. He'd understand, because he was Harold, and understanding was what Harold did best. It's one of the largest reasons that the marriage worked the way it did, and once they came to a new understanding, she'd plot her next move. Perhaps she'd start by finding a new job, or maybe hold onto to her job for the present while she looked for a softball team. She could still be competitive, and she could meet new people. She could have a new lease on life. The world was full of possibility.

Nancy parked the car and made her way into the complex's lobby, considering each new possibility in her mind. On the elevator, she started planning how she'd approach the subject, and by the time she got to the third floor and started walking down the hall toward number thirty-six, she'd planned for all of Harold's reactions and how she'd let him down gently, because he deserved that much. Within the rapid movements of her mind, she'd considered everything she could, but as the key slid into the lock and she turned the handle to her front door, Nancy was confronted by a sight that she had no way of preparing for.

Damon Alton was standing in her living room, staring at her wedding picture.

***

Rock fame was a great teacher of many things if you happened to survive at the top of the heap for longer than a single hit. For example, Damon's fame forced him to develop an acute awareness of what other people's perceptions were of him, though admittedly he only learned this trait after the sycophants had sucked him dry and The Common Miscreants were disbanded. Still, experience was the ultimate teacher, and it was nice to be able to sniff out the likes of a Brian Squires and peg him for the self-righteous prick that he was, while also remaining insusceptible to the nice-guy routine of a Harold Dancy type, who probably wanted to exploit the perception of friendship for his own personal gain. Damon disliked guys like Brian Squires, but at least they were overt about the type of person they were. Guys like Harold were to be loathed and dealt with, because nobody in the music industry was ever really your friend, and how dare someone even try to pretend to be. Damon knew the type all too well and had them pegged by their body language, right down to the posture in their everyman way of pulling up a chair to talk.

Body language was a style of communication he felt he'd mastered in his time spent traveling the world. He knew what people wanted the minute they saw him, and so it was no surprise to Damon when Nancy opened the front door and then stood in the doorway, stunned by his presence. Sure, he'd looked at Harold's wedding photo, saw the image of Nancy, and had his thought:

Piss me off enough, Harold, and I will tempt your wife like no man has ever done before.

But that was always the way it was. Sleeping with married women was more fun than sleeping with those that were single, and in a lot of cases, Damon could feel himself getting turned on just by the sight of a beautiful woman wearing a wedding ring. Of course he was always going to make a move on Harold's wife, if only as a means of shooting Harold the bird for ever thinking he could get anything over on him. The way that Nancy was regarding him from the doorway, however, put a better spin on things. This was a different dynamic, and one that almost immediately made her a sure thing.

"Did you used to have a poster of me on your bedroom wall?" he asked her.

"Excuse me?" Nancy asked, and her voice was surprisingly calm considering the odd state of shock she was feeling, seeing the lead singer of The Common Miscreants in her living room.

"You have that look," Damon said, turning his shoulders toward her and looking her over up and down. "You look like the girls that see me for the first time and realize I'm not just a poster, but a real person. It's embarrassing, really."

"I'm so sorry!" Nancy apologized, still standing in the doorway and unsure of why she felt the need to say sorry in the first place. She then shook her head, as if to admonish herself for not acting like a grown woman walking into her own home. She took one more step inside, and then said, "So you're Damon Alton? Like, *the* Damon Alton?"

"In the flesh, yes," he answered, and he smiled at her in a way that made something start to tingle.

"Why are you in my living room?" she asked, and the question came off as one of real curiosity, and not an accusation of any kind. Before Damon could answer, however, the door to Harold's office opened. First came out a stern-looking chubby guy she'd never seen before, and then her husband Harold, who appeared much happier.

"Nance!" he exclaimed, "You're home early!" He then looked her over and noticed what she was wearing. "I didn't know you started going to the gym, honey! Good for you."

"Harold," Nancy said, ignoring the gym remark and getting right to the heart of things, "what's Damon Alton doing in our living room?"

"Damon's my newest client! Can you believe it?" Harold exclaimed, thrilled with himself. "I told you I didn't price myself out of the market," he added, and it was a comment that made Nancy blush, though she wasn't sure why.

"Harold and I are nearly finished, Mrs. Dancy," the chubby man said. "I hope he isn't giving you any trouble," and he cast a weary glance toward Damon, which made the pop star roll his eyes toward the back of his head.

"Don't be ridiculous, Brian," Damon said, "She only just arrived. I haven't had a chance to misbehave."

Nancy could've giggled at his comment but kept herself in check. An overwhelming giddiness was coming over her, and it was almost too much. First the trip to the batting cages and now Damon Alton standing right in front of her, it was like the ghosts of teenage past had all come to visit, but for what purpose?

Harold carried on, unaware of any tension within his wife. "We're nearly finished with scheduling, Damon. I just need to grab my cell phone to make sure the calendar is syncing up properly. We should be done with the boring stuff in about fifteen minutes."

"Take your time, Harold," Damon said, and his eyes flashed over toward Nancy in a way that made her suddenly feel flushed. Harold saw the look but didn't read into it the way he could have.

"Nancy," he asked, picking up his phone off the coffee table in front of the couch, "you don't mind keeping Damon company while we finish up, do you? It won't take us too long."

"Take your time," Nancy echoed, and her husband smiled at her sweetly, before ushering in the chubby man, Brian, back into his office. Damon gave her another mysterious grin and then quietly went back over to the couch, sitting toward the end. Unsure if it was an invitation to sit with him, Nancy balked, and asked, "Would you like anything to drink? I think we have some beer in the fridge..."

"Some company would be just fine," Damon replied, and he patted the couch cushion next to him. "I'm still curious to know."

"Curious to know what?" Nancy asked, hesitantly sitting on the couch, and only at the furthest end to ensure that the maximum amount of space was between the two of them.

"Well, you never answered my question," Damon said. "Did you used to have a poster of me on your bedroom wall? I got the impression that the answer was yes, but you never confirmed anything."

"I mean, yeah, of course I did," Nancy replied, "but who didn't? The Common Miscreants were the biggest band you could listen to at the time..."

Her words fell short and she was almost certain that she'd just insulted the man sitting opposite of her by using the past-tense. Damon's grin didn't fade, though, and instead he playfully asked, "Which one was it? Was it one of the one's during Erin's tuxedo phase? Maybe the one where I'm in the middle, and Jenna and Erin are on either side of me?"

"Actually," Nancy clarified, "it was one that was just you, singing into a microphone while you're playing your guitar." She awkwardly pantomimed the pose, then suddenly became self-conscious and folded her arms over her chest. Damon's smile broadened.

"That was one of our top selling pieces of merchandise," he said, and right then he knew that as a young woman, Nancy must've looked at that poster in the same way a lot of young women had looked at it. He was well aware of the poster's sexual appeal, and now he was betting that Nancy was one of those girls who had stared at it nightly, at least for a period of time. In that moment, there was no doubt: Nancy had become a conquest.

Coincidentally, Nancy was exploring similar thoughts. It was all too perfect; getting back into a batting cage and then arriving home just in time to see her girlhood crush, now sitting across from her to enjoy some idle conversation. Moreover, she was certain he was flirting with her, and that was bewildering in and of itself. At that moment, she became distinctly aware of a sensation, deep within her, and it was one that she hadn't quite experienced before, at least not to this degree. She was *lustful*. She wanted Damon Alton, wanted to win him over, ravish him, and feel triumphant about it.

And then another thought came to her, and if guilt entered her mind, she buried it as quickly as she could. She'd initially left work early to talk to Harold so that they could come to an understanding about their marriage, or what was left of it, but this put a wrinkle in things. To want Damon Alton meant needing access to him, and that required Nancy to maintain the status quo. If it was unfair to do that to Harold, a man who'd never been terrible to her, whose only crime was that he simply wasn't the one for her, then she'd just have to be unfair.

For the first time since her father's death, she felt something like excitement, and she needed to capitalize on it. She needed to seize this moment, and she needed it to be in the form of the man whose poster had once been over her bed. She needed passion in her life. She needed Damon Alton.

Nancy needed a conquest.

Chapter Five

Harold Needs a Conquest (A Story About Now)

Harold left the hospital with Damon and was emphatic about going home, but Damon thought it was a terrible idea.

"It's probably still a mess!" he countered, trying hard to keep an eye on the road while giving Harold a meaningful look. "Stay with me for a few days, at least until we get a clean-up crew and a carpenter in there to set everything right."

"I appreciate that you want to do that for me," Harold demurred, "but it's been a weird couple of days, and I think I just want some space to clear my head a bit..."

Damon gave him a snort and turned his full attention to the highway. "A weird couple of days?" he grumbled. "More like a weird couple of months, or a weird year in general."

Harold digested Damon's retort, but didn't argue anything. He wasn't wrong. Strange was an understatement in this instance, and that was precisely why he needed the time to clear his head and think, though there were other issues to handle. At the forefront of his mind was the suicide note that was somewhere in the debris of his living room. The fact that it wasn't brought in as evidence to destroy Harold's auto-erotic asphyxiation story meant that no one had picked it up. Harold couldn't help but feel anxious about where it was, and in what state he'd find it in. Strange forces were at play...

Or maybe there wasn't anything at play at all. It wasn't lost on him that having a hallucination of Nancy could've been part of some massive psychotic breakdown, toward which Harold had been careening for some time now. That wasn't how it felt, though. Psychotic episodes were supposed to feel *crazy*, weren't they? Aside from his suicidal behavior and seeing the ghost of his dead wife, Harold felt perfectly normal, and anyhow there were things the insanity plea couldn't explain away.

"It's not like I glued my shoes to the chair," Harold mumbled aloud, unaware that he was thinking audibly.

"What about glue?" Damon asked, and Harold realized his faux pas, thankful that the rasp in his voice was still obscuring his speech.

"I was talking about needing glue for the chair," he answered a bit louder, hoping that would suffice. Damon gave a short laugh at that, and Harold felt relieved.

"A *new* chair is the only thing that will fix that. I don't think you realize what a shit state your place is in right now. I'm telling you, you're going to have to crash at my place for a little while. God only knows what kind of dust you still have hanging in the air! I certainly inhaled more than I would've liked before we left for the hospital, and you're the one with the throat in a sorry state. A bunch of nastiness is the last thing you need to be breathing in."

"Fine," Harold conceded, "just let me get a few things. I'll be in and out. You won't even have to get out of the car."

"Fair enough," Damon said. A victorious grin emerged over his face, and he added humorously, "Rooming with Harold Dancy! It'll be the college dorm experience I never got to have..."

Harold wanted to tell him it wouldn't be much to look forward to, but his throat was getting sore again, so he left it at that. If he could talk more, he'd tell him that the college experience wasn't everything it was made out to be. Although Harold had roomed freshman year with his best friend from high school, Jack Edwards, they hardly saw much of each other.

Their schedules never lined up, so it always felt like they were just missing each other. Toward the end of their time together, Jack really got into playing Ultimate Frisbee on campus, which was yet another activity Harold could never make work, despite Jack telling him all about the fun he was missing. In the end, Jack decided to take on a member of that club as a new roommate for his sophomore year, which was just as well for Harold. He'd opted into the Resident Assistant program to save on boarding fees and ended up having his own dorm for the last three years of school. The two had meant to stay close to each other, but they inevitably went their separate ways. After all, when Harold wasn't busy with classes or his RA duties, he mostly spent his time with Nancy; attending functions with her, going to her games, or just helping her with her own stuff, like homework and laundry. He'd been a good boyfriend; very dutiful, and that made for a seamless transition into good husband.

At any rate, there wasn't much to say about his college years, and therefore better to let Damon imagine whatever he wanted to, though that was a pretty laughable thought, too. Damon Alton had travelled around the globe and experienced nearly everything that life could have to offer, but here he was pining for the college experience he never got to have. Did *rock stars* even believe that the grass was greener on the other side?

I never thought about the grass being greener, Harold thought, and without warning his mood began to darken. *I was pretty happy with the patch of grass I had...*

After that thought, Harold tried to clear his mind and not dwell on anything by focusing on the view from the passenger side window. Within minutes, he'd dozed off, and didn't wake up until Damon gave him a nudge, telling him that they'd just arrived at the apartment complex.

"We can make another trip later," Damon told him. "Just grab what you think you'll need for the night. Quick change of clothes and a toothbrush. I've got plenty of shampoo and toothpaste and stuff."

"I told you I'd be in and out," Harold reassured him. "Keep the car running."

He got out and made his way into the building and, in the lobby, he decided on taking the stairs instead of the elevator, hoping the rigor of each flight would chip away at the emptiness he was experiencing. He wanted to feel something strong and meaningful, but all he felt was drained and numb. By the time he reached his floor and got to the end of his hallway, he wasn't even bothered by the slightest bit of foreboding: not at the thought that he was getting ready to walk into the room where he'd almost killed himself, nor at the thought that this was where he'd seen the ghost of his wife. Instead, he just opened the front door like it was any other day of the week, closed it behind him, and slowly walked into the rubble of his living room, operating on a one-track mind.

The apartment hadn't been touched since the ambulance's departure, and Damon wasn't wrong about the dust hanging in the room. Without thinking about it, Harold slipped the front of his shirt over his mouth and nose to defend his throat against the jagged air. The apartment had taken on a musky odor, and it felt less like home than it ever had before. It seemed as though the last traces of his happy life with Nancy, that thing that he'd always been trying to get back to with every attempt on his life, had finally been snuffed out by each particle of dust roaming around from the broken beam he'd tried to hang himself on. Now, with its naked walls, destroyed furniture, and bedlam covered flooring, the apartment felt like a cavernous room, devoid of life.

That feeling of nothingness gave Harold a sudden surge of determination, and he shook loose the morose quality that had hung about him since leaving the hospital. He began to fervently sift through the rubble, sweeping aside splintered wood, broken bits of chair, and stray wisps of rope, until finally, underneath the remains of the coffee table, he found his note, just as neat as when it was first written. The blue ink stood out magnificently against the stark white paper, unstained by even the slightest hint of dust, and he read back his words, chuckling at the part about his security deposit.

He took in the scope of destruction around him, and he recognized in that instant that this was his ground zero, the exact spot where he'd tried to take his life for the fourth time. Never mind any cigarette burns in the carpet, and never mind the security deposit. If his landlord had gotten word about the incident, which must've been the case by now, he was more likely to be evicted than anything else. Judging by how he felt walking into the place, that maybe wouldn't be the worst outcome in the world.

Harold folded the note, placed it in his back pocket, and went into the bedroom for his socks, underwear, shirts, and slacks. He stopped by the bathroom for his toothbrush, then left the apartment, without looking back. When he got to Damon's car, he placed his belongings on his lap and buckled his seatbelt.

"Ready for the roommate experience?" Harold asked him.

Damon smiled at that. "I'm ready for a very mild experience, Harold. No wild man stunts while you're at my place, okay? Rest and relaxation are going to do you a world of good and get your mind nice and clear. Who knows? In a couple of days, we might get productive and start hitting the list again."

Harold grinned at Damon's upbeat urge for productivity, and it made him think about what Father Ackley has said to him in the hospital. Sure, attacking Damon's list and getting back on the job could be something worth doing, but at the same time it wouldn't be enough. *Life's for the alive.* If Nancy wanted him to keep living, then he had to move forward in the service of life itself, and he knew just where he wanted to start.

✳✳✳

The Caring Hands Kitchen was a small charity in Harold's hometown. In his younger years, he'd made the occasional trip to the kitchen to complete high school service hours, which had

92

been a requirement for graduating in the honors program. In those days, he'd been positioned on the serving line with a ladle and a pot of chili, doling out portions to the homeless, the destitute, and the drug addicts that often populated the kitchen's late-lunch/early-dinner rush. Returning years later, he found that not much had changed. The same types of people crowded the cafeteria area, and the same high school aged faces were behind the counter, with ladles of chili or pieces of cornbread, serving the less fortunate while trying not to show how uncomfortable they were by the sight of toothless grins, unkempt facial hair, and clothing that smelled anything but fresh.

When Harold dropped by to volunteer his services, that's exactly where he thought he'd be positioned; alongside the younger kids, dishing out food. He was almost looking forward to it, too, hoping that his spirits might be sobered by the plight of others standing in line, grateful for whatever food they received. The serving jobs were well-covered, however, and when Harold approached the manager to offer his time, he was somewhat surprised and dismayed to be put in the back of the kitchen on dish duty. He even asked if the manager was sure there wasn't somewhere else where he could be of greater assistance, but the manager assured him that his time would best be spent making certain there were enough clean spoons and dishes for everyone to feel welcome. When it was framed like that, Harold couldn't argue, so he stationed himself in front of a sink full of dishes, with rubber gloves, hot soapy water, and the thickest steel wool he'd ever seen.

A few grandmotherly ladies milled about the back of the kitchen alongside him, baking more cornbread, heating chili, and bringing back the used dishes to add to Harold's stock. They exchanged pleasantries with him whenever they did so, but they mostly kept to each other, speaking with the familiarity of regular volunteers, making Harold feel more like a benevolent tourist than anything else. He dwelled on that thought while scrubbing at a particularly stubborn spot of burnt chili at the bottom of a large pot; He slipped into a meditative state. Father Ackley's advice was having an immediate impact, and Harold felt himself entertaining the notion that his suicidal tendencies in the name of love maybe weren't the most noble and worthy actions after all. There were lots of things he could be doing in the name of love, including dish-duty and making chili on a frequent enough basis that the old ladies in the back might soon know him on a first-name basis, too. Just as Harold was zeroing in on that conclusion, wondering if Damon Alton's profile wasn't so high that he might be able to join him, the back door of the kitchen swung open, and a flurry of activity broke his concentration altogether.

A young woman came rushing in with the largest pot of chili he'd seen yet, dropping its weight on the counter with a heavy thud. She then threw open a drawer to grab an apron, quickly said hi to the ladies, and dashed out to the serving line with the rest of the high schoolers. A second later, on the heels of the young lady's entrance, but coming in at a much more even-keeled pace while holding a tray of brownies, was none other than Nurse Shawnee from Harold's hospital visit. It had been over three weeks since that incident, though, and Harold wasn't sure if she'd remember him or not. When she put the brownies on the countertop and made the rounds with the ladies, however, her eyes fell on Harold at the kitchen sink and she greeted him with a warm, familiar smile.

"Harold, right?" she said in a pleasant, chipper voice. It was a greeting that almost made him blush, and it was a curious feeling that he had not expected to have upon hearing another woman call out his name. "What are you doing here?" she asked, catching him off guard.

"I, uh, used to volunteer here, way back in the day," he stammered, "for a high school credit thing. I haven't been back since then, so I thought it might be nice to come by and see if they needed any help. Kind of a lark, I guess."

"Well that's great to hear!" she said brightly, then added, "And your voice has healed so nicely! I don't think I ever got to really hear you speak when we first met. Do you have anyone helping you on dishes?"

Before Harold could answer, she was standing next to him, rag in hand and drying the dishes that were already dripping on the rack. "It just makes things faster," she said, smiling at him again in a way that gave him a slight pang in his chest. Harold kept his head down, obliterated by the alien feeling his hospital nurse evoked just by standing next to him and drying the dishes he washed. It was as though they were some old married couple, and the thought made him feel like he should say something, though he had no idea of what he could talk about. Wasn't it weird for her to run into the patients that she'd treated? It didn't seem so, judging by how quickly she jumped into the work, standing beside him now without the slightest hesitation. It could've been she was just very confident, or more probably that he was insecure and overanalyzing. Regardless, he couldn't just work by her in silence, and he fought his doubt to put together some semblance of conversation.

"So, Nurse Shawnee..." Harold began.

"Oh, please!" she replied. "Just call me Shawnee. I'm only 'Nurse Shawnee' when I'm in the hospital."

"Fair enough," Harold answered, and felt a slight sense of relief at her invitation to be casual. "So, Shawnee... what are you doing here?"

"The young lady that came rushing in before me is my niece, and I'm her ride today. She's here doing service hours for her high school too, just like you had to, I guess. I never knew public schools even required things like that! I graduated from a small private school in Pennsylvania, so we mainly had to do fundraisers and bake sales to try to keep the tuition cost down. Anyway, my sister and her husband both work odd hours, so I've been lending them a hand whenever I'm able, which has mainly consisted of carting my niece to and from soup kitchen duty."

"So do you come here often, then?" Harold asked, and Shawnee gave him that same warm smile.

"Not really," she said. "This is really only the third time I've had to bring her, and I've consistently been late, though in my defense, it's not easy to get a sixteen-year-old girl out the door, especially when she takes as long as she does to get ready just to go serve bowls of chili. She wants to tell me that she's taking pride in her personal appearance, but I know better, because every time we get here, she stands next to the same boy, like he's holding a serving spot there for her. Sometimes, I've caught them making eyes at each other too. It's cute, but the taking forever to get ready part is getting annoying. The old ladies in the kitchen want to give me a look every time we walk in because we can't get here when they want us to..."

"So is that why you jumped in to do dishes so quickly?" Harold asked, and Shawnee's smile widened.

"That's why," she admitted.

"And here I thought it was because I was a patient of yours," Harold added without thinking about how it might sound, and his cheeks reddened when it connected with him how it could be perceived. He hoped she wouldn't think he was being flirtatious, and to his relief, she made no indication if she did.

"Honestly, I'm just happy I got your name right," Shawnee replied, "though to your credit, you were a pretty memorable patient."

Harold cast his eyes downward at this and really focused on the bowl he'd already scrubbed clean two minutes ago. "Memorable because of the way I wound up coming into the hospital?" he asked, bashfully. Shawnee gently grabbed the bowl from his hands, brushing her shoulder and hip against his.

"Not at all," she said, lowering her voice and taking on an air of confidentiality. "Look, when you've been in the game as long as I have, you become sort of desensitized to what others would consider outrageous. I've seen all kinds of..." She paused briefly just then, as if looking for the right phrase, and when it seemed she'd found what she wanted to say, she continued on in an even lower tone. "...*sexual accidents*. Hell, in just my first year, you would've been shocked at the number of cases that came through the hospital. That's not to say your write-up wasn't adventurous, though. It's just not the *most* adventurous thing I've ever seen."

Harold wasn't sure if he should feel relieved or more embarrassed by Shawnee's candor, and admitted as much. "I don't know... If I were in your position, I think I'd have an uneasy time standing next to any guy who ends up in the emergency room for what I came in for..."

"Oh, please," she replied, and shifted her weight back to the drying rack, allowing her voice to resume a normal volume. "If you'd been here last week, you would've seen two guys arguing over a set of teeth from the lost and found area, and neither one of them looked like they could afford dentures. We're all human beings, Harold. None of us are fit to judge another. That's my big take-away from nursing, anyway."

Harold went quietly back to washing his dishes, grabbing a fistful of spoons from the bottom of the sink to spray down with hot water. He thought about what she said for a moment, and when he handed the silverware over to her, he asked, "So if my case wasn't as remarkable as I thought it was, why was I a memorable patient?"

"That's easy," Shawnee said, as if it were already obvious. "It's not every day you see a patient accompanied by a famous rock star. The whole break room was buzzing about Damon Alton being in our wing, and I was the lucky nurse that got to talk to him! I tried my best to play it cool..."

"You did a good job," Harold told her. "If you were excited to meet him, you were very professional about it."

"Well, you develop a pretty good poker face when you get into nursing, but there's no doubt I was giddy on the inside. He was *it* when I was a teenager, you know? The music was alright, and I still even listen to some of his CDs when I clean the house, but he just had that look that could turn you to jelly."

"Yeah, my wife was a fan, too," Harold said, unable to catch himself before the words left his lips. He cringed slightly, wondering if Shawnee would pick up on the reference to his wife and worried that it would lead to the awkward and ultimately depressing conversation that all widowers inevitably engage in. She didn't, though. At least, not in the way that he thought she might.

All she said was, "You'd be hard pressed to find any woman of a certain age who didn't geek out over Damon Alton at one time or another." Then she looked over him curiously and asked, "How do you know him, anyway?"

"Oh, he's a client of mine," Harold answered. "I started out as his life coach, but then moved closer to what you might consider a manager position, I guess? Basically, he liked where my head was at more than his *old* manager, Brian, so he fired him and expanded my role. He still gets decent earnings off royalties from The Common Miscreants. Likewise, his cousin Jenna had set everyone up with a good financial accountant, so he's done well with investments. Basically, he can afford to keep me on his payroll, so he's labeled me a *collaborator*, as he likes to call it."

Shawnee looked at him with piqued interest. "Collaborating musically?"

"Yeah," Harold replied. "He's taken on some of my old poems to turn into songs, and he's been fiddling with some musical arrangements for a while..."

They talked like this for the duration of their time together, and it felt really nice. When he came back the next week to do some more volunteer work, he was happy to see Shawnee already at the sink, saving a spot for him. They continued on in this way, slowly getting to know each other, and all the while, Shawnee was becoming more and more endearing to him. When they'd made it to their fourth consecutive weekend of being paired up at the dishes station, Harold emboldened himself, ready to approach unfamiliar territory.

"So, do you remember when I said that Damon Alton was working on some new material?" he asked her as she scrubbed the dried remains of cornbread from a pie tin. They'd taken to switching who'd be on scrubbing duty and who would rinse and dry each weekend, and this time it was Shawnee's turn to wear the gloves and scrape food away under the hot stream of water.

"Of course," she said, looking up from her work expectantly. "Why?"

"Well, he's going to try out some of the new songs out tonight in the city over at the 10:30 Club," Harold answered.

"Damon Alton's playing a show *tonight*?" Shawnee asked, and Harold was caught off guard by the excitement in her voice. Though he was as aware of it as he could be, the fascination that people, mainly older women, still had with Damon Alton would always be a foreign idea to Harold. It was probably one of the reasons why they worked so well together. To Harold, Damon was a normal guy, and in turn, Harold was one of the few that honestly treated him that way. Naturally, when people had a strong reaction to Damon, it always surprised him. He often had to remind himself that Damon was a global commodity, still precious to a great number of people.

"Well, it's not an *official* show," Harold said, and now he made to brush a shoulder and elbow toward Shawnee and speak in hushed tones, much like she had done on their first weekend of dish duty. Her round hips and the softness of her arm contained an undeniable warmth. When he made contact with her, Harold once again felt a giddiness within his chest. He suddenly felt younger, and without thinking about it, he found himself asking her out on a date. "It's kind of a secret thing, just to test run some of the new material. A lot of professionals will do that with smaller venues before trying out bigger stages. If you're free tonight, you could meet me at the show as my plus one."

He didn't make the offer with the sort of smug voice that others use when they brag about knowing someone famous, but with the earnestness that was just who he was. There were no unspoken strings attached to the offer, and no unfair expectations hanging over her. Shawnee looked him over, smiled again, and said, "That would be great."

"Wonderful!" Harold said, "The doors open at 7:30 and the show starts not long after that, if you're into seeing some good local opening acts."

"I'll see you at 7:30," Shawnee replied, and the two continued to work on dishes together, until the conversation naturally settled on how Shawnee's shifts at the hospital had been lately, and how her niece was no longer dating the boy she used to serve cornbread with.

***

When Harold returned from The Caring Hands Kitchen, Damon was sitting in a reclining chair with an acoustic bass in his lap. He strummed some simple note progressions to sing over, followed by a few improvisational fills for the spaces where there were no lyrics, and when Harold walked into the room, he stopped and sat up with a momentary look of concern.

"Did band practice just end?" Harold asked.

"Yeah," Damon said, "The guys just left. Where've you been? I wanted you here to listen to your lyrics and be available in case we needed to make any changes."

"Sorry," Harold replied, "I was at the soup kitchen doing work."

"*Work*?" Damon snapped. "You *work* for me!"

Harold stared at him intently for a moment, choosing not to respond, and in that silence, Damon was allowed to reflect on the tone he'd just taken. When his expression changed, Harold very calmly asked him, "Are you done?"

"Yes, I'm done," Damon answered, his voice now lower. "Sorry, man. I'm just stressed out about the show. That was Old Damon trying to make a break for it. New Damon knows better."

As a policy, Harold never engaged with Damon in a negative fashion, and it was always up to Damon to change tack. If the overall goal was to eventually rebuild the connections to his former bandmates, he'd have to be able to participate in a conversation with them that wouldn't be derailed by petty emotions. Though he could still have his flare ups, Damon had come a long way since working with Harold.

"Thank you," Harold said, acknowledging Damon's self-correction. "You know I'd never talk down to *you*. I'm a fan for life when you're not talking down to *me*. Speaking of fans, by the way, I've spent the past few weeks working alongside one of yours at the soup kitchen."

"Oh really?" Damon asked, leaning forward in his chair. He was always intrigued by the prospect of hearing about his fans and was most captivated by these moments. "Tell me more!"

"Do you remember Nurse Shawnee from the hospital?" Harold said, taking a seat on the couch opposite of Damon.

Damon looked upward thoughtfully, going through a mental catalogue of female interactions. "Yes," he said after a moment. "Sort of shortish, dark skin, long hair, with blonde highlights, if I recall correctly. Not thin, but curvaceous, right? What the kids call *thick* these days? She had a really nice smile..."

"Wow, that is impressively specific," Harold said, "and fairly accurate."

Damon smiled, taking it for a compliment, and Harold pressed on. "So as I was saying, I ran into Shawnee a few weeks ago on my first day at Helping Hands. She's been helping her family out by giving her niece a ride to the kitchen so she can finish up her community service hours."

"Community service?" Damon interrupted. "Is she an inmate somewhere?"

"What?" Harold asked, confused. "No! Her niece is a sixteen-year-old. She's doing the community service hours for high school credit. Anyway, like I was saying, we've been talking to each other for the past few weeks, and I worked up the nerve to ask her if she wanted to come to the show tonight. I'm pretty sure she's going to meet me there!"

"Yes, Harold!" Damon responded, pumping a fist victoriously into the air. "This is exactly what you need, man, and now you've got it. A conquest!"

Harold was thrown by the end of Damon's excited statement. "What exactly do you think I need?"

"You know, a *conquest*, like in that old Patty Page tune," Damon explained, before getting lost in his own thought. "Jack White did a cover of that song for The White Stripes final album, and he totally nailed it in my opinion. You know I toured with him? Not for *that* record, of course, but their first one..."

"Sorry," Harold admitted, "but I'm not familiar with the song."

"Damn shame," Damon said. "I've got the album somewhere in my vinyl stacks. You should give it a listen. However, the point remains that I think you've had a pretty good stretch as Harold the Loner, and while I can appreciate that style more than anyone else, trust me, you're too good a guy for that look. You need to get back out there and mix it up with someone! Win them over with that same Harold Dancy charm that made me a believer, you know what I mean? In short, you need a conquest! Though, I must admit, I didn't peg you as a guy who'd ask out a sixteen-year-old..."

"What?" Harold sat up, stunned. "What makes you think I asked out a sixteen-year-old?"

"Well, that's what you said, isn't it?" Damon answered, confused by Harold's reaction.

"No," Harold protested, "I asked out Shawnee. The nurse, not the niece."

"Oh," Damon replied, "I guess she's a little closer to your age then, maybe even a bit older, isn't she?"

"Is that a cliché that rock stars are really into?" Harold asked, with a trace of disgust in his voice.

"No!" Damon said, defensively. "I mean, not like that." He then grew increasingly frustrated, feeling the need to explain himself more fully. "I'm coming from a state of arrested development! Those were your words, not mine, remember? Shut up and stop trying to judge me... *I'd* never date a sixteen-year-old, for God's sakes. If anything, I was telling *you* not to do it..."

"Are you sure?" Harold asked, now needling his friend, enjoying the rise he was getting out of him. "Because the tone sounded like..."

"Don't tell me about my tone, Harold," Damon snapped, reverting back to the old voice he used when Harold first walked into the room. "Enjoy your age-appropriate evening! I have a show to get ready for," he said, and he grabbed his bass guitar and marched back into his room, shutting the door behind him.

When the mirthful feeling of watching Damon storm off dissipated, Harold was left on the couch, thinking about what his friend had told him. Was Damon right? Did he need a conquest? Was this the sort of thing that he'd have to do if he ever wanted to move on from Nancy? Did he even *want* to move on from Nancy? Was that something he was now trying to do?

Harold didn't know the answer to any of these things. Certainly seeing the specter of his wife was a life changing moment, but in what way? Was it supposed to curb his suicidal ideation, or was it more than that? If life is for the alive, had the Universe set it up so that Harold would run into Shawnee? He wasn't sure. Going out with another woman felt like a betrayal to Nancy and their marriage. It didn't seem right. After all, would Nancy have done the same thing?

Chapter Six

Nancy's Betrayal (A Story About Then)

Though she didn't know it until her first sexual experience with Damon Alton, Nancy had never experienced a full orgasm before. That's not to say that she hadn't felt something with Harold, of course, but he was the only lover she'd ever had, and she honestly didn't know what she was missing. The best she could say about Harold, at least in the early years of their marriage, was that the sex never hurt, was mildly pleasurable, and she'd always felt a certain kind of thrill on the nights that she left Harold speechless. It felt like ownership, and spoke to her competitive nature, as if she was giving him something he could never get anywhere else. In terms of actual *feeling*, however, sex was never exciting with Harold, and after her father died, their love life effectively stopped. She never gave him any signals of interest, because she wasn't, and Harold never pushed the issue, because that wasn't in his nature.

Her first encounter with Damon in the living room did produce a feeling though, and it was *the* feeling. It made her bold, allowing her to carry on a flirtation that would lead to her first real climax... and it was everything. Just two things dampened the experience, leaving her with trace amounts of sadness and anxiety beneath all that euphoria.

The first was the realization that this *really* had been her first orgasm, and she was already in her mid-thirties. When was she supposed to have experienced such a thing? Did they have a normal age for that, like freshman year of college, or was it supposed to be earlier? Shouldn't it have been with someone more meaningful to her? Was it okay that it was with a man who wasn't her husband? What about Damon? Couldn't he leave as quickly as he arrived, and if so, what would she do then?

Also mingled with the sadness of this being her first truly pleasurable sexual experience was an odd sense of shame at how quickly Damon was able to get her into bed. It wasn't a long, sordid affair. It only took a week, and probably less than that if she bothered to count the actual number of days. Was she too easy for him, or was that just some antiquated thinking messing with her head? Did he think of her as an aged groupie?

Of course she hadn't thought about any of those things during that first run-in when she saw him standing in her living room, looking at the pictures hanging on the wall. Why would she? It wasn't as though she could think straight anyhow, becoming so enraptured by the way he turned his attention toward her. Harold had looked at her that way, too, naturally, but it didn't mean the same thing, because he was *Harold Dancy,* and this was *Damon Alton* giving her the eye. And she *had* touched herself to that poster of him hanging on her bedroom wall, watching his picture stare down at her passionately, sweating in front of the microphone, clutching his guitar in a way that she herself wanted to be gripped...

It was only twice that she could remember: once late at night and once just after a practice when the house was still empty. She was never really comfortable with the idea of that sort of touching. It always felt too awkward when she tried, so she never went beyond that bit of youthful experimentation. In the end, that only made her tryst with Damon even more powerful.

How they got to that point required a fair bit of deception that Nancy, surprisingly, did not mind. She'd officially come to the conclusion that her relationship with Harold was over, and had been over for some time. She'd married him for all the wrong reasons, mainly to begrudge a father who didn't even live long enough to say, "I told you so," when she'd realized the truth. Was it right to stay as a matter of fairness? To whom was she supposed to be fairer; her husband, or herself?

Occasionally, she tried to think from Harold's perspective, but she never got very far. She knew she didn't always treat him kindly, but he never complained or got angry, and his patience was limitless. He only looked at her with love in his eyes, and when he talked about their relationship, he made things sound so great. He had a habit of describing their marriage like they were this fantastic team, and it was heartbreaking to her. She couldn't look at him the same way that he looked at her and couldn't understand how he did it.

In those instances, when she would dwell on that thought she'd find herself overcome with some form of guilt, as though he were suffering cheerfully for some defect she brought into their relationship; that's when she'd initiate sex. It was her way to alleviate the guilt. On the nights she left him breathless, a sense of absolution coupled itself with her sense of power and ownership, and she could forgive herself for beginning the cycle again, so long as Harold's patience held up.

This was the basis for the physical aspect of their relationship, and it had stayed that way until it was broken by the death of her father. Since then, Nancy had gone through the process of divorcing herself both physically and emotionally from Harold, although not fully aware that she was doing so. She now viewed him more like a roommate than a husband, and lying to your roommate was nothing like lying to your spouse. It was sufficiently easier and required no recognition, forgiveness, or absolution.

Her first lie to Harold came as a suggestion from Damon, when Harold had gone back into his office with Damon's manager, and it was just the two of them sitting on the couch.

Nancy had just admitted that she'd owned a poster of him when she was a teenager, and privately decided not to tell Harold that their marriage was over, having been swayed by Damon's flirtatious demeanor and her desire to have him. When Damon first leaned in on her, just as she was having those thoughts, it was like he could read her mind.

"Listen," he had told her, lowering his voice when the room was clear, moving close enough to her that she could feel the heat coming off of his arms. "It's not often that I get the opportunity to talk with a long-time fan of the music. Would you like to go out with me and grab some lunch sometime? I'd love to hear what you thought of my old band's songs..."

"Yes!" she'd said immediately, the word nearly erupting from her, and then trying to regain some sense of composure, "I mean, if you want to clear a time that will work for Harold, too..."

"Harold doesn't strike me as a fan, though," Damon had replied, casually, as if he was of little importance. "Why have him tag along and ruin the fun? We'd have to constantly explain the music to him just to make him feel included, and the whole thing would turn into a drag, wouldn't it?"

It wasn't lost on her that he was laying it on thick, and she was smart enough to know a come-on when it so obviously presented itself. All the same, she was taken aback by the force of it and from whom it was coming. The most she could muster in response was a passive, "Okay." In her entire life, Nancy had never sounded less forceful, nor been more excited by the prospect of the unknown.

That was the beginning of her fling with Damon Alton, and it started not with an outright lie, but a lie by omission. She went out to lunch with him two days later, and Harold didn't know the first thing about it. From that singular omission, however, came the necessity to tell *real* lies, usually in response to one of the innocent questions that Harold would pepper her with as they got ready for bed. On the same night as her first lunch date with Damon, for example, before Harold had begun brushing his teeth, he peeked his head out of the bathroom as Nancy got under the covers and caught her off guard.

"Hey," he asked her, as if a curious thought had just come to his mind, "What did you end up doing for lunch today?"

The question made her feel a burst of warmth rush through her cheeks, but if Harold saw her turning red, he didn't mention it. Nancy reacted quickly and deflected, choosing to respond with humorous confusion. "That's a weird question to ask me before bed," she chuckled, and concentrated on adjusting her pillow rather than look Harold in the eye. "What made you want to ask?"

"Oh, I made your lunch this morning using last night's leftovers, and I threw in a tangerine just in case it wasn't enough. It was in a grocery bag with your name on it. Did you not see it before you left?"

"I guess I just didn't notice it," she replied, which actually was true. She'd been so fixated on her date with Damon that she hardly remembered opening the refrigerator to pour milk into her coffee. Harold frowned at the thought.

"You didn't go hungry, did you?" he asked, and that's when she felt herself cross a threshold. She looked away from her pillow, locked eyes with him, and gave him a smile that suggested he was sweet for thinking of her.

"I can take care of myself, Harold. I ran out and got a smoothie."

The coldness of that lie was belied by her delivery, and Harold, who couldn't have thought anything of it, smiled right back at her before returning to his nightly dental routine. In reality, she'd taken a long lunch break, telling her staff that she was courting a potential client that might lock their branch down for long-term rental services, before meeting Damon at a coffee house in a town twenty miles over, where he insisted it would be easier for him to keep a low-profile.

It was a quaint little spot within a historic town, and when Nancy asked Damon why he chose that place, he answered candidly: "It doesn't happen to me like it used to, but on the off chance that I get photographed and someone does a write-up,

I'd get slammed for going to a chain restaurant. You get a picture snapped in a place like that, and all the mags would run a story about how you've hit rock bottom because you obviously can't afford to go out to the upscale places where the photographers typically perch out front like a bunch of vultures. It's better to be seen in a cute little mom and pop place like this. Readers will think you're hip and trendy, and everyone automatically loves you for supporting local business."

He shrugged his shoulders after he said this, as if he was indicating that he didn't make the rules for being famous, but he knew them well enough to follow them, and that was good enough for Nancy. They sat together at a small table, drank slightly above-average lattes, and enjoyed a warmed croissant each, all while talking about the music. Nancy would rattle off the names of a few songs or talk about the first album, and Damon would come back with some light-hearted story that involved its creation. They were very human responses, and his willingness to be so open only deepened the feelings that Nancy was experiencing, as if he were revealing some private pieces of information just for her. Their exchanges went something like this:

"So why'd you name your first album *Adventure Avenue*?" Nancy asked.

"It's a John Lennon reference," Damon answered. "but not because we're big Lennon fans. Really, we wanted the people recording our LP at Electric Records to take us seriously, and we thought the best way to do that was with a Lennon reference. He had this album, *Menlove Avenue*, that we knew about because Erin's dad had an old record collection and that was in it. Apparently, the record was named after the street Lennon grew up on, so we figured we'd do the same thing, thus we called our first full album *Adventure Avenue*, which was the street Jenna and Erin grew up on."

"That's so cool," Nancy replied, enthusiastically. "Did you get a bunch of John Lennon fans to start listening to your music after that?"

"That's the funny part," Damon said, maintaining his remarkable air of candor, *"Menlove Avenue* is the worst received Lennon album of all time. Very few people know that's what inspired our album name, least of all any John Lennon fans. It's since become this weird bit of trivia that only the die-hard fans really know, which makes me kind of surprised that *you* didn't know that..."

Nancy would blush or smile at his flirtations, and a new song or topic would be brought up, and the cycle of conversation would continue. In sum, they spent more than ninety minutes together, long after the coffee was drained, and the croissants were down to crumbs. When things seemed to be drawing to a close, Damon took the next step, essentially laying the groundwork for what was to come, and Nancy was all too ready to acquiesce.

"You know, I really have to thank you," he began as they got up from the table and made their way out of the shop. "It's been nice to just have a conversation and be normal for a change, instead of what I typically get from someone who calls themselves a fan."

"You're an easy person to talk to," Nancy responded, flattered by his sincerity.

"Let me thank you by taking you out to dinner this Friday night," Damon said, "so we can enjoy some more of this casual conversation, only somewhere more upscale. It'll give us an excuse to dress nicely."

"Sure!" she answered, then added with just a note of hesitancy, "Did you want me to check to see if Harold was free to join us?"

"Do you really want Harold to be there?" he asked. The way that he said it, with such confidence, had made her heart beat just a bit faster, and she could feel herself getting light-headed.

"I guess I don't mind if it's just the two of us," she responded, and Damon's smile grew wide enough to show his teeth.

"Good," he said. "Then it will be dinner for two."

A late-night dinner, however, was more difficult to lie about than lunch, and it required Nancy to invent a tale about a manager's retreat that she forgot to put in her calendar. Still, she ended up delivering a performance that was disturbingly convincing, despite one moment of hesitation and a reaction from Harold that was so casual it came off as unnerving.

That same Friday as the week of her lunch date, she'd left work early. When she got home, she stood outside of their apartment for just a second, composed herself, and then burst into the room, slamming the door behind her loudly enough for Harold to hear it in his office. Before he could come out to investigate though, she made sure to race through their living room and into their bedroom, where she slammed that door, too, and then threw open her closet doors to dramatically toss clothes onto their bed. Not a moment too late, Harold slowly opened the door to their bedroom and cautiously approached, as predicted.

"Nance, hon, you okay?" he asked her, watching her manically throw an open suitcase onto the bed, scattering the laundry that had already began to pile.

She stopped what she was doing, looked at him viciously, and snapped, "Does it *look* like I'm okay, Harold?"

Her husband, never one to raise his voice in kind, only held his palms in the air like he was getting ready to surrender. Calmly and deliberately, he asked her, "Why don't you slow down for a second and tell me what's going on?"

"I can't slow down," Nancy spat, although secretly relieved at how quickly he had set her up to deliver the well-crafted alibi. "It's bad enough I had to look like an asshole in front of the staff today when they asked me about the manager's retreat, and all I could do was stare at them like I hadn't the slightest clue as to what they were talking about, *because I didn't!*"

"So you've got a manager's retreat?" Harold replied, and he sounded like he was relieved that that's all it was, but Nancy knew better. That was one of the tricks of his trade. When a client came to him with the force of all their stress, it was his habit to respond in that exact tone. Whatever he was saying, the subtext was always, *"Is that all you're worried about? We can handle that!"*

Even though it was never his intention, Nancy always felt like it was condescending, and whenever he directed that tone toward her, her response was typical. This time, however, the situation was all artifice. When she reacted the way she thought she would if it were all real, it forced her to acknowledge just how normal her bitterness toward Harold was, and it produced the only private moment of hesitation in their entire exchange. Even still, it wasn't enough to derail her dinner plans with Damon, and she remained in character, stone-faced with stress.

"Don't give me any of your life-coach bullshit, Harold," she cursed at him. "Not right now! I don't want to hear about *lists*, or *schedules*, or any of it. I know you want to help me, but I've got to be in New York in less than three hours and I have no idea how I'm going to make it in time for the keynote speaker's address!" Nancy hadn't even planned on saying anything about a keynote speaker. That was a detail that had just come to her, and she said it, hoping it would help her sell the lie. She watched Harold shift slightly in his stance and peer down at his wrist watch to calculate the time. When he looked back up at her, there was a deeper look of concern on his face.

"That's at least a three-hour drive, Nancy," he said. "You weren't planning on coming home tonight, were you?"

"What?" Nancy asked, and she paused momentarily, dumbfounded by his response.

"Well, it's nearly two o'clock now," Harold explained, and then he raised his hands again defensively. "I know you don't want to hear about scheduling, but come on, Nance! If that retreat starts this evening, and it's over three hours just to get to the city, you wouldn't get home until well after midnight. If you're going to go to this thing, I think you should get a room."

"Get a room?" Nancy echoed, and now she felt just the slightest palpitation. Did Harold know she was going to go out with Damon? Was he toying with her in some weird,

Shakespearean way, or was he truly ignorant and telling her to get a room out of genuine concern?

"I mean it," Harold reiterated, completely unaware of the thoughts that his wife was processing. "You can put it on the credit card. Now that we've got Damon Alton in our lives, we can actually afford to put things on the card!" He smiled at her when he said this and then turned to leave her to her things. Just before he shut the door behind him, he looked back at her and said, "Seriously, Nancy, everything's going to be fine."

If there was ever going to be a moment that made her pause before going to dinner with another man, this was that moment. The simplicity of his sentiment reinforced how unerringly decent he was, and just as a feeling crept up in Nancy that could allow her to be moved by his words, she recognized what that feeling was before it was too late, and it almost made her sick. She wasn't being moved by passion, or even some milquetoast version of romantic love for Harold. It was pity, and purely that.

She shook herself out of it and continued to pack the suitcase. It was time to take ownership of her life and not worry about what was fair or unfair to Harold; not if being fair to him meant being unfair to herself. It didn't matter that she was essentially using him, delaying the inevitable with Harold to take advantage of his connection to Damon. She felt she owed it to herself to see how far things could go. It was *lady's choice*, and this was what she was choosing. When her bag was packed, she left the apartment quietly, and without saying goodbye to Harold.

Chapter Seven

Damon vs Harold (A Story About Now)

Harold felt so apprehensive about going out with someone other than his wife that he almost skipped his date entirely. Had it not been for the fact that he was also going to support the debut of Damon's new material, he probably would have cancelled. He was so certain that he was going to have a terrible time, or worse, that Shawnee wouldn't show up, that as soon as he got to the 10:30 Club, he immediately went over to the bar and bought two draft beers, one for each hand. Damon gave Harold a bemused look when he saw him holding his drinks, chalked it up to Harold's erratic post-Nancy behavior, and retired to the green room to tune his bass and run through the set to quell any last-minute doubts.

Harold posted up near the back corner of the main concert floor, in what he thought was an ideal spot. It was just far enough from the speakers so he didn't have to worry about ear plugs, and close enough to see Damon in full view. Admittedly, it was Harold's first time seeing him in concert, and he wondered if he would live up to the hype that so many of his fans perpetuated. After all, the crowd was fairly sparse, seeing as how it wasn't marketed as a "Damon Alton of The Common Miscreants" show (much to the chagrin of the Charm City

Sounds label, hungry to capitalize on their investment), and Harold wasn't sure if a thing like that might subdue Damon's performance. Could crowd size have an impact on a performer who's sold out major concert halls, or does a sense of professionalism grant rock stars the ability to thrill a crowd regardless of attendance numbers? Harold assumed he'd get to find out, and he tried his best to concentrate on *that*, instead of the nerves he felt, wondering whether or not Shawnee would show.

Shawnee did show up, however, just as Harold was about to raise one of the two beers to his lips. He first heard her call out to him and was nearly dumbstruck by the sound of another woman saying his name. When he looked over to the direction of the club's entrance, he saw Shawnee striding toward him, wearing a beautiful blue dress and gold hoop earrings that stood out against her skin and the length of her neck. A woman's neck had always been a weak spot for Harold, though he couldn't explain why he found it so irresistibly beautiful. The sight made him lapse into a thought about the way Nancy's neck looked, and he felt the briefest shift in mood toward the melancholy before Shawnee spoke again and brought him back to the living.

"Are one of those for me?" she asked, and Harold became bashful.

"No, I had plans to drink both of these," he answered truthfully, but with a smile. "If you're thirsty and you like draft beer, you can have one."

Shawnee laughed, taking it for a joke at face value, and accepted the beer that he offered her. From there they struck up a conversation that only paused when she offered to buy the next round, and then again later when Damon came on stage to perform his songs, though their talking didn't cease altogether. After each number, Shawnee would lean in to Harold and ask him if that was one of the songs he helped write. Whenever he answered positively, her smile would widen, and she'd gently grab him by the elbow to either tell him how good it sounded or ask him how cool it was to hear it performed. For his part, Harold accepted her excitement, but didn't try to think too much about what it felt like to hear his own words set to music, because all of his lyrics were tied to Nancy in some fashion, and he struggled with the subject matter.

If he was projecting any feelings of loss and mourning, however, Shawnee couldn't read them in the shadows of the concert venue, nor was she trying. She stayed tuned to the music, swaying gently from side to side at the ballads, or nodding her head enthusiastically at the up-tempo stuff, and always nudging Harold in a way that encouraged him to move with her as well. It was these subtle movements, a brush of her hand against his, or her shoulder against his arm, that carried him away from thoughts of Nancy. By the end of Damon's set, he was shuffling around in his own rhythmless two-step, eliciting a look of approval from Shawnee, who moved with him as a willing dance partner in the dark.

When the show was over, Harold fully expected Shawnee to ask him for a second introduction to Damon, but it never came. Instead, she suggested they sit at the bar and have another drink, so Harold gladly accepted, and they sat together for another hour, talking until the house music went off and the lights came up. By then, Harold noticed that Damon had already left without him. When he checked his phone, he saw an encouraging text message from him that simply read, "Good luck."

Harold looked back over to Shawnee and asked, "You don't have work tomorrow, do you? I didn't realize how late we'd be out."

"I got the day off, actually," she explained. "I switched shifts with a friend so that I could make sure I had a good time at the show tonight."

"So... did you have a good time?" Harold asked, unable to restrain the hint of doubt that had risen up with the question. Shawnee responded to his insecurity with a playful shove, and it put his fear to rest.

"I had a *great* time," she answered, "although it would've been nice to hear some of his old material. The new songs don't sound bad at all, musically, anyway. If I'm being honest, I couldn't always understand what he was singing. It's like the guitars were too loud sometimes."

"I think that happens with some of these local clubs," Harold explained. "I don't know anything about running a soundboard myself, but Damon says it's always crucial to get the right mix. If he didn't get that tonight, I'm sure I'll hear about it later. Still, it's not all bad that you couldn't hear the words..."

"And why is that?" Shawnee asked, and she raised a suggestive eyebrow at Harold that almost made him blush.

"It's nothing inappropriate or anything," he said, "They're just some personal songs, I guess. It's weird to be out on a date and have to listen to someone else sing your poems..."

"Is this a date?" Shawnee asked playfully, but before Harold could get himself worked up over a response, she relented immediately. "I'm just kidding. Of course it's a date, and it's been a pretty good one, so far. It's nice to go out with a guy that's put together, anyway."

"Well, looks can be deceiving," Harold replied, but Shawnee cut off what she presumed would be a self-deprecating rant.

"Please, Harold," she said, "you've got a job, a permanent address, and you volunteer at a soup kitchen. On top of that, you write songs for famous people. Spare me your sob story."

She didn't mince her words, and in that instance, Harold was reminded of the best parts of Nancy. He didn't want to keep thinking of his wife, but he couldn't help himself. This time, however, it was a pleasant thought, and it spurred him toward a bolder sense of confidence.

"You know, if you're having a good time, we don't have to call it a wrap on the night just yet," he said, and Shawnee tilted her head in interest.

"What did you have in mind?" she asked.

"Well," Harold ventured, "neither one of us had anything to eat tonight, unless you count the beer as food. Did you want to go to a late-night spot and grab a bite?"

"There's a diner on Broadway," Shawnee replied, sliding off of her bar stool. "No time like the present, either. We can leave our cars here for now and cab it over there. That will give us time to sober up."

"Great!" Harold said. "I'll settle the tab and then meet you out front."

When Shawnee left, Harold gave himself a small pep talk, reminding himself of the good things to focus on, and his thoughts formed a sort of mental checklist. Shawnee saw him as a man with a respectable job, which was a refreshing perspective when compared to what Nancy used to say about the life-coaching business. She also liked that he was helping out in the community, though if pressed he'd sheepishly have to admit that that was his first foray into public service as an adult. Still, the impression she had of him was strong, and it synced up with what Damon thought of him. "Harold Dancy is a nice guy," he said to himself. "It's time for Harold to stop being a loner. Get back out there, don't talk about Nancy, and don't make it weird. You can do this." He tipped the bartender and walked out with confidence.

Before they even got seated at the diner, however, Harold had managed to bring Nancy up twice, with each instance making the night progressively more awkward. The first time was when they got into the cab that Shawnee had called for them. Harold marveled at the interior and said, "I'm impressed how clean it is in here."

"Have you had bad experiences with cabs?" Shawnee asked, innocently enough.

"I've never been inside one before," he replied without thinking "Nancy always insisted on one of us being a responsible driver whenever we'd go out. She said our car was guaranteed to be the cleaner vehicle and wherever we were going, we always knew we'd arrive safely."

The last sentence struck him as being poorly phrased, and if it wasn't the name that brought attention to what he'd said, surely it was the look on his face.

"Who's Nancy?" Shawnee asked. The look on her face was flirtatious at first, a playful attempt to gesture at mock jealousy, but the look faded rather quickly when she saw Harold's pensive expression.

"Nancy's my wife," Harold said bluntly, glancing over at his date with a self-conscious look. Shawnee misread the statement as an omission of guilt.

"Are you saying you're married?" she asked, and though there was a subtle flare of temper in her voice, Harold was unaffected. His eyes fell downward, and as he was fully prepared for things to get awkward, he answered quietly.

"I *was* married," he said, "but my wife has since passed on. It's been a little over a year now."

Shawnee's demeanor shifted once again. "Oh, God," she replied, laying a comforting hand on Harold's forearm. "I'm so sorry! The doctor's notes referenced you were a widower, too. I can't believe I'd forget something like that!"

"You're totally fine," Harold said, but as the cab ride went on, more apologies were made. Both of them protested that they were sorrier than the other, until their back and forth became a gentle form of bickering, and they didn't stop until the cab reached their destination. Harold seized the opportunity to pay the fare, and in the silence that ensued, he took the opportunity to put a cap on the subject.

"Look," he explained, "it's really not something I try to bring up. It feels like I'm creating some weird expectation of sympathy, and that's not how I want things to go with you. I didn't mean to bring up my wife. It legitimately slipped out." He gave Shawnee a meaningful look, and his mouth formed a half-smile. Quietly, but firmly, he said, "No pity parties, right?"

Shawnee returned the look, and as they got out of the cab, she kept her hand on his arm. "No pity," she relented. "You've got it."

The walk up to the diner helped to drain away some of the tension from the ride over, and when Harold opened the door for Shawnee, she'd successfully shifted the trajectory of the conversation.

"I've always wanted to go here," Shawnee admitted as they walked inside, "but I never made time to do it. Have you eaten here before?"

"Nope," Harold answered once again, and with unfiltered candor, he added, "but like you, I've always wanted to. Diners were just never really Nancy's thing." He flinched when he said this, and then looked bashfully over to Shawnee. A look was already starting to form on her face; the natural expression of pity that Harold had become aware of whenever he talked publicly about his deceased wife. It was such a typical expression that it had encouraged his silence and his eventual reclusiveness of the past several months, in which he only made time for Damon Alton's comeback while plotting his own demise on the side.

As an afterthought, he added, "Sorry. I really don't mean to keep bringing her up."

Shawnee wrapped a hand around his elbow and hugged his bicep to her side. "You don't have to apologize for a thing," she assured him, and they grabbed a booth by the window closest to the door.

They sat for a moment in silence as they waited for someone to come and take their order, and while they did so, it was hard not to feel that something in the atmosphere had turned the night away from Harold's favor. Mercifully, Shawnee broke the silence, and without the slightest hint of apprehension from their most recent topic of discussion.

"So this is Broadway's Diner," she said as she looked around and took in the décor. She then added with some bemusement, "I see it's appropriately named."

Harold looked around, too, and marveled at the posters of old Broadway productions mounted around the room, as well as the collage of playbills, hundreds of them, that served as a makeshift ceiling border. "I guess it wasn't enough to just name the place after the street it's on," he said, "but if you're going to run with a theme, nostalgia never fails."

"I don't know," Shawnee replied, sounding somewhat disappointed. "Sometimes that whole nostalgia thing falls flat. The biggest reason I've wanted to come here is because my parents were actually huge Broadway fans, like down to knowing some serious trivia and history. I was always lucky enough to get to go with them to see whatever shows they had tickets for, though when you're a kid, that doesn't always feel like luck. I'm just looking around at some of the playbills and posters that are on these walls, and it's surprising to see how many of them are from mediocre or just plain bad productions. You'd only know it if you were someone who paid attention to that industry, though. I guess they figure they get a pass because it all still fits in with the Broadway history vibe, right?"

Harold shrugged his shoulders. "I think it's a nice look," he said, and Shawnee considered his words for a moment before softly rebutting him.

"If that's what you're into, sure. It might be a nice look on the surface, but if you're paying attention to the finer details, nobody in their right mind puts up a poster of *Taboo*. That was one of the worst shows my mom ever made me sit through."

Harold glanced over in the direction of Shawnee's gaze and noticed the framed poster advertising *Taboo*, with a garish cartoon image of Boy George on the front. "That bad?" he asked.

"Bad enough that I couldn't commit any of it to memory," Shawnee answered. "If you asked me what it was about, I wouldn't be able to tell you the first thing."

"Well, what shows did you get to see that you liked?" Harold asked

"That's a pretty big question," Shawnee replied, and her answer became thorough enough to dominate the conversation. Harold didn't mind at all, and he relished the opportunity to sit quietly and listen while she steadily filled him in on all of it: the well-known productions like *Les Miserables* and *Rent*; her love of Broadway's oldest shows, like *Oklahoma!*

and *Hello, Dolly!*; and newer productions he'd never heard of before, like *Legally Blonde* or *The Drowsy Chaperone*. It was a good conversation, and Harold found himself comfortable with her taking the reins. He liked hearing her talk. Moreover, he thought it would create an opportunity to avoid talking about Nancy, until Shawnee brought the subject up directly, much to his dismay.

They'd each just finished a slice of pie and were working on their second cup of coffee, and the conversation had been going strong. Shawnee was describing the plot of *The Book of Mormon* and Harold had laughed at all the parts she'd detailed. It had been a charming experience up to that point, and then the conversation hung a left.

"You know you can see most of these shows locally through Broadway tours now, don't you?" Shawnee asked. "The Hippodrome has them come through all the time. Did you and your wife ever go there for anything?"

"Nancy?" Harold asked, and he knew the expression was draining from his face, in spite of the fact that he tried to will from himself a sense of good humor. The question caught him off-guard, and Shawnee immediately picked up on his reaction.

"I'm sorry if that was upsetting," she said, slightly alarmed. "When you brought her up last time, you said something about it bothering me. I just didn't want to seem like it did, and I thought the question might put you at ease."

"No, you're totally fine," Harold said, staring into his cup of coffee to avoid Shawnee's expression. He'd found it hard to deal with the way people looked at him when he talked about Nancy, and if he was going to talk about her now, he didn't want to see that look from Shawnee any more than he had to. "It's just weird to talk about," he admitted. "It's been a little over a year, and I still..."

Shawnee picked up on his loss for words and interjected her own. "How did she pass, if you don't mind my asking?" She spoke softly when she broached the subject, and when Harold raised his eyes to her, he saw that her expression was soft, encouraging an openness that, true to his initial request, didn't have a trace of someone who pitied him. He could've been coy about the subject, or at least tried to wade into things slowly. Instead, he took a breath, and told the whole story as plainly as his heart would allow.

"We were on the highway together," Harold began. "I was driving, and she was in the passenger seat. It was one of those big SUVs we were riding in, the kind built like a tank to make you feel safe. I don't remember it clearly, but I feel like something must've jumped out into the middle of the road. I think Nancy tried to jerk the wheel, but we were so spread out that she couldn't reach it without unbuckling her seatbelt, so she did. When she jerked the wheel, I lost control and we hit the median wall. She was thrown through the windshield and went head first into the concrete. The SUV had one of those emergency GPS things built into it, so an EMT came pretty quickly. The driver-side door was pretty smashed up, which meant I had to crawl over the passenger seat to get out. By the time I reached her, I had just enough time to see her take her last breath."

Shawnee sat in silence, completely dumbfounded. Harold let out a long, slow breath.

"I know," he said, feeling the weight of the moment. "That's a pretty intense story."

"That's a terrible way to lose a loved one," Shawnee said, clearly moved, and Harold felt himself fully impressed. She never looked away from him as he told the story, not even once. Regardless of how awkward he may have felt about telling it, she didn't seem to feel that way about listening, and now the most Harold could do was smile awkwardly, unsure of where to go with conversation.

"Pretty terrible," Harold agreed after a short pause, "or pretty romantic, if you want to view it another way. She died trying to save my life." Then abruptly, he said, "Hey, working as a nurse, how often do you hear a story like that?" Shawnee raised her eyebrows at the question and took a second to consider her thoughts.

"Well, it's not so often that you become desensitized to it," she answered, "but a sad story is a sad story. You end up hearing so many of them and if you let each one have an effect on you, you'll burn out from the stress. When I hear stories like yours, I try to channel them into a humble appreciation for life and not take for granted how fragile our situations truly are."

Harold sat quietly, absorbing his thoughts for a moment, and then drained his cup of coffee. "Thank you for not making my Nancy story feel weird. I stopped telling it to people because it kept feeling like a bad thing to do. You're the first person I've told it to where it didn't feel like I ruined something."

"You haven't ruined anything, Harold," Shawnee said, and brought her coffee toward her lips, smiling at him in a way that made him believe she was telling the truth. As she began to take the last sip of her cup, though, Harold felt a familiar sensation come rushing past him, like a quick burst of air that gave him goosebumps all over. At the moment that feeling registered, Shawnee's cup slipped from her hands and fell to the table, shattering to pieces and spraying the last bit of coffee onto Harold's shirt.

They sat stunned for a moment, and then both burst out laughing. Harold grabbed napkins and started to clean the shards of the cup and a waitress came over to help them with the mess. When the commotion had settled down, Shawnee quietly whispered to Harold, "I have no idea how that slipped out of my hands like that. I promise I've sobered up since we left the club."

"You're good," Harold reassured her. "The damage was minimal. I'm okay and you're okay, right?"

The broken cup ended up being the signal to put an end to their evening. Harold settled the check and they took a cab back to the club to retrieve their cars. Internally, Harold went back and forth with himself as to whether or not things had gone well, and ultimately, Shawnee settled the argument. Just before Harold parted from her, she leaned in, gave him a kiss on the cheek, and wished him a good night. Harold smiled at her, nearly embarrassed by the affection, and wished her the same, before watching her get into her car and safely drive away. His date had ended on a euphoric note, but the feeling was short lived. When Harold got home, Damon was still up waiting for him, and the expression he wore was not the one of a friend looking for details.

"What's going on?" Harold asked.

"It was laundry day," Damon said. "Turns out, my cleaning ladies found a neglected basket of laundry that hadn't been done in quite a while. Guess what they found when they went through the pockets?"

"I have no idea," Harold said, apprehensively. He knew Damon was building toward some dramatic moment, but hadn't a clue as to what it could be until he saw Damon pull out a piece of paper he had tucked behind him. Harold recognized it immediately and felt his heart drop.

"Should I read it out loud?" Damon asked.

Without thinking about it, Harold lunged toward the paper, grazing it with outstretched fingers just as Damon side-stepped away from him.

"I'll take that as a 'yes' then, Harold," Damon continued, and Harold felt himself become suddenly infuriated.

"Don't!" he demanded and heard a tone in his voice that he'd never had before. Harold Dancy didn't lose his temper, because Harold Dancy didn't have a temper to lose. The expression of anger was for the most part a foreign concept to him. On the rare occasions he experienced an angry moment, he found it gave him an uncomfortable, chaotic energy. He continued to lunge at Damon, who for his part, had seamlessly transitioned into an adolescent bully, holding the note high in the air, just out of Harold's reach, where he could look up and recite the lines while playing his game of Keep Away.

"To whom it may concern," he announced in a broad voice, as if he was reading it to some large invisible audience, "this should not be a surprise to any of you. The only thing that is surprising about this situation is that it's taken four tries to get it done..."

Harold swung a wild kick and struck Damon in the shin. Damon's knee buckled with the pain, and Harold seized the opportunity, jumping onto his shoulder and making a play for the outstretched hand holding the note. Damon recovered quickly, threw Harold off his back, and kept the paper aloft. By the time Harold had found his feet, Damon had created some space for himself by jumping over a chair, and the game boiled down to going in circles while Damon read and Harold kept sporadically lunging at him.

"My reasons for doing this are my own," Damon continued, "but since you must know, it's because I miss my wife very much, and I am determined to be with her again. You can disagree with my choice, but that's your business, and what's yours is yours and mine will be mine..."

At these words, Harold changed tactics and threw a semi-closed fist into Damon's teeth. Damon recoiled, instantly bringing his hands down around his mouth, and Harold snatched the note from Damon's grasp, immediately tearing it to shreds. He then jumped back several feet and cowered behind the couch, suddenly aware that he just punched a paying client in the mouth.

Damon had stumbled backward, checked his fingers for blood, and then glared at him angrily. Harold assumed it was because he'd been hit, but when he spoke, Harold was surprised by the true source of Damon's ire.

"All of the shit these past few months!" Damon shouted. "Your stupid behavior and the reckless stunts! I figured you were acting out because your wife died, but I chalked it up to going crazy in a rock and roll sort of way. Hell, I've been there! Who hasn't wanted to break some shit when they felt the walls closing in on them?"

Harold stood there silently, and Damon stopped staring at him for a moment to dab his lips with his fingers again, checking a second time for any blood. When he continued to speak, he was quieter, but with the same intensity as before.

"My God, Harold. All those stunts you pulled... These weren't the actions of a man gone wild, were they? I mean, you haven't gone crazy at all, have you? I'll bet you don't even masturbate..."

There wasn't a trace of humor in Damon's voice on his last point, and Harold understood what conclusion he was coming to. "No, not really," Harold admitted.

"Not really you don't masturbate, or not really about having gone crazy..." Damon asked, and as ridiculous as the question may have been, there was an air of desperation in his voice that made Harold take him seriously.

"No, I don't masturbate, and no, it's not the kind of crazy you first thought it was... but it is the kind of crazy you're probably understanding it to be now," Harold answered.

Damon looked away from Harold, and he let out a long breath. Harold felt like he should get closer to him, but traces of residual fear kept him standing safely behind the couch while he watched his friend process the information.

"They were suicide attempts?" Damon asked, heartbroken in voice. "For her?"

"Yes," Harold answered quietly. They stood in silence for a moment after he said this. Although they were just vaguely aware of it, they were both experiencing the same sense of shame, only Harold had yet to discover the root of Damon's guilt.

"She's not worth it," Damon whispered.

"You couldn't possibly understand what she's worth to me," Harold replied. "I loved her."

"Yeah?" Damon replied. "Well, I fucked her."

Stunned, Harold felt the air slip from his lungs. The word Damon used was violent and searing. It brought a sharp pain to Harold's ears, clouded his sight, and numbed his remaining senses. A white-hot surge of anger rushed through his veins. Without thought, he leapt over the couch, ready to claw out Damon's eyes, but Damon had prior experience from his rock star life on the road. The wrath of an angry husband could be formidable, but it was also predictable. He kept his forearms up and adopted the footwork of an experienced fighter. Harold attempted to throw wild punches, but none of them successfully landed, outside of grazing the meat of a bicep or the edge of an elbow.

All the while, Damon kept repeating himself: "That was Old Damon. New Damon doesn't do that to his friends. That was Old Damon..."

But the mantra was not getting through to Harold, and even if Damon had no intentions of hitting Harold, he had to do something to calm the situation. Without meaning to put too much power behind it, Damon let his right hand fly out, and the back of it caught the bridge of Harold's nose. Harold reeled backward, tripped over the cord of a floor lamp, and landed on his back, smacking his head hard against the floor.

What happened next could only be described as sense memory. The exact spot where Damon's hand landed was the same spot Harold recalled hitting the night of the car accident. Without warning, he had total recall of every detail of when Nancy had grabbed the wheel. As Damon cautiously approached him to pick him up off the floor, Harold grabbed him by the wrist, and looked into his eyes with the sheer terror of his realization.

"Damon," he trembled, "I remember everything!"

"You remember what?" Damon asked, apprehensively.

"The accident," Harold answered, "Nancy was trying to kill me."

Chapter Eight

Nancy, Dying (A Story About Then)

For Nancy, there was a certain thrill in sleeping with Damon Alton. Even as the affair carried on from weeks to months, the excitement of bedding her rock star idol never lost its luster. She felt happier at work, and the guys like Duke, Jake, and Clayton over at the rental branch noticed the change in her demeanor. Things were less tense, and just like her husband had, they attributed it to Nancy taking time out for herself. It wasn't so far back that the thought of their boss with a baseball bat in her hands would make them shudder. Now, they were relieved.

Harold had eventually gotten the full story about Nancy revisiting the cages over at Herlihy's, and how she'd bought some new gear and was going to work on her timing. To Nancy's surprise, he seemed elated to hear that she was in training to join a rec league.

"I mean it," he'd told her when she explained to him where her extra time had been going. "I'm so happy you're doing this, and it will be fun for both of us! I'll be able to go to your games, grab a spot on the bleachers, and watch you get back behind the plate..."

Going to Herlihy's was a half-truth, of course, though she really did *sometimes*, and was actually starting to perfect the timing of her swing. She would've preferred to have a live pitcher who could put a little movement on the ball, but that would come when she found a team to join. Baltimore had all kinds of weekend leagues at varying levels of competitiveness, and Nancy wanted to find the most competitive. She'd work to make herself the best on the team, and it was with that thought in mind that she kept going to Herlihy's as often as she did. When she didn't go, however, it was because she was stealing time with Damon: sometimes at his place and sometimes at a hotel, but rarely at her apartment. She thought it was too risky, and whenever they used her apartment for one of their secret rendezvouses, it had to be carefully orchestrated, with little room for doubt. If she was going to be caught, she knew she still had enough feeling for her husband that being discovered in their bed with Damon was the last thing she'd want him to see.

***

Damon, however, *did* have a preference on how he wanted to be caught, and in Harold's bed with Harold's wife was exactly the way he thought it ought to be. Certainly, his thoughts on the affair differed from Nancy's. He knew what this was for her, and he'd long been accustomed to the fantasy that women developed in these situations. She wasn't having sex with *him* as much as she was having sex with a concept – *Damon Alton, of The Common Miscreants*. That's how everyone saw him, even Jenna and Erin at the end of everything. He was a commodity, and when it worked for him, he was okay with it. Sleeping with Nancy happened to be one of those times where it worked for him. She'd become a balm to his secretly bruised ego; proof that his brand of sexual appeal still had some value. Furthermore, the two of them meshed quite well in the bedroom. She was a lot of fun, and it was a nice arrangement. He got to feel like he was twenty again, and the joy of sex combined with the joy of sticking it to management was wholly satisfying.

When he thought about it, however, his spite for Harold Dancy was nearly startling. On the surface, it appeared completely unwarranted, but Damon felt that Harold was cloyingly nice, to the point where he could not be trusted. He smiled too much, and who could put faith in someone who didn't lose their temper once in a while? Damon was rude to him at nearly every turn, and still, the nice guy persona persisted! Harold Dancy was a con artist playing the long game, and Damon was steadfast in his refusal to fall for it. It was with this in mind that Damon derived his purest joy from sleeping with Nancy, and if they had to be caught with each other, please God let it be in Harold's bed. For that reason alone, he pushed hard for meeting up at her place, and a break in Harold's schedule finally offered up the chance to do just that.

The opportunity presented itself when Nancy noticed Harold's calendar had him scheduled to meet with one of his needier clients. According to his notes, it was someone he'd helped set up a retirement lifestyle for, who was now fretting over whether or not it was a mistake to leave the workforce. Harold must've anticipated that the meeting would run a little long, as he had agreed to a two-hour block at the client's place, for the sake of their comfort. Immediately following that meeting, he'd have to come back for his scheduled goal-setting session with Damon in the home office. When Nancy explained all of this, Damon sold it to her as the perfect setup for a frisky afternoon. By his logic, they'd have at least a solid hour together, with plenty of time afterward to straighten up and grab a shower before Harold made it back. Though Nancy was leery at the idea of meeting in the apartment, it was the thought of showering with Damon that eventually won her over.

When Damon arrived, just a half hour after Harold had left, Nancy answered the door, and without exchanging greetings, the two immediately started kissing each other passionately, clumsily knocking into furniture as they made their way into the bedroom. Once inside, Nancy began to undress, and Damon dug into his front pockets, then patted the back of his pants. A panicked look crossed his face and he uttered a frustrated, "Shit!"

"What is it?" Nancy asked, half-naked and slightly alarmed. She froze in place clutching the bottom of her shirt that was ready to come off, her anxiety heightened by the prospect of any hiccup in their plans.

"You don't have a condom, do you?" Damon asked, innocently. In truth, he intentionally hadn't brought one, as that was his preference and he'd felt that things had gone far enough with Nancy to try something new. Still, experience taught him that it was better to pretend to have forgotten the protection and gauge the woman's reaction, rather than to willfully declare he'd rather go without. The latter could spur uncomfortable conversations about pregnancy and fatherhood, and that was a talk he wanted no part of. It was easier to set the situation up as accidental and hope the heat of the moment would carry their activities toward a more natural conclusion.

To her credit, Nancy had never been anyone's fool, and she wouldn't be one to allow for any *natural* conclusion. As much as she didn't want Harold walking in on them, she just as strongly didn't want her husband finding out about the affair through an unwanted pregnancy. It had been long enough since they'd last been physical that it would be pretty obvious to know who *wasn't* the father. Very slowly, she started to pull her shirt back down, eying him suspiciously. "Why didn't you bring one?" she asked directly, and her tone was unmistakably forceful. "You've had condoms ready when you *didn't* know we were going to have sex, but you forget on a day when you know it's going to be a sure thing? What kind of stunt are you trying to pull here?"

Damon's expression twisted. This was a new experience for him. Rarely had he been called out by a woman in any of his sexual exploits, and never so openly. In that instance, he could feel their dynamic begin to shift, and it was disquieting. Just like that, she was getting dressed again, and it was almost

132

an affront that anyone could think to turn him down after they'd already taken their pants off.

"Relax," he insisted, and he took a step toward her, gently taking her by the waist, both to comfort her and to ensure her hips remained blissfully bare. "It was an honest mistake. Surely you have something around that we could use?"

Nancy looked into his eyes, as though she were ultimately judging whether or not she'd give him the time, and then said, "Harold and I don't use condoms, but I think he keeps some in his office."

"Why would Harold have condoms in his office?" Damon asked, confusedly.

"I think he likes to encourage his clients to practice safe sex," Nancy said, suddenly suppressing a grin, "and yes, I am well aware of the irony." Damon felt his own smile widen at the mischievous look on her face, one that he found fully arousing. She playfully slapped him on the ass and bid him to make a quick search. "Go in his office and look for one. If you find something we can use, then we can play ball. If you don't, then you can just settle for going down on me."

"My god, you are forward, woman," Damon said, and regarded her with a devilish look. "Get on the bed and don't put your pants back on. Knowing Harold, he probably keeps them on a table in a glass bowl." Nancy laughed at the comment and shooed him out of the bedroom. Damon dashed quickly into Harold's office, hell-bent as a man on a mission.

Obviously, it wouldn't be so easy as to discover a bowl of condoms presenting itself center table, but Damon was not one to just accept the fate of keeping things strictly to foreplay. He rummaged through every inch of the office in search of anything covered in foiled wrapping, but nothing turned up. The desk drawers contained a myriad of pens and an assortment of different colored sticky notes, more than likely for Harold's infamous 'lists'. The top of the desk was neat enough to know there'd be no condoms found there, and the tables were indeed empty, as were the spaces in-between the couch cushions. Having grown fully desperate at the prospect of a missing good sex, Damon started scanning the bookshelf against the back wall, hoping to see something in the least likely of places. He found no condoms there either, but something did catch his eye.

Sandwiched by a massive text on life-coaching and a heavy volume on psychology was a slim book so mismatched in size that it grabbed Damon's attention. Curious, Damon pulled it from the shelf and glanced down at the cover, made of a smooth leather binding that bore no markings of a title or anything to indicate what it was. He opened the first few pages, and just as he realized what he had in his hands, the door opened behind him.

Expecting to see Nancy, he whirled around with a smile on his face. Instead, he saw Harold standing there, wearing a bemused expression while he glanced down at his wrist watch.

"I know I've told you 'early is on time' but arriving an hour before we're set to meet might be going overboard," Harold chuckled. Then he glanced up at Damon with an expression of concern, "I didn't mark it down early in the calendar, did I?"

"No," Damon replied, keeping things casual and maintaining the smile. He hadn't been caught doing anything wrong, so there was no need to rouse Harold's suspicion. Instead, he told a version of the truth. "I was bored, so Nancy let me in. She told me to go into your office."

"She puts up with a lot, doesn't she?" Harold said, and then a look of confusion swept over his face. "Though she ought to be at work right now..."

An inexperienced man would've panicked at this moment, but Damon had slept with married women before, and he knew how to conduct himself. After all, being caught alone in Harold's office was not the same as being caught in bed with Nancy, and he wasn't ready to be discovered just yet. To that end, he maintained his air of casual boredom, and let Harold process things for himself. Should it turn out that Harold might put the pieces together, it obviously wouldn't be ideal, but Damon would more than survive. He'd encountered threatening husbands before, and Harold didn't fit the bill. As if to underscore Damon's assumption, Harold delivered.

"I guess she came home for lunch," he said, thoughtfully. "She does that sometimes, which is lucky for you! Otherwise, you would've been stuck out in the hallway!"

"Or I would've just cancelled on you, Harold," Damon replied, his surly tone belying his smile, "let's be honest."

"Right," Harold sighed. He thought for the briefest of moments that Damon's early arrival was a sign of their relationship improving, but the familiar note of disgust in his client's voice made such hope evaporate. He motioned for Damon to have a seat, knowing that another grudging session laid before him in which he'd continue to work on Damon buying into the program. Then he saw the book in Damon's hands.

"What are you doing with that?" Harold asked, and Damon took note of the mild shift in Harold's voice.

"It looks like a diary of sorts," Damon said, eying the leather journal with disinterest. "I grabbed it off the bookshelf. It's not yours, is it?"

"It is mine," Harold confirmed, and there was a testiness in his voice that intrigued Damon, as if he was about to see the world's nicest man finally let his mask slip off. "My wife gave it to me when I graduated. If you wouldn't mind putting it back, we can get started!"

Damon's smiled widened. He could see Harold trying to gain control of the situation, but it was fun to see him off balance. He began taunting him.

"It's not private, is it? I mean, if it were, you wouldn't have put it on a bookshelf for just anyone to see, would you?"

"Normally, people don't pay any attention to the bookshelf," Harold replied, and he tried to force a casual smile on his face, but he wasn't as practiced as Damon was. "If you could just please put it back, we can get started with our goal-setting session."

"Well, now I'm more interested in what you've got in here, Harold," Damon said, as his smile became a bullying sort of leer. "You don't mind if I read a few pages, do you?"

Harold's voice dropped to a lower register, just short of anger. In as firm a tone as he'd ever produced in front of Damon, he said, "Don't."

Damon held the journal aloft, so that it would be out of reach if Harold attempted to grab at it, though Harold had made no sudden moves toward his direction and glanced up at the first page he turned to.

"Oh, so you're a poet?" he asked, with the snarky quality in his voice having grown thick. Harold only stood there with his eyes cast downward like a wounded animal, waiting for the moment to pass. Damon looked back up at the lines of poetry, ready to mock the first few, but didn't. Instead, he read the full poem. When he finished, he read it again, and the smile from his face faded. Harold took notice of the change in Damon's expression, and for whatever reason, it caused him momentary panic.

"What?" he asked, and the feeling deepened when he saw Damon lower the book to chest level, staring pensively at the pages.

"This isn't bad, Harold," Damon said. He looked up at Harold with a fresh set of eyes, as though he was seeing him for the first time. "I actually think this is pretty good." Damon held onto the book and took a seat on the couch, continuing to flip through the pages.

"I minored in English," Harold explained, "mainly studying poetry."

"It shows," Damon said, as he used his finger to guide through the lines on a page in the middle of the book. "I especially like this one."

"Which one?" Harold asked, and Damon took it as an invitation to recite the work aloud:

I'm tired of talking about the little things,
It often gets too loud to speak.

Whatever happened to the bigger picture?
We used to stare at it constantly.
Seems now the only things we'll ever say out loud are lies,
Like when I ask you if you'll love me tomorrow,
But the promise isn't there in your eyes.
You just nod your head,
And turn away.
We're lying in bed together,
Drifting slowly away.

Harold began to bristle at the sound of his own words being repeated back to him, and he raised a hand in deference toward Damon. "I'm very glad that you like it," he said, "but I think that's enough for now."

Damon immediately objected, and the hint of excitement in his voice ultimately won Harold over. "No," he replied, "let me finish reading it. The second verse is where I think it gets really good. I'm hearing music in my head right now."

"Really?" Harold asked, surprised and genuinely perplexed by Damon's interest in his work. He viewed his poetry as a trifling attempt at art, so much so that he didn't share his work, not even with Nancy. Especially not with Nancy.

"Really," Damon answered, without a trace of insincerity. "It's like I can feel a moment coming on. I have to read it out loud."

"Well, if you must," Harold said bemusedly, still caught up in the idea that anyone might appreciate his work, let alone Damon Alton, of all people. Damon continued:

I never meant to be a disappointment.
I often wonder how I got this way.
It's never kept me from a moment with you;
Old habits, they're all hard to break.
Seems like the only things we ever do are what is routine,
Like when I ask you if you'll love me tomorrow,
Always right before we go down to sleep.
You just nod your head

And turn away.
We're lying in bed together,
Drifting slowly away.

Damon shut the book and looked thoughtfully up at Harold. "Shit, Harold! Is this supposed to be about you and Nancy?"

"Well, not exactly," Harold said, shifting uncomfortably in his stance. He didn't know whether to sit down and take Damon seriously, or keep his guard up, and so he aimed to dismiss the conversation altogether. "It's just a poem, right?"

"Yeah, but you just said, 'not exactly'," Damon pressed. "Which parts are true?"

"I don't know," Harold replied, and his anxiety began to increase. He'd almost rather Damon make fun of him and be done with it, but he was taking his work so seriously. It would've been complimentary if the poem he chose to read hadn't been so personal. If there was a silver lining to his discomfort, he hoped it would be in the form of a breakthrough with his obstinate rock star client, who until now had yet to take their sessions seriously. "I don't think it's a big deal," Harold confessed, "but sometimes I ask Nancy if she'll love me tomorrow when we go to bed. I'm just trying to be cute when I do that, though..."

"Sure, but what does she say?" Damon asked, further intrigued. Without realizing it was happening, Damon's entire understanding of Harold was being recalibrated in this moment of naked honesty, and he couldn't let it stop now. Never mind that Harold's wife had just been waiting for him back in their bedroom - Harold Dancy was becoming real to him.

"Nothing," Harold answered, plainly. "She doesn't say anything. She just smiles at me, I guess. Then she goes to bed."

"Wow, Harold," Damon said, with real pity in his voice. "That might be the saddest thing I've ever heard."

"Oh, don't be ridiculous," Harold replied, as he finally took a seat next to him on the couch. His tone became light-hearted in a clear effort to shrug off his client's assessment of the situation. "It's just married couple stuff," he explained, and then jokingly added, "A guy with your libido might not understand that." Damon didn't laugh at that, however, and Harold felt compelled to explain further to avoid the awkward silence. "You don't understand the context. Nancy's father passed a little over a year ago, and I think she's been taking some time to process her grief. I'd be a real jerk if I were to complain about anything, especially considering I wasn't her dad's biggest fan. It would come off as pretty cold-hearted if I did..."

"So is that what the bit about being a bastard is all about then?" Damon asked, still digging for information.

Harold was thrown by Damon's attention to detail, and could only shrug his shoulders, failing to come up with a response that felt adequate. Words fumbled around in his head before he caught himself repeating his previous line. "Like I said, it's just poetry..."

Damon would not be dissuaded though, and he continued on, going so far as to reopen Harold's journal to scan the lines of his work. "Maybe," he said, "but the hook doesn't sound right to me. I mean, poetically it works, but if I asked my wife if she'll love me tomorrow, I'd prefer an answer."

"It's not like she says she *doesn't* love me," Harold protested. "She might not say *yes*, but she doesn't say *no*, either."

"Forgive me if I'm overstepping boundaries, Harold," Damon said, "but I've been with a lot of women, and I've learned a fair bit. As a rule, just because a woman doesn't say *no*, it doesn't mean she's said *yes*, either."

He thought about what Damon said, and without meaning to, Harold's thoughts went back to the first time he asked Nancy to the dance. He'd waited for her in the parking lot and had offered her his second ticket, but she hadn't said one way or the other what she'd do. It wasn't like she had ignored him, either. She acknowledged him with her eyes, heard what he had to say, and then silently, she'd gotten into her car and drove away without answering. Yesterday, Harold would've remembered that fondly, as though there was a bit of mystery surrounding their initial date. Now, Damon had cast that memory into a new and discomforting light.

Damon, at the same time, was having his own breakthrough. All this time, he had Harold pegged as just another music industry goon - someone who would eventually try to manipulate him the way they all did, using the nice-guy routine as his means of doing so. In a certain respect, he was right that this shtick was masking something, but Damon had thought it a disguise for a shark. Now he saw it for what it was: a defense mechanism for some underlying sadness. It was a toppling realization, and he found himself keenly aware of his own terrible behavior, now completely unwarranted and unjustifiable. It further led him to wonder what really made Nancy tick, and why she'd cheat on a legitimately nice guy like Harold.

"I'm sorry for the way I've treated you, Harold," Damon said, and Harold gave him an apprehensive expression of surprise. Damon noted his reaction and became emphatic. "Really," he explained, "I think I've misjudged you terribly." He flipped through Harold's journal once more, taking in the bits and pieces of poetry that were there. "I've dealt with so many different suits in this business, and guys like Brian Squires. I call them *wranglers*, because that's all they seem to want to do. It's like management to the point of control, you know? Given enough time, all of those bastards slip up and expose themselves for the heartless and creatively bereft creatures that they are. I had you lumped in as one of them, and I've just been waiting for the other shoe to drop. Now I think you might've been legitimate this whole time."

"And reading just one of my poems gave you this big realization?" Harold laughed in moderate disbelief. Damon remained completely sincere, however.

"Not just the poem, but the conversation that came with it," he answered. "I mean, you really opened up to me, you know? Those other guys in the business aren't interested in anything but giving orders. Even after all the shit I've given you, you still had that conversation with me, like we were two normal human beings."

"That's all I've been trying to do this whole time," Harold said, settling into the moment. Sensing inspiration, he got up to grab a pen and the empty notebook he had dedicated to Damon, initiating the start of their actual session.

"If I had words like these," Damon told him, brandishing the journal, "I might be able to do something. Jenna and Erin were always the lyricists. I was just good at bass riffs and mugging on stage. I was young, you know? I felt like it was my job to sell the rock star image, like it was a meaningful contribution. Since the Miscreants split, every writer I've ever been paired up with gets caught up in that reputation and wants to write me generic songs about sex, drugs, and destructive tendencies, like they're writing for that aura and not for me, right?"

Harold couldn't help his look of incredulity, and Damon caught on to it with a half-grin.

"Look, just because I like having sex and drinking, that doesn't mean it's the only thing I want to sing about," he continued. "I think about other things, too. I'm tired of celebrating the life of a kid. I want something real, mature. If I had a set of lyrics like that poem of yours I just read, I could show the industry that I'm not some strung out has-been, you know? I'm someone who should've been taken seriously from the get-go."

"Is that what you really want?" Harold asked, and that's when Damon became aware of Harold writing down everything he'd just said.

"What are you writing?" Damon asked, alarmed and balking at the question. "What are you doing?"

"We're having our session," Harold said, as if it was obvious that this is what it had been this whole time.

"No, Harold," Damon demurred. "The moment's passed. You're ruining it."

"Oh, come on," Harold replied. "Getting personal is a two-way street. You just admitted something big, and I'm into it. If being taken seriously is your aspiration, then we just made that our mission." Damon tried to laugh it off, seeing Harold go into his full life coach routine, but Harold persisted.

"Honestly, Damon, if your goal is to be taken seriously in the music industry, what would it take for you to feel like you've accomplished that?"

Damon studied Harold for a moment, and then let slip a truth that he had subconsciously buried deep beneath layers of rock and roll avarice, pride, and self-pity, but was now ready to admit to Harold and to himself.

"It's more than just the industry," he said. "It's Jenna and Erin, really. They've gone off and done their own thing, and it's like it was proof they were the talent and they didn't need me."

"So then a reunion is what you want?" Harold asked, and it was like a revelation to Damon. That's exactly what he wanted, and though he didn't know it until now, maybe what he'd always wanted.

"Yes," Damon answered. "I want my old band back. I want to make good with my cousin. I want Erin to look me in the eye again. I want a new album, and I want to be back on the road."

"Then we'll make that our goal," Harold smilef, and the conversation continued further down that path. In the excitement of their big breakthrough, however, neither of them noticed that the door to Harold's office was still slightly ajar, and that Nancy was on the other side, listening in on everything.

* * *

When Harold walked into the apartment, Nancy's breath got caught in her throat, and she felt a certain hitch there that made it difficult to exhale. He wasn't supposed to be home yet, and there was no warning of his arrival. Quickly and quietly, she jumped off the bed and immediately put her pants on, fearful that he'd burst in on her at any moment. When that didn't happen, she stood by the door and waited for the outburst of emotion that she knew was coming at any moment, but it never did. Horror gave way to confusion. He'd walked right past their bedroom and went straight into his office. He most certainly happened upon Damon searching his office for condoms, and how Damon would respond was beyond her guess. She couldn't help but assume the worst, and so she stood on her toes, waiting for his reaction.

But the seconds elongated to minutes, and after enough time had passed, Nancy realized the explosion might not occur after all. Hesitantly, she stuck her head out from behind the bedroom door and looked over to the living room, but no one was there. She made her way out entirely and looked back over to the kitchen, which was also empty. Finally, she slowly walked toward Harold's office door, still on guard and waiting for some eruption of anger. She peered in through the doorway and saw Damon and Harold sitting next to each other, like it was one of Harold's typical sessions, only Damon looked remarkably receptive to the conversation. In that instance, a near sense of panic crept into her, and her hand came forward, as if beyond her willpower, pushing the door open to steal her husband's attention.

"Hey, Nance!" Harold said, looking up at her with his usual smile. "Thanks for letting Damon in. He got here early and as luck would have it, my meeting cancelled. Fortunately for the both of us you were home. Are you on your lunch break?"

"Yes," Nancy said, automatically, as she looked over to Damon to try and make sense of what she was seeing. He glanced up at her, shrugged his shoulders, and looked back down at a book he was holding in his lap. She then looked back over to Harold, who was peering at his watch.

"Your lunch hour is probably almost up by now, hon," Harold said. "Are you headed back to your branch?"

"I am," Nancy said. The anxiety she was experiencing started to work its way up into a knot in the back of her throat. She looked at Damon and could see a difference in his expression. He normally couldn't stand to be around Harold, but that didn't seem so obvious to look at them now, and she got the sense that something had changed. She cleared her throat, looked back at her husband, and said, "I was just checking in on you two. I'll see you later tonight."

"Drive safe, Nance," Harold said. Nancy looked over to Damon one more time, only to see that his eyes would not meet hers. She left the apartment and drove back to work, where the rest of her staff was surprised to see her return.

"I thought you were taking a half-day?" Duke asked upon seeing her walk back into the branch. "Is everything okay?"

"I made a mistake," Nancy replied, though her voice made it sound as if she were not all there. "I got mixed up. I'll be back in my office if you need me."

Duke Franklin was used to his manager's mercurial nature. He'd definitely seen her angry before, and lately he'd seen her happy more often than not, but the way she sounded now was off-putting. It was like she'd somehow gone numb. He could've dwelled further on it, too, had time allowed, but the branch was soon swamped. Everyone in the office, Duke, Clayton, and Jake, hadn't a minute to sit down, even for a break. For all the rush they had to deal with, Nancy never once came out of her office for support. By 5 o'clock, their entire fleet of cars had been rented, and they were sitting on an empty lot. Jake and Clayton went to clock out for the day, and before Duke followed along, he knocked timidly on Nancy's office door.

"We're all set here, boss," he said through the door. He was too afraid to open it, and too afraid to ask his next question, but his sense of concern overcame his nerves, and he put it out there. "Are you okay, Nancy?"

"I'm fine, Mr. Franklin," she answered curtly, acknowledging his presence with her voice only. "Good job managing the fleet today. Go home. I'll lock up when I'm finished going over my paperwork."

Mr. Franklin was a return to her old form, and Duke knew better than to press further. Instead, he simply replied, "You got it, boss," and left quietly, still worried that he might disturb her in some way.

In reality, Duke Franklin being a nuisance was the last thing on Nancy's mind. The entire time she spent inside her office had been dedicated to researching places to go, new areas to live, and the average cost of a divorce lawyer. It was time to pull the trigger and move on with her life. She was ready, and when she called up Damon, asking him to meet her at the branch, it was to discuss their future together.

But Damon seemed hesitant when he answered the phone, and even reluctant to meet with her, which sent a quaking feeling through the core of Nancy's being. She knew the minute she saw Damon's expression talking to Harold that he was slipping away from her. She'd hoped what she saw was a mistake, but the more she thought about it, the more she knew she wasn't wrong. It was a total departure from the detached and almost comical expression Damon tended to wear whenever he was in a meeting with Harold, listening to him drone on and on about purpose and goal-setting and list-making. This time around, he looked engaged, really tuned into what Harold was saying, and it made her worry.

For the most part, she'd done well to keep her wits about her and wasn't completely ignorant of her romantic situation. She'd realized quickly after their first time together that Damon had bedded her more out of an interest in having something over on Harold, and not solely on her own merits. She could tell from his insistence on wanting to attempt things in the apartment. To Damon, discretion seemed to be a secondary concern, as if he wasn't at all bothered by the idea of being caught, and although she understood his mindset, she persisted with the affair, knowing it was a calculated risk. Foolishly or not, she'd allowed herself to hope that he'd sincerely fall for her, and for an instant, that hope was elevated by the way he acquiesced to her demand to search for a condom, lest he only be allowed to perform oral sex on her. In that moment, she'd stopped feeling like a groupie around him, and instead felt herself getting stronger. Could one meeting with Harold really have changed their dynamic entirely?

She persisted on the phone, and when Damon finally arrived, Nancy was waiting by her car, having already locked up the branch for the evening. She was resolute and ready to go at a moment's notice. She had the credit cards, and he was most certainly on solid financial ground. They could leave with each other immediately, without any cash on hand, and figure it out. Nancy felt like she was a talented and resourceful woman; starting over from scratch couldn't be all that hard, especially if she was with Damon Alton. When he finally arrived, she said as much to him as he got out of his car to approach her. His response was less than ideal.

"Oh God, Nancy!" he moaned, "You haven't gone all bunny-boiler on me, have you?"

"Bunny-boiler?" she asked, dumbfounded by the response. "What in the hell is that supposed to mean?"

"Bunny-boiler," Damon explained, "from that movie where the woman falls for the guy she's sleeping with, and then goes crazy and boils the family bunny."

"You mean *Fatal Attraction*?" Nancy protested. "What makes me the bunny-boiler, Damon? I'm the married one in this scenario. You're the homewrecker. If anything, you'd be the bunny-boiler!"

"Homewrecker, maybe," Damon countered, "but I'm not the one being irrational right now. You're talking about throwing your entire marriage away over a *fling*! A fun fling, granted, but a fling nonetheless. Think about what you're proposing!"

"I'm proposing that we keep the fun going!" Nancy said, but her words and mannerisms were not in sync. All of her muscles felt like they were starting to tighten, and the level of her voice was elevating alongside her heart rate. She knew she'd lost him the minute she saw the look on his face when he'd gotten out of his car, but she couldn't help fighting all the same, and the further she took things, the more difficult it was to mask the tone of desperation becoming more apparent with each word that passed over her lips.

"You don't build your life around 'fun', Nancy," Damon said. "You build it around boring, responsible people like Harold, who really isn't all that bad a guy, by the way. Honestly, what's so terrible about him that you'd want to leave him?"

The question unleashed an unreasonable flood of anger into her being. She no longer gave the slightest shit as to how *nice* a guy Harold Dancy was. He could end hunger and find a cure for cancer, but at the end of the day, he'd still be Harold Dancy: a guy she'd never been into and had only married out of spite. She'd been young and immature when she made that decision, but now she knew better. She couldn't *un*know the things she'd come to realize about her marriage since her father's passing. Damon wasn't wrong in the sense that Harold wasn't a terrible man, but why did that entitle him to the best years of *her* life, when she just didn't connect with him in the same way that she did with Damon? To make matters worse, why did she need to explain herself to Damon Alton, of all people?

"Look," Nancy said, flustered, "you and I work together in a way that Harold and I can't. Don't just dismiss the chemistry we have! I know you've felt it, too!"

"Wow," Damon replied, flatly. "You've really put everything into this one basket, haven't you?" He looked hard into her eyes for a second, and then continued, bluntly. "Let me set you straight. You're great, but you're not the first woman to come at me with the *whole new life together* bit, and I've walked that path one too many times to want to walk it again. You're not thinking of the consequences!"

"I have -" Nancy protested, but Damon cut her off.

"For yourself, Nancy!" he snapped. "You've only thought about yourself. It's all well and good for you to uproot your whole life, get a new job with a famous new boyfriend that you can have loads of sex with, but what about me? I belong to a management company! I'm under contract, and Harold's a part of that contract! You'd get to run away, but I wouldn't.

Regardless of what passes between us, I'm still beholden to him and to the record company. Likewise, let's not forget the media frenzy a scandal like this would attract!"

Everything was falling to pieces, right in front of her eyes, and dreams of running away with Damon were slowly evaporating into an air of bitterness. His words hurt, and all she could think to do was to lash out at him, so she did.

"Oh, get over yourself, Damon!" she yelled. "You're not even newsworthy anymore."

The expression on his face changed immediately, going completely slack. He was stunned by what he'd just heard, and Nancy, knowing immediately what she'd done, didn't hesitate to do more. She seized on the opportunity and continued to put him in his place.

"Everything you do," she growled, "like visiting the out-of-the-way places for coffee, and always with your need to be 'discreet' in public, is all part of your delusional fantasy that you're more than a has-been! Well guess what, Damon? Nobody cares!"

Damon stared at her, hearing everything she said, becoming more stoic with each passing second. A silence grew between them when she finished, and he let it settle there for a moment, thinking of what to say. When he spoke next, what he said was more statement than question.

"So," he said slowly, "you think I'm a *has-been*."

"I think," Nancy replied carefully, "that you could be happier with me than you are right now, alone and by yourself."

"Tempting," Damon replied, "but I don't know that I could be happy with someone who thought so little of me. Unlike you, I tend not to commit to relationships built on such little substance. So, if you'll excuse me, I'll be on my way now."

"Really?" Nancy called out to him as he turned toward his car. "You're going to choose Harold over me?"

"It's not a choice between the two of you," Damon answered, turning back to look at her. "It's me continuing on with the life that I've spent the better part of twenty years building. Since you bring it up, though, Harold's the first guy in a long time to actually talk to me like a musician and not a product. He sees what I want to do, and he's going to help me get there. It's actually kind of refreshing!"

"Well, what are you going to do if he finds out about us?" Nancy asked, grasping at the edge of a point to stand upon.

Damon tilted his head to the side in thought, regarded her for a moment, as though he were making an evaluation, then said simply, "I won't tell if you won't."

"Don't think we'll be sleeping with each other again!" Nancy said, defiantly, but it failed to impact him the way she wanted it to.

"I wouldn't have it any other way," he said as he walked to his car, got in, and drove away, leaving Nancy alone with her thoughts.

She stood there in the emptiness of the parking lot, the sweeping landscape of barren black asphalt totally bereft of cars, save her own, and she felt like she could scream. This was not what she wanted, and she didn't know what to do next. She only knew where she didn't want to be, and so she got into her car and slammed the door shut.

From her vantage behind the steering wheel, she could see that she was back to where she'd been all those weeks ago, back to thinking about her father and her failure of a marriage. She was back to being stuck again. If it really was *lady's choice*, at what point was she going to make the right decision?

Not wanting to think anything more about it, she slipped her key into the ignition and turned it, only to hear the worst and most inconvenient sound the engine could possibly utter. She'd worked in the rental business long enough to know what that noise meant. Instinctively, she looked over to her headlight switch to see that she had, in fact, left it on. Her battery was dead.

She should've thought to unlock the branch, get the emergency jump kit, and take care of matters on her own, but she didn't. Instead, she called Harold, angrily explained the situation, and demanded that he come and pick her up.

Sensing trouble, Harold said he would drop everything and come to her. True to his word, he was there in less than fifteen minutes, pulling up beside her car in his oversized SUV. Having to climb into it reminded Nancy of how much she hated Harold's vehicle, how he referred to it as *The Tank*, and how he defended its purchase by saying it was to protect 'precious cargo', as though she were cargo that needed protecting. Her feelings of quiet rage were suddenly compounded. She fumed miserably to herself, buckled her seatbelt, and folded her arms over her chest.

Harold read her body language and felt it better to say nothing. He put the SUV into drive and pulled away from Nancy's car, assuming it was safe to leave it there for the night. By the time they were on the highway, a tense atmosphere had slowly built inside the vehicle's cabin, and he felt unsure of what to do next. Finally, he broke the silence and asked her, "Is everything okay?"

Nancy stared straight ahead and said nothing.

"Bad afternoon at work?" Harold persisted, and Nancy turned her head slightly to glare at him, which Harold mistook as confirmation. "Well, if that's all..." he said, and it was in that familiar tone that Nancy had grown to despise, the one he'd used on all of his helpless clients, and the one he was using on her now. It was a tone that suggested he could help fix this.

"Damon chose you," she said under her breath, but Harold didn't hear her completely.

"What's that?" he asked.

The question itself broke open the gates of some closely kept pit of rage that dwelled deep within her. Nancy could feel herself starting to slip into the darkest form of anger she'd ever felt.

"You took Damon," she answered. Her voice was louder now, and she cast a look of seething anger in Harold's direction. Oblivious to the root of her hostility, he kept his own eyes steady on the road.

"I'm not sure I follow your meaning," Harold replied, navigating through traffic. He was more focused on getting around a rather large box truck that was going under the speed limit. He slipped into the left lane to try to zip past him. "Do you mean like I took Damon on as a client?"

Whether it was because of the sheer cluelessness of his statement, or that she felt like she'd lost something to Harold Dancy, of all people, Nancy reached a breaking point. She glanced out the driver side window and watched the median's concrete embankment glide past them as the SUV picked up speed, coming up even with the box truck. Nancy felt hypnotized by the mass of stone, moving so fast she could hardly follow it with her eyes, and in that moment she fantasized of thrusting Harold into it.

What occurred next happened in the breath of an instance. It passed too quickly for consequences to be considered. Impulsively, Nancy rocked forward, and jerked her hand outward to reach for the steering wheel, but the shoulder strap of her seatbelt locked into place and cut her just short of the mark. She reached down to unbuckle herself, just as Harold swung his head over to her direction. The last thing he saw was the wild look in her eye as she came out of her seat and grabbed hold of the steering wheel, jerking hard to the left.

The front end of the SUV's bumper caught the jagged edge of where two sections of the concrete barrier met unevenly, and the back end swung to the right. The driver side airbag deployed, but the passenger's side didn't, as it had been automatically turned off from Nancy leaving her seat. In the chaos, Harold went face first into what felt like a canvas wall, and an unpleasant popping noise came from the bridge of his nose. As for Nancy, her body was thrown forward through the windshield, with the back of her head, neck, and the top of her shoulders making first contact. She flew over the hood, coming full force into the median barrier, and the bones in her body broke instantly in countless places, creating waves of pain that put her in an immediate state of shock. A cacophony of shattering glass, screaming brakes, and squealing tires deafened her. The air was strong with the scent of burning rubber and old motor oil.

It was quick. In that second she touched the steering wheel, she'd been immersed in an all-encompassing darkness that robbed her of all her senses. Nancy couldn't even feel what it was like to take her last breath.

Chapter Nine

Harold Comes Clean (A Story About Now)

"What do you mean she was trying to kill you?" Damon asked, stunned by Harold's words. Harold steadied himself on his feet and shut his eyes against the swirling pain still present from the two knocks to the head he sustained; first from Damon's quick jab to the nose, and then from the resultant trip and fall that landed him on the back of his head. His mind was suddenly filled with images and phrases from the night of the accident, newly resurfaced and not to be ignored. They were the sharpest memories he'd ever recalled. Thinking about them clearly for the first time in a year, he wondered how he ever convinced himself that something had jumped out in front of his SUV on the highway. Had he been so desperate to avoid some semblance of truth?

"All this time," Harold said, looking for the words to match his racing mind, "I thought she was protecting me from something. Why else would she have removed her seatbelt to get to the steering wheel? Nothing else would've made any sense!"

"Slow down," Damon cautioned. "Just sit down a minute. How did we go from 'you trying to kill yourself' to 'Nancy tried to kill you'?" He was just as bewildered as Harold was with the turn of events. This was supposed to be a one-man intervention, where he'd call out his friend on his suicidal tendencies, with the result being that they'd agree he'd get help, so that they could continue down this new path of making music together, culminating in the reunion of The Common Miscreants.

He hadn't meant to let slip the fact that he'd slept with Nancy; he would've gladly taken that secret with him to his grave. It came out, however, and in the form of a tasteless retort that he immediately regretted as soon as it left his lips, especially considering Harold's reaction and the way he came after him. He'd never intended to lay a hand on his friend, but it was all he could think to do to stop the rush of flailing limbs bearing down on him. The aftermath of it all was absolutely surreal. Of all the reactions to a stiff backhand to the side of the head, the last thing Damon thought would happen was for Harold to come up from the floor, saying his wife had tried to murder him. A new layer of guilt was already starting to form over the old one he'd done his best to ignore, and he hoped that Harold was just rattled and talking nonsense. Harold, however, was more than convinced.

"The last thing she said to me," Harold recalled, holding his fingers to his temples and shutting his eyes tightly, "was your name."

"*My* name?" Damon asked defensively, put off by this new information. "What did she say about me?"

"I didn't know what to think of it at the time," Harold continued, and now he opened his eyes and threw a look toward Damon that was like a dagger to the chest, "but now that I know you two were sleeping with each other, it makes every bit of sense!"

"What did she say?" Damon repeated, now with a touch of fear in his voice.

"She said I *took* you. She looked at me and literally said, 'You took Damon.' It was the last thing I heard her say before she grabbed the wheel." Then the reality of it came upon him instantly, and in disgust, he added, "Oh God... those were her dying words."

The color drained from Damon's face. There was nothing he could say to that, as he'd long been in a state of denial, himself. Of course it was suspicious that the day he ended things with her, she and Harold would be in a car accident only an hour later, but he willed himself to believe that it was a coincidence, much like Harold willed himself to believe that Nancy had grabbed the wheel for altruistic reasons. He'd even taken solace in that version of the story, wanting it to be the truth as much as Harold did, because if it *was* true, it meant that he'd done nothing wrong in ending the affair and that her death had nothing to do with him. This new revelation washed all of that away. He felt himself getting sick at the thought of what happened to Nancy, and what Harold had been going through since then.

Abruptly, Harold stood up, grabbed his keys, and walked briskly toward the door. Damon reacted quickly, came around the furniture, and wedged himself between Harold and his exit, delivering his protest in the process. "Come on, Harold!" he pleaded. "Where are you going to go."

Harold stopped in place and glared at Damon. "I don't know," he said, "but it'll probably be a motel room. I'm sure you could suggest which places are the classiest to hole up in for a day or two."

"And why would you be so desperate to leave?" Damon countered, ignoring the obvious jab. "You want to write a new note before you finish the job?"

"No!" Harold said, raising his voice and rolling his eyes to look away in frustration. "I just want to get away from you!"

"So... you don't want to die anymore?" The question came out of Damon in such a small way. The shift in tone, from accusatory to vulnerable, robbed Harold of his present sense of anger. Even the expression on Damon's face had changed, and when Harold acknowledged him again, he could see he was looking at someone who really thought himself a friend. The concern was obvious.

Feeling defeated, Harold answered, "No... at least I don't plan on it. Not today, anyway. I can't shake the feeling of being lost, man. I was having hallucinations, or I'm having them, and somedays I feel like I'm losing my damn mind. Right now, you're not helping things."

He didn't wait to hear what Damon had to say after that. He brushed past him, bumping his shoulder as he made his way out the door, and didn't look back. He went down to his car but paused when he got to it. It had been a simple choice; a used sedan bought after the SUV was wrecked. Though the accident hadn't totaled it, Harold naturally had no desire to ever drive it again. He'd bought the smallest, cheapest replacement he could find, if not for any other reason than just the contrast it provided. Standing next to it now, it was like revisiting all of the decisions he'd made since the accident. Everything was subject to this new context, and it sent chills through him. He knew if he wasn't careful, he was liable to start picking every little instance of his life to pieces, and not just the years with Nancy, but the months after her death, too. The questions were already starting to form a list in his head:

Did she really want to kill him?
Had he wronged her so terribly to justify murder?
Was he a bad person and just didn't realize it?

There were so many answers he didn't have, and all he really wanted to do was just put an end to the night. So much had happened in the last few moments that it was hard to believe he'd just had a nice time with Shawnee not one hour ago. If he wasn't already unhinged, he was well on his way, and before he could even conceive of what he was doing, he was in the car and driving. When he became cognizant of his actions, he was already halfway to a stretch of highway motels nearby, and he was repeating out loud, like a mantra, "I just need to get some sleep. I just need to get some sleep..."

Harold glanced in the rearview mirror and was immediately aware of Damon's car following him from behind, but he lacked the energy to care. He needed to put a cap on the night and pulled up to the first place with a vacancy sign.

Getting through the check-in process as fast as he could, Harold paid up front for a five-day stay. Tomorrow, he would try to make sense of his life. Tonight, he just needed a bed to lie in.

On his way out of the motel office and to his room, Harold glanced over toward the parking lot and saw Damon's car idling in a spot not far from where he'd parked. Harold shook his head and kept moving. Damon could wait.

When he got to his room, he stood in the doorway for a moment to take a good look at his surroundings. He started by flipping a switch to the left, illuminating a small wall-mounted lamp light that cast dark shadows on the room's drab, beige paint job. The only thing that offered even a hint of vibrancy was a single framed print of a floral painting that hung on the wall opposite of the door. The bathroom was directly to his right, and with the lights on, it looked remarkably sterile, as though no one had ever used it before. The air had the faint odor of potpourri, and for a cheap motel room, Harold was impressed. A few steps inside gave him a full view of two twin beds, neatly made with floral-patterned comforters that *almost* matched the framed print on the wall. A solitary nightstand stood between the two beds, complete with a second lamp and a digital alarm clock with large red numbers that blinked midnight, though it was well past two in the morning. Opposite the beds was a large, box-shaped television that looked like a relic of the early 90s. It sat on top of a long dresser housing empty drawers meant for long-term inhabitants.

Harold had nothing with him to put in the drawers and had no real sense of a plan. Considering the hour of the night and the information he'd just processed, it was fair to say he was in a mild state of shock and in dire need of anything that could offer comfort. The room itself, bereft of Nancy's touch (which, try as he did, could not be scrubbed from their old apartment), offered him a blank space with which to rest his mind. He collapsed face-first onto the bed closest to him, and within minutes was in a deep sleep.

***

Harold rarely dreamt vividly, and typically only ever woke up with vague notions of obscure visions, but when he passed out on top of the floral covered twin-bed in his motel, he had the subconscious notion of being transported someplace that was otherworldly. It was as if he were somehow outside the realm of time itself, and if felt bizarrely familiar.

In his dream, he was seated alone at the top of a bleacher and in his hands he held a paperback book. He looked at its cover, stark white and featureless, then flipped through its pages; all of them were blank. Part of him felt disappointed by this, but he also knew it probably wouldn't have made any difference to him. Had there been anything printed on the pages, he still wouldn't have been able to read anything. He looked up and around and noticed everything around him seemed to be slightly blurred. Colors were muted, edges were softened, and the hard, smooth surface of the bleachers on either side of him took on a rough texture. Harold, who'd had perfect vision his whole life, thought to himself, *this must be what it's like to need glasses*, as though he needed to make a mental note for some future instance when old age or life in general would make a play for his sight.

He blinked a few times in an effort to see more clearly, and he looked up at the sky above him, which was unnaturally purple with pink puffy clouds. He inhaled deeply through his nose, expecting fresh air, but was instead treated to the odor of dust mixed with the smell of a mild, feminine perspiration. It stung him in a way he had not expected. *I know that smell*, he thought to himself, and then his attention was drawn to the sound of a hard smack, like a ball hitting a leather glove, followed seconds later by the plunking sound of something being dropped into a plastic bucket.

He blinked again, harder this time, as though trying to bring things into focus, concentrating on what was in front of him. He heard a familiar voice yell, "Coming down!" and then the smacking leather sound, followed by the plastic being plunked again.

That's Nancy, his thoughts continued, and he tried to speak, but found he couldn't. His lips were too dry and stuck together, like they'd been fused by some incredible thirst. The feeling made him panic, and he tried to call out, but couldn't. It suddenly felt like he was suffocating. He squeezed his eyes shut as hard as he could, and when he opened them again, instantaneously, everything came into clear view:

Nancy *was* behind the plate, wearing her old college softball uniform and catcher's gear, the equipment she used to playfully call *the tools of ignorance*. Even her hair was braided and pulled back like she used to wear it during the season. This sight gave his heartstrings a youthful twist, and he remembered that he hadn't seen her hair kept like that since their last year in college together, when she'd played her final games as a serious athlete. It made him wonder just how much of her had stopped *being* after they'd graduated, and the thought only worsened the twisting sensation.

Across from her, he saw a fire-engine red pitching machine mounted to a tripod standing at the center of the mound. Its large cylindrical clip of yellow softballs jutted out from the back end. A small cord ran from it all the way down to home plate and attached to a controller that Nancy held in her right hand. The device looked like a joystick with a red button on top, and when she pressed it, a softball launched out from the machine, moving faster than his eyes could follow. Nancy would catch it cleanly, drop the controller, pop up into her perfected stance, and rocket the softball toward second base. Harold watched her throw it on a line that broke just ahead of the bucket so that the ball dropped neatly inside, landing with the familiar plastic plunking sound. Nancy would look on, evaluate her throw, and when seemingly satisfied, she would give a quick fist pump before squatting back down to pick up the device and do it all over again.

The sight was too much, and he couldn't understand why he'd brought so much of the real world into a dream. Seeing her in the flesh made him heartbroken with longing, and his love for Nancy made him happy to find her doing what she'd been the best at for so long. And yet, he could not escape the echo of Damon Alton's voice in the back of his ears and the crass thing that he'd said, or the vision of Nancy's hand thrusting toward the steering wheel. There were too many thoughts happening at once, too many feelings to bear, even in a dream world, and without warning, Harold had found his voice.

A long, feral roar, unlike anything a human should produce, shook the ground beneath them, and the sky's mild purple hues grew several shades darker. A nasty wind kicked up from behind, whipping the dust up from the infield to blow the bucket of balls backwards. Nancy leapt up from her position and ripped off her mask to look in Harold's direction, and Harold caught full view of her face. She looked younger than he remembered, almost the age before they got married, but her skin had a ghostly luminous tint. Only the milky whites of her eyes showed themselves, as if he were looking into the open stare of his dead wife, and without moving her lips, her voice echoed inside his mind.

"Harold?"

Harold rose up from his sleeping position, gasping for air; his body was covered in sweat. A large wet spot was at the center of the pillow, and he quickly deduced that at some point in the night, he'd rolled face down, accounting for his difficulty breathing. He looked at the alarm clock to see that it was still blinking midnight. He checked his phone and was stunned by what he saw. He'd slept for twelve hours straight and had woken up just shy of 3 p.m. The luminescence of the wall light was washed out by the sunlight pouring in through the open blinds of the windows, and it was all too disorienting.

The dream had been so vivid that it was hard to negotiate where he'd woken up and where sleep had taken him. When he fully recalled *where* he was, and *why* he was there, a momentary pang of grief hit him. It threatened a wave of despondence, and just before it could, Harold recalled an important aspect of his dream. It was so clear in his memory, and so uncharacteristic of him in reality, that it made his feeling of heartache vanish into nothing.

Harold had *roared*. It had happened, and Nancy took notice. Sure, he told himself, it'd only been a dream, but it still must have meant something, right? His sleeping mind had been wrestling with Damon's admission, some new aspect of his marriage had been processed, and a fundamentally different understanding of his life's trajectory had taken root from deep within.

Now he stood up, resolute, and felt himself smiling as he walked to the bathroom. He stripped down, and allowed himself a very long, hot shower with which to thoroughly cleanse himself, body and mind. He was so thorough, in fact, that he used both complimentary bottles of shampoo and conditioner in their *entirety*, even though his thinning red hair didn't need quite so much. Likewise, he wore the mini bar of soap down to just a bare sliver of its former self, going so far as to even scrub behind his ears and between his toes, places which typically only received the benefit of runoff suds from his hair or general body wash. When he got out of the shower, he trimmed his fingernails, combed his hair, flossed, and brushed his teeth. Even the complimentary razor was put to use. When his impromptu deep cleansing was complete, he stood before the motel's bathroom mirror and evaluated himself.

It was like coming out of a tailspin. Harold looked deep into his own eyes, and said something out loud that he'd never said before, something he'd long denied, even in his own private thoughts:

"I didn't kill my wife."

His expression didn't change. He didn't break away from his reflection, and his words did not falter. He hadn't felt so confident about anything since the accident, nor so clear headed. Everything up to this point, his work with Damon on his life plan and comeback album, the random excursions into soup kitchen work, and even his one date with Shawnee felt like a distraction from the one prevailing thought that was with him both day and night - that he had survived something he didn't deserve to survive, and therefore didn't deserve to live when Nancy had died. Whether he was conscious of it or not, he had tried his best to mask his survivor's guilt and suicidal ideation with the trappings of a grand romantic gesture: *Harold's suicide in the name of love*. It was such a powerful thought that it had spurred him on to try and try again.

His new perspective forced a look backwards. What about all those botched attempts? What about that last time? Hadn't he seen Nancy's ghost? Wasn't he certain of it? He had to think. Was her appearance in the living room the same as it had been in his dream?

"If she didn't love me, and she tried to kill me, then there's no way she's been trying to save me..." and just like that, his doubt returned. The moment of resolution passed quickly, and confusion flirted with his mind once again. This time had to be different though. He couldn't spend another moment dwelling on why he had survived the SUV wreck; he had to dwell on why he'd survived his suicide attempts. He needed someone to talk to, and he knew it couldn't be Damon.

He got dressed, and his feelings of cleanliness were slightly diminished by having to wear yesterday's clothes, but not enough to dissuade him from what he was about to do next. He looked at his phone and noted the time. It was five o'clock - a totally appropriate time to call Shawnee and ask her to come over. She felt like somebody he could trust to get things off his chest, and she'd maybe even help him make better sense of everything, but just as he was ready to dial her number, he got cold feet and sent her a text message instead: *"Are you interested in dinner?"*

He sat down on the bed and placed his phone next to him, unsure of what to expect. It might be hours before she saw the message, and they'd already spent time with each other the night before...

His phone went off almost immediately, much to his surprise. Shawnee had messaged him back with, *"Ur place or mine?"*

Harold, who hadn't had a lot of experience texting with people back and forth, answered honestly, *"Actually, I've got a motel room. I could get us a pizza if that's okay with you."*

Again, not more than two minutes after the message had been sent, Harold's phone lit up with Shawnee's response. *"Send me the address"* his phone read, so he replied and included the motel room number. She messaged him back saying she'd be there by six.

Harold was a little surprised with how quickly she was willing to come over, so he left the room in a hurry to grab some necessities. On the way to his car, he was happy to see that Damon had since left the parking lot but didn't put much more thought into it than that. He drove away from the motel and went five miles south to a mini mall that housed a laundromat, a pizza and sub shop, and a convenience store.

He took note of the laundromat for later use, especially if he was going to be staying for the full five days at the motel. It forced him to think about how he'd need to get a change of clothes from his spot at Damon's without having to deal with Damon himself, which was another thought for later. At present, he focused on dinner with Shawnee and put in an order at the shop for a medium cheese pizza. While he waited for the food, he headed over to the convenience store for some essentials, like more shampoo and soap, as well as napkins, paper plates, and plastic spoons. His room didn't have a mini-fridge, but he'd seen an ice machine on the way to his car, so he picked up a small cooler and a six pack of beer to keep cold for his impromptu date. It might be nice, he thought, to just sit on the bed quietly with her and eat a slice while sharing a beer, before he tried to work up the nerve to talk about his experiences after Nancy's death. In her line of work, he was certain she'd seen her fair share of weirdness, and he hoped she'd might judge things better than he could.

When the pizza was ready for pick up, he paid the bill, made his way back to the motel, and had just enough time to make sure the bathroom was tidy and his bed was made before he heard a knock on the door. He glanced at his phone and saw it was six on the dot. Smiling at her punctuality, Harold opened the door, and what he saw made him immediately take a step back.

Shawnee stood before him, looking just as gorgeous as she did the night before, if not more so. It was almost embarrassing, as he quickly realized he had on the same thing from yesterday, and he hoped desperately she wouldn't notice. Obviously, it was one thing to see her made up to go out to a music venue with him, but now she wore a tight black dress that complimented her beautiful brown complexion, while amplifying her curves and breasts in a way that was impossible for him to ignore. Her hair was pulled back again, and he could see the red rubies of her earrings were a near match to her color of lipstick. He barely had time to process the raised eyebrow expression on her face. No sooner had he opened the door and said, "Wow," she was on him, lips fully locked onto his, a hand on his ass, and moving their bodies toward the bed. Her back heel came up as she entered, kicking the door closed, and just before Harold fell over onto the mattress, a clear thought entered his mind:

She thinks I got a motel room for sex...

Instantly, Harold was squirming to get out from under her. He made it to a seated position on the edge of the bed while Shawnee, still on her feet, continued to lean into him, with her knees pressed against his inner thighs. He felt like he needed to clarify his intent, but it was hard to break away, having never experienced a woman coming at him with such force before. His mind screamed that he should confess to her that he'd only ever had sex with one woman, and that he should stop things now before she found out he wasn't any good at it. A strong sense of performance anxiety was beginning to churn within him, and before he could help it, his mind went to thinking about Nancy and Damon, and (God help him) whether or not this was what it had been like for them.

Shawnee, however, gave no hint that she was aware of what was going on in Harold's mind. Arched up against him, she passionately kissed his neck and worked her lips up to his ear, while she pressed her left hand against Harold's crotch. Harold's eyes widened and his entire body went rigid with the sensation, which Shawnee must've taken to be a good sign. She leaned into him, and he leaned with her, propping himself up on his elbows while arguing internally as to whether or not he should remove her hand from his pants. As he was thinking about this, he was caught off guard by Shawnee's right hand, which glided up his chest on its way to his throat, where he felt her fingers tighten slightly against his neck.

It was sensory overload. Her lips on his ear, one hand on his crotch, and the other around his neck was more than he knew what to do with. He brought a hand up to lightly brush away what was happening with his throat, but she was undeterred. Her hand came back up so forcefully that his forearm slipped from underneath of him, and he fell onto his back. Shawnee jumped on top of him, straddling his waist while choking him harder as her other hand worked to unzip his pants. Harold meant to protest, but couldn't find his voice, and in spite of everything, found himself being aroused anyway.

The small lamp mounted to the wall, casting a dim light over their activities, suddenly grew very bright. The bulb underneath the lamp shade shattered with the wave of electricity, creating a loud pop that made Shawnee stop and look behind her, startled.

"What the hell was that?" she asked, while Harold, also alarmed at the room's sudden darkness, reached for the drawstring of the light beside the bed. It clicked on, and they were both able to see a small black stain on the wall behind the shade, like evidence of a miniature explosion.

"It must've been a power surge," Harold suggested, and Shawnee looked back at him with a satisfied grin.

"Or maybe we're just *electric*," she said playfully, and she made to go back to kissing him when Harold used the opportunity to stop her entirely.

"Wait, please, just one second?" he asked her, and Shawnee pulled away from him with a look of worry on her face.

"Was I being too hard?" she replied. Although Harold could hear the note of concern in her voice, he still felt compelled to say something.

"Too hard?" he echoed, squirming again to pull himself up into a seated position. "It was more like too much! Why were you trying to choke me?"

"I thought that's what you were into," Shawnee said, shifting back away from Harold. "You know... the asphyxiation stuff. I'm an open minded woman, Harold, and it certainly *felt* like you liked it..."

Flustered, Harold could feel his face turn red for a moment. "That was more from the stuff you were doing with the other hand, not the one that was around my neck."

"I don't understand," Shawnee said. "If that's not what you're into, then why..."

"That's actually why we have to stop," Harold quickly replied, cutting her off. "I realize now that it probably looks like I had certain intentions by getting a motel room, and it goes without saying that I'm completely flattered that you'd come over with that in mind! It's just not the reason I asked you to come here..."

"So then why am I here?" Shawnee asked, and he could see that she was beginning to take offense. He couldn't beat around the bush and risk losing her, so he dove right into it.

"The reason I was in the hospital," Harold began, "wasn't because of what you think. That was just something Damon came up with. I wanted to talk to you about the real reason I wound up in the hospital... all of it. The full story." He hesitated, and then added in a softer voice, "It might get a little weird."

Harold looked at her anxiously, and Shawnee studied him closely. "Okay then," she said, after a moment of silence. "Tell it to me."

Chapter Ten

Nancy, Dead (A Story About Four Attempts)

When she hit the concrete embankment and her last breath escaped, collapsing her lungs for good, she did not experience a montage of all her life's greatest moments, nor did she feel any warm light pouring over her, beckoning her towards some set of pearly gates, beset by ponderous clouds.

For Nancy, there was no previous experience that could prepare her for dying.

She had been wrapped up in the total darkness of the moment. A panic crept into her sense of *being*, whatever it now was, and it made her want to hyperventilate, but there was no air to breathe for her to do so. She felt tethered to something, stuck, and bobbing in an atmosphere of nothingness, like a balloon tied to a child's wrist; there was just enough movement to suggest freedom, but any attempt to explore space was met with an anchor of frustration. It was an attack on senses that no longer existed, and the paradoxical nature of her situation was maddening: She was simultaneously aware and unaware. She knew she was dead, and understood the circumstances of her death, but had no idea what new state she was in now. She'd become a mind without a body. She wanted to clench her eyes shut and run her fingers through her hair like she did when things were stressful, but she lacked the means to do these things.

She was an abstract, and nothing more. She continued to float along in that void of despondency, until a voice, *her* voice, called out of the darkness, like some kind of repetitive mantra:

I just need to get some sleep... I just need to get some sleep... I just need...

She suddenly felt the need to dream, and with the sound of her own voice pouring over her again and again, the panic that had threatened to tear at her slowly faded into a dull background noise. It was not entirely gone but had mellowed out in the same way that the pain in her knees had after all her years of catching. It became manageable.

As the tension faded, the darkness surrounding her turned to a dark purple. "It's almost my favorite color," she heard her own voice say, and it was bewildering to hear herself speaking without conscientiously using a mouth, or lungs, or vocal cords. "If only it were just a bit lighter," the voice continued, and instantly it was. She saw before her an exaggerated version of all the twilights from her youth, and a memory began to take form.

This was the sky she remembered from being behind home plate, when there was just enough light from the setting sun to see the shape of the softball as it left the pitcher's hand. The sunset painted the clouds a pale pink that stood out in contrast to the purple sky that further darkened with every passing minute. She remembered the smell of dust and sweat mingled with the cool breeze coming off the river near the ball field; air that always smelt of the marshy shores by the waterways, but not so pungent as to be displeasing. It smelled like home.

Now, Nancy found she could blink through a set of eyes she'd already lived through. Her body was from her sophomore year of college, when she felt her strongest and at the peak of her physical capabilities, but her surroundings resembled that of a more distant memory, of being thirteen and fighting for a coveted prize: the starting spot behind the plate, calling plays and commanding the infield. In that moment, her awareness of everything became total: there she was, fully equipped in her catcher's gear, feet standing in their practiced position behind home plate, softball clutched firmly in her right hand, and the catcher's mitt hanging on her left.

"I'm making this happen," she heard her own voice say, though her lips stayed firmly in place. They would not shift, because they could not move, not even to form a smile, but it didn't matter. It was enough to have her thoughts become audible, as though her mind's words could not be deterred from taking form, despite what other senses seemed frozen in time.

"This will do just fine," Nancy thought approvingly, and she took in the full scenery that was borne from the darkness of her mind. The infield dirt was finely groomed, more-so than it ever had been in real life, and the chalk-white outlines of the batter's boxes looked symmetrical and perfect, with their first and third base foul lines extending outward like two taut and immaculate rays. Hadn't that always seemed impossible in real life? How many times had she watched all of the volunteer coaches and dads struggle to wheel out powdered lime over a loose string connected haphazardly to a paint-can opener staked down behind home plate, with everything hurried in their effort to get the field ready by game time? Now, with the sheer power of her will, she could summon up perfection. Even the bases themselves looked bleached white, untouched by the cleats of young girls tagging-up, sliding in, or standing over to cover the steal. The grass of the outfield was startlingly green, almost glowing in the low darkness of twilight, and was so well manicured that it could've been the fairway for a professional golf course. The dugouts, well off to either side of the foul lines, were in excellent condition, and fully stocked with bats, gloves, helmets, and large orange jugs of water. For Nancy, these were the most perfect playing conditions, for practices or games. The only thing missing was the rest of her teammates.

"It's because practice is already over," she heard herself say. "This is me just getting my extra reps, just the way I used to insist after rough days..."

And with the power of that one thought, a pitching machine appeared on the mound, precisely forty-three feet away from her, the exact distance she would've demanded even as a kid. The only difference now was in the superior quality of what had just materialized before her, which wasn't anything like the machine she'd first used from way back when. That thing had been a rusted-out affair carted around by her old coach... what had his name been? She couldn't recall. She could only vaguely remember a slim man feeding softballs in manually, one at a time, and making constant adjustments to the tripod it sat on, as he could never find the perfect strike zone. Secretly, Nancy had liked that old machine's unpredictability, and thought it made her a better catcher; it certainly forced her to work on framing a bad pitch so that it looked like it might've hit the edge of a strike zone, or just close enough to make an umpire second guess himself. Funny that she could remember the detail but couldn't summon it now.

What stood before her in its stead was not at all what she'd been used to. This was a brand-new pitching machine, fire-engine red, more like the ones from her high school years, only better. Nancy walked out to the mound and examined it from all angles. The machine looked gorgeous, sat evenly on the hill, and even came with a push-button trigger attached to a long wire. Nancy picked up the control, pressed the button, and was surprised by the yellow blur of a softball that shot out of the machine, impressed with its speed and accuracy. It whistled as it cut through the air and hit the backstop so hard that the smack of metal echoed into the outfield, and a small impression was left behind. Most catchers would've been intimidated by a fast pitch softball coming in that hot, but this was the product of Nancy's mind, and she naturally relished the opportunity to get behind a pitch of such magnitude.

She kept the controller in her hand and jogged back to her spot behind home plate. She placed the controller in the dirt beside her and looked around the softball diamond. Where once there was nothing, there was now a large plastic bucket by second base, and Nancy's eyes lit up with a fiery passion. She knew exactly what this was a setup for, and she lowered the catcher's mask sitting atop her head, squatted into position, and picked up the controller that laid beside her.

"Coming down!" her voice rang out into the empty softball diamond, and she pressed the button of the controller. A bullet of a softball came whizzing into her glove, but she felt no fear. In spite of the fact that it was going too fast for her to even perceive where it would impact, she sensed its location and caught it squarely in the webbing of her mitt, so that she felt no sting in the palm of her hand.

She jumped up into position, pulled the ball out of her glove, brought it back behind her ear, and launched it forward with a motion that felt both powerful and easy, like she could make that throw infinitely and never feel exhausted. The softball cut a straight path forward and dropped into the bucket with a satisfying plunk, with only the smallest bounce that defied the laws of physics.

None of this is real, she felt herself thinking, but this particular thought didn't take the form of audible speech like all the other ones had. Instead, she became aware of a sensation, like being the balloon on the child's wrist, and she registered the faint odor associated with hospitals and emergency rooms, mixed in with the scent of outdoor air and dust and sweat. This dreadful thought became more palpable, and the vision of the field and her catcher's equipment started to fade away into that sense of permanent darkness.

With all of the concentration she could muster, she forced her mind to call out, "Coming down!" The softball world snapped back into place with a sharp focus, and the odor along with the feeling of being tethered vanished instantly. Empowered by this moment, she understood what she must do to avoid the darkness. She would practice, get stronger, and learn the rules of this new existence. She would never return to that tethered feeling. She squatted back into place, picked up the pitching machine's controller, and pressed the button...

* * *

The hypnotic rhythm of squatting into position, calling the play, pushing the button, catching the pitch, and launching the throw-down (always punctuated by the plunking sound of the softball landing in the plastic bucket) consumed Nancy's being. It never got boring to her, in spite of the fact that the velocity of the pitching machine, or its pinpoint accuracy, never wavered, or that her throws were always consistent, and never once missed or bounced out of the bucket. The machine could launch a maximum of twenty pitches, and then Nancy would walk out from behind the plate, take the bucket from second base, load the balls back into their clip, and begin again with her post-practice routine, creating a perpetual full circle. Her determination superseded the mundanity of the activity, because she knew that it kept the darkness at bay. She thought about nothing except the game, and with every push of the button on the pitching machine control, it was like resetting her mind. She could've gone on this way for the rest of eternity, too, if it hadn't been for Harold, standing out in left field.

She saw him, just as she popped up into her stance, and froze. He was not looking at her, but turned slightly away toward center field, rocking lightly on his toes while staring at the dirt in front of him. A familiar smell, different from the ones she'd grown accustomed to, drifted toward her on a light breeze blowing from his direction, but it was too subtle to be completely identified. Feeling compelled, Nancy let the ball and her mitt slip from her hands and walked over to her husband. The closer she got to him, the heavier the scent became, while other sensations gained strength with each passing step as well.

Nearer and nearer still, it was the feeling of being the balloon on the string that was becoming ever powerful. What kept her tethered felt shorter now, crippling her sense of

172

freedom, until she was moving toward her husband with the immutable pull of some magnetic force, completely against her will. When her feet touched the grass of the outfield, the softball diamond disappeared completely, dissolving into a mist of air that revealed the apartment she shared with Harold when she was alive. It felt like it had been ages ago, but judging by her husband's looks, it hadn't seemed as though much time had passed at all. He stood outside the window of their bedroom, on the small balcony that overlooked the community area behind their complex, and he was nearly the same in appearance, except a little thinner and a bit more haggard than she'd ever recalled him being. She came closer to him, and when she was within arm's reach, she caught full sight of his face, and could see he'd been crying.

A momentary wave of compassion hit her, like a phantom vibration running through her being. Nancy wanted to speak but had no means to do so in this place, finding that her mental voice had gone silent inside their apartment. She could still think, though, and she tried to take in every detail that she could, hoping to make sense of it all. It was strange, and she couldn't understand how Harold's presence made its way onto her softball diamond, or how he was able to draw her into what she assumed was the real world, but here she was, unsure of what would happen next, until Harold spoke:

"You're doing this for Nancy," he uttered, as he slowly climbed over the handrail of their balcony, one foot at a time, until he was turned around and facing forward, with just the edge of his heels on the ledge, and his hands gripping the railing.

Horrorstruck, Nancy understood the situation, and not just what was obviously Harold's attempt at suicide. She understood why she was there, what the meaning of the balloon feeling was, and more importantly, what would happen if she watched Harold die. She was in the apartment, because *he* was in the apartment, just like when she caught the odor of the hospital, Harold must've been in treatment. They were connected. It wasn't a child's wrist she was attached to, but

173

Harold's soul. If he jumped from the balcony now, he would join her in whatever state of existential limbo this had been. It would be Nancy and Harold and the darkness, forever.

The compassion she initially felt turned to panic as soon as the connection with her husband became clear to her, and more than a hint of anger was mixed in with it. She had died trying to kill him, and in that instance found a place of peace without him. The solitude of her softball diamond, the perfect pitching machine, and the rhythm of her throwing drill would be lost with Harold in tow, and she couldn't stand the thought of how he might make an impression on their new existence together. He could ruin everything in death, as much as he had in life.

Harold was looking down at the sidewalk below, as though he was working up the nerve. He wasn't faking anything, either. Nancy was certain of that, in as much as she could *feel* his sincerity. Fifteen feet ahead of the spot where he'd land was the edge of the deep end of the complex's public pool, completely uninhabited, save a few people sunbathing on the deck with their eyes closed, oblivious to the man above them ready to take his own life. Desperation overcame her. Nancy thrust her hands forward and was surprised to find that she'd made contact with her husband. Not just a slight touch, either, but a full push with enough force to launch Harold forward.

He screamed as he sailed through the air, and cleared the sidewalk entirely, landing squarely and safely in the water. The splash he caused was so massive that it soaked the sunbathers lying innocently on their towels, and as the commotion of his landing garnered their attention, Nancy felt herself fade from her vantage point on the balcony.

She was standing alone in left field again, as though she'd never left the diamond, and Harold was nowhere to be seen. The sky above her was still the same twilight purple as it had been, and she felt a strange happiness as she considered her perpetual evening on the ball field. She'd discovered the nature of her new existence and felt a kinetic energy coursing through her that she'd previously been unaware of. This was *her* world, and she demanded ownership. That meant keeping Harold out, and to keep him out meant she'd have to keep him alive. As she made her way back to her position behind home plate to pick up her drill, she was struck by the notion that this suicide attempt would not be Harold's last. She couldn't explain why, except to say that she felt it within that connection to him.

***

It could've been after the hundredth pitch, or it could've been after the thousandth; Nancy didn't know. There wasn't any concept of time in this place, save for the routine and its unending repetition. The only thing she could be sure of was that once she'd started, she wouldn't stop until Harold appeared again, just as she thought he would.

The second time she saw him on the diamond, he was pacing around just behind first base, looking as though he was talking to himself. He had on a sweater that she distinctly remembered hating when she was living, worn on days when he told her he wanted to feel "comfortable and lazy." Only now, his sleeves were rolled up, which was never how she could recall him wearing them, and he held a paper in one hand, and a pencil in the other. With a sigh, she removed her catcher's mitt, placed it on home plate, and walked over to investigate the situation.

The feeling was much the same as it had been before. As she got closer to him, she could feel something in her tighten. Within a few feet of his presence, the field once again vanished, and she found herself inside their old kitchen. As if in response to her being there, he stopped pacing and placed the note down next to the sink, near a pack of razors.

Nancy examined the scene: plastic had been laid across the kitchen floor, and Harold was resting his arms on the sink. She glanced over at the note, read its one sentence, and shook her head at how ridiculous it was. *How ridiculous*, she thought,

175

glad she could make no sound in the real world. If she could laugh in this place, she would've done so.

She continued to watch him and could see that Harold was changing things up for his next suicide attempt. Jumping didn't work, so now he had to try a new method. Oddly enough, she respected him for that, as she herself was never one to chew her food twice. It also made things interesting for her, trying to figure out how to disrupt this next go.

The razors were obviously for his wrists, the kitchen sink was to keep the blood, and the plastic on the floor was probably to catch any residual blood spatter, so as to not stain their floors. It was classic Harold, and as hard as she wanted to laugh at his note, she would've laughed even harder at his devotion to being fastidious. Since she could not, she tried for the next best thing.

Feeling confident from the outcome of her poolside "shove", Nancy decided to further test her abilities. She looked hard at the box of razors, and concentrated on the composition of them, the coolness of the steel, and how they might feel in the palm of her hand. At first, there was nothing, but then, little by little, she could sense their presence, almost as though she was touching them without making any contact whatsoever. Soon, she felt the edge of a single razor, and with her focus, concentrated on making it dull, like folding the thinnest layer of molecules onto themselves, until the blade was no sharper than a ballpoint pen would've been. Satisfied with the results, she worked on the next sharp edge she could sense, until there were no more sharp edges she could pick up on.

When Harold went for the box, he took a deep breath and grabbed the first razor out of the pack. He pressed the corner of the edge against the flesh high up on his forearm, with his wrist angled downward into the sink. He solemnly whispered, "For Nancy," and thrust the razor downward, but to no real effect. His eyes had been clenched tightly in anticipation of the pain he thought he'd have to endure, and as he slowly opened them, the look was replaced by one of confusion. Harold saw that the best the razor could produce was a weak mark down the length of his arm, barely on the level of what a trimmed fingernail could do. Nancy watched him try a second time, a more emphatic third time, and then throw the razor down into the sink with disappointment. He grabbed a different razor from the box, reset himself in position, tried again, and still only achieved the same results. Angry, he started running the razor up and down his arm vigorously, like a child trying to erase a mistake on their homework, but the best he could produce was a harsh rash, and nothing more.

By the time her view of Harold faded away, replaced by her home on the softball field, Nancy felt incredibly satisfied, and almost looked forward to the next time she'd see her husband. As she picked up her mitt to resume her throwing drill, she wondered where he might reappear on the diamond, if in fact he did show up again...

$* * *$

The third time Harold appeared, he was not found on the field, but in the dugout. Nancy had become aware of his presence when the sounds of splashing mixed in with the sounds of her drill. She looked over at the home team side of the field and saw the dugout had taken on the qualities of a bathtub, filled with a muddy water made murky by the infield dirt, soaking the softball equipment housed inside. Nancy thought she'd be amused seeing Harold again, but not at the expense of the gear she so loved to glance at it in between pitches, especially the way the bats always looked in their rack, shining and unblemished.

Grudgingly, she shook loose her gear, and once more marched over to Harold, feeling his presence becoming a chore. She still couldn't get used to the pulling sensation within her whenever she'd get close to him, as each new encounter felt stronger than the last. When she approached the edge of the dugout, the field dissolved itself into their bathroom, and she saw Harold sitting in the tub, holding aloft the toaster that'd been given to them by his parents on their wedding day.

The bath had been fully drawn, and steam came off the water where the caps of his knee just barely broke through. Nancy evaluated the scene and judged by the angle where the toaster would fall, that it would land directly in his lap. A devious thought entered her mind, and she patiently waited for Harold to complete his ritual. His eyes were closed, he took a deep breath, and then exhaled it, whispering her name along with it. "Nancy," he said, relaxing his grip, and letting the toaster drop.

It was then that she focused all her concentration on the electricity running through the house, and right when the toaster was about to hit the water, she willed the circuit breaker to shut off. The lights went dark right as a loud splash was created. Harold leapt forward in the bathtub, howling with pain at having dropped a toaster directly onto his crotch...

* * *

For his fourth attempt, Harold appeared standing on second base, as Nancy had just let the ball release from her throw, dropping directly into the bucket as it always did. She felt a surge of energy run through her upon seeing him again, angry and annoyed that Harold could be so persistent. She tossed her glove aside and jogged toward second, feeling that the gravitational pull toward her husband was the strongest it had ever been.

Within seconds, the field was gone, and she was inside her living room, looking at Harold on top of a chair with a noose around his neck, ready to jump. Having realized the full scope of her power, Nancy was supremely confident in what she could do within Harold's presence. She concentrated on the soles of his shoes, binding their structure with the wood of the chair, feeling their molecules dance with each other until they were inextricably bonded. Then she watched in amusement as Harold made to step off, only to flounder around and shuffle with his feet glued to the chair. His face contorted, and she heard him say, "It's happening again... I don't understand why this keeps happening?"

Their connection, whatever the nature of it was, gave her a glimpse into his mind, and as quick as he thought to slip his foot out from his shoe, she was already ahead of him, concentrating on the laces so they would tighten in on themselves. When he thrust his knee forward and failed to kick out of his shoes, he looked down and made an expression of wonder, almost as if he could see Nancy's work playing out in real time.

Enjoying herself now, Nancy watched Harold remove his head from the noose and attempt to bend down to untie his laces. When he did so, she concentrated on the chair he stood on, focusing on creating a looseness of the joints holding it together that gave it a wobble when Harold doubled over. The effect was comic in nature, and she watched her husband stand upright and declare to no one in particular, "This isn't a deal-breaker! I can get through this. I *will* die today. You're not going to stop me."

It was doubtful Harold knew that Nancy was the "you're" in question, yet it kept her in the room to see how determined he really was, ignoring the counter-pull of her softball field, beckoning her to return to her hypnotic state of existence. The voyeuristic nature of it all struck her in a way she hadn't considered before. She was fascinated seeing the way Harold was *without* her. It suddenly made him more interesting than he'd ever been before.

The comedy of the scene continued, with Harold attempting again to untie his shoes and negotiate the chair's newfound wobble, muttering "What the *hell*?" as he found his efforts fruitless. When he tried to just squat into a point of tension, Nancy focused on stretching the fibers of the rope, elongating it just enough so that there was too much slack for his airway to be restricted. His reaction to this was more entertaining than she could've expected, and it was highly amusing to watch him then hug his knees to his chest and pick the chair up off of the ground. Even though it was working,

Nancy was confident his arms wouldn't hold out, and gave an extra pull against his grip for good measure, just to ensure he'd release his knees before his life was seriously in danger. He lasted only a few seconds, and the chair came back to the ground forcefully as her husband struggled to catch his breath.

"I can still do this!" she watched him say to the empty living room. There was a wild look in his eyes, unusual for someone who'd always prided themselves on being well-composed, but then again here he was attempting to take his own life for the fourth time. "Shoes glued to the chair?" he continued, "Fine! Laces too tight to untie? Fine! Can't hold a pose long enough to die? That's fine, too! We'll see how much I survive when I murder this chair!"

Then Nancy watched him do something she had not anticipated and had inadvertently helped him with. She'd focused on making the chair weaker, structurally, and he used that to his advantage. He jumped once, twice, and on the third attempt, the chair shattered, in spite of Nancy's attempts to hold it together. It was beyond her abilities to mend the things she had done to the chair while he was jumping on it, and an awful way to discover her limitations. She barely had enough time to soften the impact of his drop, stopping his spine from being severed. With the chair gone, the little extra length she gave to the rope was inconsequential; he still had enough room to put full tension into the line, and it was working. He was suffocating.

Nancy could immediately sense the bond between them grow stronger. She could feel him really dying now, like his soul was attempting to leave his body and join her in this new existence. She felt overwhelmed by panic and focused all of her efforts on the beam over his head, putting as much pulling force into it as she could manage. It was her greatest effort yet. When the beam above him finally gave way, she had no kinetic strength left to bring herself back to the ball field. Nancy could feel the horror of the darkness envelope her instead, knowing that it would feel like an eternity before she could draw the will to recreate her idyllic paradise.

Just as her surroundings started to fade and the sensation of nothingness began to swallow her whole, she swore she could hear Harold call out her name. Did he know? Could he have been aware of her presence preventing him from taking his life? Her name, *"Nancy?"*, said in the sound of Harold's rasping voice, was all that she could take with her into the darkness. The echo of it faded long before she was able to make her way out again.

Chapter Eleven

Amends (A Story About Now)

By the time Harold finished telling Shawnee about his life post-Nancy, including Damon's sordid revelation, the pizza had gone cold and the beer had turned warm. Shawnee sat and listened attentively, occasionally asking a question to clarify, but never interjecting with her own opinions. She simply took in all of the information that Harold gave to her and processed it quietly. It was that quietude they both sat in now, side by side with their feet dangling over the edge of the twin bed.

"You're ready to bolt, aren't you?" Harold asked with a nervous laugh. "I said too much, didn't I?"

Shawnee didn't respond right away, but instead reached into her purse and started rummaging through her things. Harold watched her anxiously, wondering what she was looking for.

"I don't want you to take this the wrong way," she finally said, still searching through her purse, "but I think it's pretty obvious that we aren't going to sleep with each other tonight. That was a lot of information to take in, and it goes without saying that the mood is ruined." She looked up at Harold after she said this, pausing in her search through her purse, and insisted, "This isn't me running away though, seriously. Let's be real, just the fact that I even came over for what I thought was a booty call should tell you a lot about how I feel."

She smiled at Harold and unearthed a weathered business card from the bottom of her bag, bent in one corner and creased through the center. She grabbed Harold by the wrist and pressed it purposefully into the palm of his hand and held it there. The sense of intimacy gave Harold a slight internal spasm. In spite of himself and the context of their ruined sexual encounter, the simple act of holding her hand made him feel good. He couldn't remember the last time Nancy took his hand in such a way. It was nice.

"I wish you would've been more honest with Doctor Pruss," Shawnee continued. "She's a fantastic professional, but she can only work with the facts that she's given. She had her doubts about how sincere you were with your story, and I'm sorry I didn't pay her observations more attention in the details of her medical report. It should've been a red flag when you told me about your wife last night, but I was too caught up in the way you were looking at me. I liked it."

Harold's cheeks reddened slightly, and although it was a nice compliment to receive, it was attached to a commentary about his hospital visit. He suddenly worried that she might be tactfully ending something that had yet to truly begin. "I don't think you did anything wrong, or unprofessional," he said, consolingly. "Willful ignorance gets us all in trouble."

"Doesn't it, though?" Shawnee asked, with a small laugh. It made Harold feel a bit better about the situation, as if things weren't as dire as they could be.

"Still, it's not a very good excuse," she continued, giving Harold's hand a slight squeeze before letting it go. He looked over the business card she left behind and examined the lettering carefully. It was the information for a therapist, and just as quickly as Shawnee's laugh had eased the sinking feeling in his chest, her suggestion with this card made it return with an even greater force. She could see Harold becoming tense and placed her comforting hand on his knee. "I think you're suffering from some kind of survivor's guilt," she told him. "That kind of anxiety can cause a great deal of stress - to the point of experiencing hallucinations, even."

Harold looked at her and felt a great surge of anxiety mixed with despair, almost to the point of making him break. He sighed heavily and asked her in a wry tone, "Are you *sure* you're not running away?"

"We all go to dark places for our own reasons, Harold," she told him gently. "You're complicated, but you're not a bad guy, which is why I think you need to talk to somebody before we take things further." Harold gave a second hesitant look at the card in the palm of his hand, but Shawnee read his body language, and emphasized her point.

"Look, I'm not a doctor," she said, standing up with a finality that signaled the end of their night. "I can only tell you what I've seen as a nurse. You either want help, or you don't. I gave you the contact information of someone you can trust, so use it. You're sweet, but sweet only gets you so far. I'm not looking for perfect, but I do want someone who takes their health seriously. You should think about what you really want, okay?"

Shawnee's quick shift into a forceful tone was impressive. Harold, worried about ending the night on such a daunting note, cycled through a dozen different responses he could've used to bait her into staying a little bit longer, but in the moment, he settled on the wisest choice, answering her with a meager, "Okay."

Clutching her purse under her arm, Shawnee looked him over, as if she were reassessing everything from the night, starting with his initial text message. Harold worried that her look would turn to one of disgust, or regret for having come to his motel room in the first place, but it wasn't either of those things. Instead, she gave him that same smile he'd come to admire, and said, "Good night, Harold."

Harold returned the smile, wished her the same, and watched her walk away. When she was gone, he laid back in bed with his hands folded behind his head, thinking about the bizarre circumstances of his day. He grinned, imagining the way Shawnee burst into his room, and the smile widened as he thought about where it all could've gone had he just let things happen.

He looked over toward the burnt-out wall light, and the black stain behind it. Without realizing he was doing it, he stared at that spot for the rest of the night, wondering how a power surge could've caused that one bulb to blow, but leave the other light fixtures unaffected. Lost in his thoughts, Harold eventually fell into a light sleep. He did not dream.

***

A frantic knock on the door startled him from sleep, and for a moment he forgot where he was, until he saw the floral print of the comforter he was sleeping on. The natural light in the room suggested it was early, but he glanced at his phone plugged into the wall, just to be sure. It was a quarter after six, and he knew it couldn't be Shawnee returning to his room. It was too early, and besides that, what more was there to say? Then it occurred to him who was actually standing outside, and he couldn't help but feel a spark of anger, so soon after just waking up.

"There's no way," he said to himself, but he felt confident. He leaned over the bed and groped around the floor for anything he could throw. He felt a shoe, grabbed it, sat up in bed, and chucked it as hard as he could against the door.

"Go away, Damon," Harold yelled. "You've never been up this early in your life. Why start now?"

"I demand to speak to my life coach," Damon replied in a clear voice through the door.

"I quit," Harold fired back. "Go home."

"You can't quit," Damon said, emphatically. "The program's just starting to work."

"I don't recall you sleeping with my wife being part of the life coach program," Harold said, "unless you're just looking for more material."

185

"I deserve all of that," Damon replied. "You have every right to be pissed at me as a friend, but I'm not talking to that Harold Dancy right now. I'm talking to Harold Dancy, the life coach."

At this, Harold got out of bed, threw the chain lock on the door, and opened it for the few inches the chain would allow. Immediately, Damon's hand came inside, clutching a piece of paper.

"What the hell is this supposed to be?" Harold asked, without taking it. Damon's hand continued to brandish it, waving it back and forth.

"I made a list, Harold," Damon answered, "and as my life coach, you are obligated to respect the list. Your words, not mine."

Begrudgingly, Harold snatched the paper from Damon, and the hand disappeared from the door frame. Harold scanned over the list, saw a series of famous names, and at the bottom, saw his own, alongside Damon and Nancy. He wanted to crumple the list into a tight little ball, throw it out the door, and tell Damon to leave, but his curiosity was too strong, so he relented.

"Good job," Harold said. "You've made a list of names. I'll bet there's a good explanation for it, too."

"There is," Damon said, "and if you'll let me in, I'll tell you what it all means."

"I'll open the door," Harold conceded, "but you're not coming in. You can stand outside and explain the names, and we'll see what I say when you're done."

He closed the door, unfastened the chain lock, then opened it wide. Damon stood in the frame with a suitcase next to his feet. Harold recognized it as his own luggage.

"Is that my bag?" he asked, and Damon nodded.

"I'm so glad you noticed," he said, "but I want to get to this list first, and then we'll talk about the bag." He reached a finger over the paper and tapped the first set of names on the list.

"That's George Harrison of *The Beatles*, and Eric Clapton, who at the time was most well known for being a member of the bands *Cream,* and *The Yardbirds*. They were best friends, but that didn't stop Eric Clapton from ultimately falling in love with George's wife, Pattie Boyd. Thanks to that bit of unrequited love, we've got Clapton's song *Layla.* He wrote *Wonderful Tonight* after Pattie left George to be with him."

"Are you serious right now?" Harold uttered, knowing full well where the conversation was going, but Damon continued, undeterred.

"Second on the list are Denny Doherty, Michelle Phillips, and Cass Elliot, all members of *The Mamas and The Papas*. Mama Cass was pissed at Michelle for stealing Denny, and the tension within the band helped the creative process."

"And it also caused them to break up," Harold replied, but Damon threw a finger up to silence him.

"Had Mama Cass not died, I'm sure there would've been a reunion - much like the third group on the list: Lindsey Buckingham, Stevie Nicks, and Mick Fleetwood. Thanks to that love triangle, we got *The Chain, Go Your Own Way*, and the rest of that album, *Rumours*. Before you say anything more," Damon said, pre-empting a response from Harold, "the fourth on the list are Joey and Johnny Ramone, who both dated Linda Danielle. We can thank her for some classic *Ramones* jams, including *KKK Took My Baby Away*."

"Would that explain why our names are at the bottom of this list?" Harold asked. "Isn't that a bit presumptuous?"

"Nonsense," Damon declared confidently. "I'm Damon Alton, one-third of *The Common Miscreants*. I slept with my life coach's wife and ended up using his poetry to turn into songs, and it's those songs that I'm going to record so I can win my old bandmates back. It's the stuff of rock and roll legend, Harold."

It was that kind of charm that justified Damon's whole existence. It was both maddening and delightful. Harold kept trying to hold on to his anger, but it was anger in relation to an already broken marriage. He couldn't just erase the past year of friendship that he'd created with Damon Alton. Had things with Nancy been better, then maybe his contempt for Damon would be strong enough to withstand such a persuasive nature, but as it was, Damon's appeal was too winning. The most Harold could conjure up in the way of self-defense was a half-hearted response.

"I seriously hate you, Damon."

"And I wouldn't have it any other way," Damon replied. "If we can never be friends again, I understand, but I'm telling you, that was the *old Damon* who did those things, and I'll always be sorry for that. I'll never be able to make it right, but I can at least take your words, put them on an album, and we can try to make a legacy out of this whole thing. Not as a solo project, but as the source material for The Common Miscreants reunion album. Help me do it, Harold. I can't do it without you."

Harold stared at him for a moment. He couldn't decide whether to keep the door open, slam it shut, or take another swing at the man standing in front of him. In the end, there was no longer enough love for Nancy to fuel a hatred for someone who'd become one of his greatest friends.

"What's the bag for then?" Harold asked, relenting.

Damon smiled.

***

Damon booked time at a recording studio near Johns Hopkins University, on a less than amiable street. For convenience, he made arrangements to stay in the small vacant apartment above the studio with Harold. The deal was to record and get a rough mix of ten songs. Damon insisted on using female session musicians to get him as close as possible to the mind space of what it was like to create that first Miscreants album with Jenna and Erin. Initially, Harold felt like a tourist, and wasn't sure why he was there, but then Damon threw new ideas for songs at him, pressed him for rhythm changes, and leaned heavily into recording new verses on the fly, requiring Harold to scratch out new words onto a piece of paper to run into the booth. Sometimes Damon took them immediately, humming to himself to create a melody, and sometimes he'd crumple them and demand a rewrite, telling Harold bluntly, "This is shit. Try again."

When they weren't working, Damon listened to music, and started studying all of Erin and Jenna's newer stuff. He'd write out bass parts by ear and work up vocal harmonies that didn't exist. Harold, having no role to fill in that particular process, thought about Shawnee, Nancy, and the card with the therapist's information that was tucked safely inside his wallet.

After a few days, he worked up the nerve and made the phone call to Dr. Allen Calm's office. A receptionist answered, looked over their calendar, and found an empty spot that had recently opened up. Three days later, Harold was sitting in a chair, talking to a man with a friendly demeanor, who insisted on beginning their session only after they'd taken their shoes off.

"You want me to do what?" Harold asked.

"Take your shoes off," Dr. Calm reiterated, then smiled at him. "That is, if you don't think your feet have an offensive odor." His voice was a deep baritone, and he spoke so evenly that it was hard to feel on guard. As if it was an ordinary thing to do amongst strangers, Dr. Calm himself leaned over in his chair and began removing his own shoes.

"I would've already had mine off," he explained, "but I went out for lunch, and I'm sure you're familiar with the old adage, 'No shirt, no shoes, no service.'" He looked up from his laces and smiled again. "Please, Mr. Dancy. I insist."

"Well, okay then," Harold said, and although he hesitated briefly, he began to take off his shoes, too. It made him think about how easy they were to untie, in contrast with how impossible it was only several weeks ago, when he was standing on a chair in his living room.

"It was my mother's rule," Dr. Calm explained. "When I was growing up, shoes came off when you entered the house, and it wasn't to save the floors, either. They were hardwood and we owned three dogs. It was almost safer sometimes to keep your shoes on, there were so many splinters just waiting to get into your toes. I used to complain to my mom and ask her why we couldn't just keep our sneakers on in the downstairs area, but she wouldn't budge. She'd tell us that you're not at home until your shoes are off and your jacket's hung up in the closet." Then playfully, he added, "Good thing you're not wearing a jacket, Mr. Dancy. It saves us the extra step."

Harold laughed politely at the remark and felt himself becoming more comfortable in the doctor's presence. As he slid off his left shoe, the doctor started peppering him with questions, but not in any way that made him feel like he was being interrogated. It was all conversational in nature.

"Did your mother have any rules like that growing up?"

"Well, we had two dogs, so I definitely relate to the whole shoes off thing," Harold said, working on his right shoe, and it occurred to him that he hadn't thought about his childhood pets in a long time. "Tank and Bailey. God, I loved those dogs. They were the best for a kid to have and take care of – not any trouble at all. Mom and Dad weren't around a lot. They both taught, but they didn't work at the same school I attended, and they were both pretty involved with extracurricular activities for the extra pay."

"Teachers don't make a lot of money, do they?" Dr. Calm asked, and Harold shrugged his shoulders.

"Not much," he conceded. With his shoes finally off, he was able to ease back into his chair, and there really was a palpable effect to removing them. His felt free to be open and didn't mind this little pretext to their session.

"Everyone had to pull their weight," Harold continued. "When I got home, there was always a list waiting for me. That was *our* big rule, I guess you could say. Respect your parents and respect the list."

Dr. Calm leaned back in his chair too and went on in his genial way. "What kinds of things were on the list?"

"Oh, you know, odds and ends. Walk the dogs and clean up the backyard. Finish homework and cook dinner. Do the dishes. Things like that."

"Anything crazy happen if you didn't finish the list?" Dr. Calm asked.

Harold scoffed at the idea. "No," he answered quickly. "My parents were very even-keeled. Besides that, it was in my nature to be obedient anyway. I'd hear them argue with each other sometimes at night, when I was really young, over bills and stuff like that. They were very frugal, to the point of being stingy, but I didn't mind, because I knew how hard they were working. I recognized pretty quickly in life the importance of just falling in line and not rocking the boat. They had enough to worry about, so they didn't need any more to worry about from me."

"That's good," Dr. Calm replied. "So, where are your parents now?"

"They're in Germany, working on a military base, still teaching. We don't really keep in touch, but that's just kind of how it's always been. We've never been the kind of family that calls each other up on the phone."

"Do you exchange emails? What about social media?"

"I'm pretty sure they still use typewriters," Harold laughed. "And I know they still use a landline. They've got a serious aversion to cellular technology and never really tried to adapt when mobile phones came on the scene."

"That's very interesting," Dr. Calm said, and only then was Harold aware that he was making notes in a small book. "Does it ever bother you that you and your parents don't keep in touch?"

Distracted, Harold managed only to reply, "Well... like I said, I've never been one to rock the boat," before asking, "I'm sorry, but have we officially started the session?"

"The session began as soon as we took off our shoes, Mr. Dancy," Dr. Calm answered. "Harold, if you prefer."

Dr. Calm had a way about him that was disarming. Harold had expected to dive right into talking about Nancy, but that wasn't the case. He hadn't talked much about his parents before, but only because no one ever really asked about them. Here he was now, opening up completely without realizing he was saying anything of significance at all. Dr. Calm's demeanor made it possible to just speak, and Harold had no idea he'd be so eager to talk.

"You don't have to call me Mr. Dancy," Harold said, and they continued on, chatting freely for the duration of their first one-hour session. By the end of it, Harold had opened up to Dr. Calm more than he thought he would, mainly about his existing relationships with his parents, Damon, and Shawnee, and had yet to say a word about Nancy. When he left Dr. Calm's office, Harold gladly discussed scheduling options with the receptionist at the front desk, settling on a weekly slot for ongoing appointments.

✳✳✳

Within three weeks, Damon had a working demo. Harold was handed one of the first copies.

"Why don't you call up that super-fan?" Damon asked, innocently. "The nurse you brought to that last show?"

"You mean Shawnee?" Harold said, seeing right through Damon's motivations. "The woman you saw walking out of my motel room the night before you convinced me to live above a recording studio for a month?"

"That's the one," Damon said. "Have her give the new material a listen and see what she thinks. If you guys get naked in the process, that's up to you. It's not my job to pass judgement."

Harold felt he should explain that they hadn't actually had sex, but then saw no point in it and let it pass. Instead, he took Damon's advice, the spirit of it anyway, and gave Shawnee a call, though his first instinct was to be a coward and send her a text message. The phone rang, and just as he anticipated reaching her voicemail, Shawnee answered. Her voice was warm, like she was happy to hear from him, and they exchanged pleasantries. Afterward, Harold confessed that he started seeing the therapist she'd recommended.

"That's great, Harold!" Shawnee said, "I'm really happy to hear that."

"Yeah, it's been good," Harold said, "though the shoe thing takes a second to get used to..."

Shawnee laughed audibly through the phone and said, "Oh I am so glad to hear you say that!"

"Why?" Harold asked, confused, yet pleased by her reaction.

"Well," Shawnee said, and the humor in her voice subsided a bit, "not that I thought you'd lie, but Dr. Calm's made that a common practice in all of his sessions, though only his patients would really know that."

"Wait," Harold said. "Are you telling me that you see Dr. Calm, too?"

"Why do you think I had his card?" Shawnee answered. "Honestly, I went to him because I thought his name was part of some kind of clever gimmick, so I figured I'd give him a shot based on that alone. I'd been in therapy for several years, but at the time, I was in-between doctors. I've worked with Dr. Calm for well over a year now."

"Have you really been in therapy for years?" Harold asked. He felt a sense of relief he didn't know that he needed from the admission.

"Why not? You see a lot of things you sometimes wish you didn't when you're a nurse," she answered. "I take my mental health very seriously, Harold. I wouldn't encourage you to do something I didn't also believe in."

"You are just ridiculously cool," Harold admitted, and then was flustered that those words had left his lips without more forethought. Shawnee was receptive to it, though, and replied in kind.

"That means a lot coming from someone who travels in the inner circle of a famous rock star," she said, and Harold jumped on the opportunity to bring up the demo.

"Well, that's actually why I called," he said, broaching the subject. "I wanted to know if you'd be interested in listening to the new tracks we recorded. Damon's always looking for feedback from fans of his early stuff."

"Sure," Shawnee replied, and Harold felt a rush of confidence at how quickly she accepted. "I'm working the night shift tonight, so I was planning on grabbing something to eat before going into work. Are you free now?"

"You are a very 'no time like the present' type of woman, aren't you?'" Harold asked.

"Never put off until tomorrow what you can do today," Shawnee answered, and Harold once again felt the familiar swoon deep within himself.

"That's a Thomas Jefferson quote!" he said excitedly. "It's one of my favorites. I often share it with my clients."

"Well then, it sounds like we're on the same page," Shawnee continued. "Do you mind picking me up? We can listen to the demo in your car, stop somewhere for a bite to catch up, and then you could drop me off at the hospital, if you don't mind."

"That sounds great to me," Harold replied. After getting the details and ending the call, he showered quickly, then argued with himself for twenty minutes over what he should wear to their casual meeting.

***

Unlike their last two encounters, Shawnee was not made up for any type of night out. Instead, she was in her plain pink nursing scrubs, with her hair pulled back in a series of tight braids, and she wore little in the way of makeup, allowing herself a very natural look, save for the gloss of the lip balm she applied meticulously in the car. Still, Harold found her absolutely beautiful.

An awkward moment befell them once they were inside the vehicle, as if they were both silently considering the circumstances of their last conversation. As if in response, Harold awkwardly waved the demo in the space between them.

"We all know why we're here," he offered as a clumsy preamble, "so let's not waste any time, shall we?"

"Let's not," Shawnee agreed, and she sat quietly through the first two tracks, nodding along with the rhythm of each song.

"It's so nice to actually be able to hear the words," she offered when the third track was midway through. Harold kept his eyes on the road as he drove through the city, for fear of seeing something in her expression that suggested the music was less than listenable. "The lyrics are really good," she commented, and Harold felt a wave of reassurance run through his body at the mere mention of them. They were the same lyrics that Damon had read aloud from his journal, on the same day as his accident with Nancy.

Shawnee glanced at the small watch that hung from her wrist and said, "There's a parking lot up ahead on your left. We've got some time. Do you want to just let the car idle while we listen to the rest of the CD?"

"Sure!" Harold said, trying hard to not sound too excited. If she was willing to stay inside a parked car with him to listen to the demo, it either meant she was into the music, or into the company. Harold wished very much that it was the latter of the two.

When they found a parking spot, he continued to stare straight ahead, listening to the words he'd allowed Damon to put to music. He tried hard not to pay attention to Shawnee's reaction to each song, but he couldn't help himself. She had a way of listening to music that made it obvious which songs resonated with her, and which ones fell flat. Coincidentally, she reacted most favorably to the songs that Harold had penned lyrics for.

When the CD was finished, she pressed the pause button on the stereo, and turned toward Harold, looking him in the eye. "Why don't you play that one slow jam again from early in the demo?" she asked. "I think it was the third track. The one where he's singing about asking someone if they'll love him tomorrow..."

"Do you really like that one?" Harold asked, drawing his eyes toward hers. Shawnee smiled at him. It was a very inviting smile.

"Yes I do," she replied.

"Why?" Harold asked.

"Because on the surface it sounds nice, right? Then you realize he's saying these things to somebody who's not interested in hearing that from him, and it's kinda sad. Who wouldn't want to have someone tell them they'll love them tomorrow every night before they go to bed?"

"Is that something you'd want?" Harold asked, and for a moment he became unaware of himself, and the fact he was leaning into her, as if drawn by a natural connection. To his excitement, Shawnee leaned toward him as well. Their lips touched, and right as they did, an ear-piercing burst of static erupted from the stereo, and they split apart from each other. Instinctively, Harold looked toward the center console. As he did, the sight of a luminous green light glided over the car windshield. It was familiar to him for the most terrible reason.

"What the *hell* was that?" Shawnee asked.

"I don't know," Harold replied, trying to keep calm and not allude to experiencing another hallucination. "I thought the stereo was on pause. I guess there's just a bad track at the tail end of the demo."

"I'm not talking about the stereo," Shawnee said in a tone that was somewhere between confusion and fear.

"Then what are you talking about?" Harold asked, afraid of what she might say.

"That green light that just flew over the car! Didn't you see it just now?" Shawnee answered.

Harold's mouth fell open. "Great," he heard himself say. "Then you saw it, too."

Chapter Twelve

Nancy Out of Darkness (A Story About Harold's 3 Appearances)

It was a very long time before Nancy could return to the world she'd made for herself. When she finally did, it was clear that her time spent bobbing up and down in the realm of darkness made a drastic impact on her psyche. Her softball diamond was no longer an idyllic paradise, but was now infuriatingly realistic, containing almost every imperfection she'd ever come across in all her years of playing her favorite sport.

The foul lines were washed out and uneven, the outfield grass was overgrown, and the infield dirt looked like it hadn't been dragged in ages. Moreover, it was so dry, Nancy could see cracks forming in several areas from extreme drought. When she moved around behind home plate, the ground beneath her feet felt hard and unforgiving. They were the worst field conditions she'd ever seen, and if that wasn't enough, she could no longer visualize her fire-engine red, top-of-the-line pitching machine with the perfect accuracy and lightning quick speed. Instead, she could only conjure the pitching machine from her youth, rusted and uneven, looking like it might fall to pieces after the first pitch, or under the pressure of a strong gust of wind.

It didn't have any type of device controlling it, but ran off an electric switch that, once turned on, would keep throwing until it had nothing left to launch, and then windmilled in place until the power was cut. Without anyone to help her execute the drill, Nancy had to load the balls, flip the machine on, and then run back to her position, typically missing the first two pitches. On two occasions, she'd been clipped by one of the machine's errant throws on her way back: once on her shoulder blade, and once on her spine just above the tailbone. Both times stung ferociously.

The first instance was too much of a surprise to think about anything else, but the second time she was hit, it occurred to her that up to that point she had not felt any actual pain since dying, and this realization became an unwavering distraction that would only multiply her miseries.

She missed pitches, overthrew the bucket consistently, and after six haymaker throws, a sharp pain began emanating from the base of her elbow into the meat of her triceps. Her change in existence didn't make any sense, and when the pitching machine ran out of balls for the sixth time, Nancy threw down her mask and her glove in disgust, much like she had on the days when she just couldn't recover a terrible practice session. It was no longer enjoyable to carry on with the routine.

Before Harold's last suicide attempt, this place had been paradise. Now she could barely make a catch, and when she did, she couldn't hit the bucket on the throw down. What used to be a simple system of catch, throw, and reload, now felt like an eternity of collecting the missed balls behind home plate and scouring the tall grass of the outfield for everything else she'd overthrown.

Even the sky looked different. The sun beat oppressively overhead whenever she searched center field, and Nancy couldn't stop sweating profusely inside her catching equipment. The large orange jugs of water she used to marvel at were now nowhere to be seen inside the dugouts, and an irrepressible thirst became more pronounced with each movement she made. Everything was terrible now, even the softballs themselves. Every one of them felt heavy and weathered in her grip, the way they always got when left out overnight to soak in some terrible storm, refusing to yield up the water that made them bloat so terribly.

Standing behind home plate with her catcher's mask and glove in the dirt beside her, Nancy slumped forward in a state of lament over her current conditions. Since coming out of the darkness, she couldn't feel the same drive and motivation within her to recreate her original place of peace, and this thing that she was settling for was far removed from the source of comfort she'd once known. Her body ached, and the field was harsh and unforgiving. Caught up in her moment of self-pity, a thought crossed her mind, and it brought with it a sickening feeling, deep within the pit of her soul. Without meaning to, she heard herself think it out loud, and the sound of it made her quiver with fear.

"I think this is Hell."

Nearly ready to collapse at such a suggestion, Nancy looked wildly around herself, hoping to see some change on the ball field that might spark some sense of relief or happiness, but the outfield contained nothing for her, and the infield was as barren as it had been since she'd returned. But then, out of the corner of her eye, Nancy saw something new take shape, and she quickly turned to see what was there.

Harold had appeared again and was now sitting in the visitor's section of the bleachers. Nancy felt nauseous at the sight, and not just because of who she was seeing, but *where* she was seeing him. She'd made the connection instantly, and it was too much to be coincidence. Harold was seated in the exact spot that her father used to sit when he'd watch her play from behind home plate, and anytime her father had watched her, it put her on edge. Some games, that edge could motivate her to complete a highlight reel worth of plays in a single game, but sometimes, it did just the opposite. The errors would mount so quickly that she'd take herself out of the game before the coach could get the chance. Why was Harold now sitting there, and what was with the curious look on his face? Nancy had to know.

She walked out from behind home plate and began to approach him, crossing over the foul line on her way toward the bleachers. As she got closer, she could once again feel that bond with him growing stronger with each step she took, but it wasn't quite the same as it had been. Instead of the usual pull associated with some light gravitational force, it now felt like she was riding toward him on a heavy wave of nausea, growing in magnitude with the closing proximity. Closer still, she could see that Harold was different, too.

His body was turned slightly away from her, and his mouth moved inaudibly, as if he was engaged in conversation with someone sitting next to him that she couldn't see or hear. Nancy tried, but could not read the active dance of his lips, and to add to her confusion, he'd occasionally stop and flash a smile that looked so unfamiliar to her, it was disconcerting. It was a lively smile, and it made her angry. How had he gone from trying to end his life to be with her, to smiling idiotically while carrying on a conversation? It made no sense, and she reached out to grab him by the shoulder, meaning to find the answers to her questions.

Instantly, the world around her dissolved, replaced by a dimly lit diner with the tackiest décor ever conceived. The smell of fried foods mixed with strong coffee was overpowering, and it intensified the feeling of queasiness she was already experiencing. There were so many foreign sensations acting as terrible distractions, and a deep dislike of where she was had begun to foment within her. She focused her attention on Harold and was stricken by what she saw.

There he sat, actively talking to a woman she'd never seen before, and it was all too conspicuous to be one of Harold's coaching sessions. For one thing, it looked like it was the middle of the night, as the bright fluorescent lights of the diner starkly contrasted the dark skyline shown through the windows. The woman sitting across from him didn't look the part, either. The majority of Harold's clients dressed way too casually to ever be successful in life; they portrayed little in the way of confidence, save for Damon Alton, and in hindsight, he was just as much a loser as the rest of them, unworthy of the time she'd given him.

This woman was a different story. The blue dress she wore accentuated her brown skin and highlighted a voluptuous figure. She carried herself with confidence and held Harold's stare in her own. She didn't look like the kind of woman who needed help, but the kind that gave help. The way she looked at Harold was almost as irritating as the way Harold looked at her.

Something was different with him, and for the first time, she wondered just how long she had floundered in the darkness. To see him now, she believed it must have been a considerable stretch. The last time she was around Harold, he was standing on a chair, looking worse than ever. Now it seemed like he'd recovered. He was clean, and his posture was different. He was dressed nicely, like he'd just been somewhere important, and they were talking in a way that suggested intimacy.

They'd been conversing with each other since she'd arrived, but the sound had been dull and faint. By the time it came into clarity, however, she caught Harold saying the words,

"Thank you for not making my Nancy story feel weird. I stopped telling it to people because it kept feeling like it was a bad thing to do. You're the first person I've told it to where it didn't feel like I ruined something."

Ruined something? The words stabbed at her, though she didn't understand why. She only knew that the context of what they meant definitively confirmed this woman was not one of Harold's clients, and it infuriated her. Nancy's old competitive spirit began to stir, and a low energy pulsated within her, like the power she hadn't felt since coming out of the darkness. She turned her attention to the woman in blue, and listened to her reply:

"You haven't ruined anything, Harold."

A thought crossed Nancy's mind, and though it caught her off guard, she couldn't deny its truth. If she could say anything in this place, she would've told the woman to back off. Harold belonged to her, and he couldn't be won away so easily. He was literally *dying* to be with Nancy again. This woman was nothing, and now even stronger feelings of animosity were conjured up within Nancy's being. The pulse of energy let out a flare, and she used it to lash out at the woman, knocking the steaming cup of coffee from her hands and shattering it to pieces on the table in front of them. The shards scattered all over, and some of the coffee managed to spray on Harold's shirt.

It didn't have the impact that she wanted it to have, however. Instead, they both started laughing, and Harold began to clean up the mess in good humor, which was too much for Nancy to see. Feeling more than disgusted, she left them, and went back to her softball field.

That feeling of new energy was still burning within her, like a moment of reckoning. If Harold was moving on, she was just fine with that. She'd already moved on, hadn't she? Feeling like she'd regained some of the power she'd lost in her last foray with Harold's suicide attempts, Nancy decided she was going to put all of her focus into bringing her softball field back to what it was, and she wouldn't go back to her position behind home plate until everything was just the way it had been. She was confident, now. This didn't have to be Hell. She could make it her own private paradise once more. All she had to do was change one thing at a time, and she began by focusing on the sky above her.

* * *

Nancy had no concept of how long the whole process had taken, but true to her own will, she did not get back down behind home plate with her gear on until everything was just the way she wanted it to be. She had transformed the sky into the deep purple of twilight by channeling happy memories of the past, when she'd practice until there was barely enough light to see. Then the grass in the outfield shortened itself into a lush and vibrantly green uniform of thin carpeting that would allow a line drive ball to roll all the way to the fencing. Soon, the foul lines were back to being perfectly linear, bright white against the soft brown dirt of the infield that was raked smooth. The bases were clean, the softballs light, and the air around her was no longer stale and hot, but temperate with the light breeze that brought with it the scent of running water.

The last thing to change was the pitching machine itself. Like witnessing a chameleon in the act of changing colors, she watched it slowly roll from its dull rusted steel to a bright, polished red. The legs of the tripod, taking on a life of their own, straightened themselves and readjusted their position so the machine sat level. A hand-held control unfurled itself from the back of the machine, unrolling gracefully onto the pitcher's mound, inviting Nancy to come and pick it up.

She walked out to the mound and glanced over every feature of the field and her surroundings. The field looked right, and even the dugouts were stocked once again with the orange coolers of water and now that they were available to her, she no longer felt the need for them. The feeling of thirst had faded away in her concentration, and now she realized she no longer felt any shooting pain in her elbow either. To be sure, she looked over at both the home and away side bleachers and was relieved to see them both empty. With everything how it should be, she reassured herself it would stay that way if she just willed it to be so.

"We make our own Hell," she heard her voice say out loud, putting into words the unconscious thought. If that was true, then the opposite must be true, too. She could make her own

Heaven. She just needed the will to make it so, and she had it now, in spite of Harold.

She picked up the pitching machine's controller, walked it down to home plate, and gave the infield one last glance, as though she were reading the play before the next pitch. She slipped the mitt onto her left hand, squatted into position, and heard her voice call out, "Coming down!" She pressed the button, and watched the pitch fire out, straight and true, smacking into the webbing of her glove, as it had before. She leapt up into her stance, her feet in their perfect position, and she fired the ball forward, effortlessly. It did not sail this time in some high arc, where it would land somewhere off into center field, but travelled on a straight shot, dropping directly into the bucket, just as she wanted it to. A thrill came over her, and it almost felt like it was too good to be true. She repeated the process, again hearing her own voice, completely independent of her lips, call out, "Coming down!" The pitch came, just as straight and just as true. She caught it cleanly, popped up, and made the throw. The ball cut through the air with a whistle, and dropped squarely into the bucket, landing with a *plunk*. She did it a third time and got the same results.

Everything was back to normal, and Nancy pumped her fist in her moment of satisfaction. The thing to do now was to lose herself in the drill and forget that she'd ever lost anything in the first place. There would be no more trips into the darkness, and she would no longer pay the threat of it any mind. There would be no more transgressions, and no more interruptions. She would focus on the rhythm of this place: catch, throw, and reset... catch, throw, and reset. It was a satisfying thought.

She squatted back into position, put the controller in her hand, and was ready to squeeze the button again, when the ground suddenly began shaking beneath her feet. An explosion of sound came from her left - a loud, deafening roar. She popped up into her stance, ripping free her mask to look toward its direction.

She saw a blurry vision of someone sitting in her father's spot on the bleachers, wearing his clothes and holding a paperback book, just as her father always had when he'd come to her games. In that moment, a feeling of dread fell upon her. She wondered if it really could be him, because if it was, she didn't think she could handle it. The man then came into better focus, as if he was sitting behind a fog that was slowly rolling away, and then she realized who she was looking at.

"*Harold?*" she heard her voice say aloud, and her dread was quickly replaced with a surge of anger. Harold had come back, disrupting the peace and quiet she'd fought so hard to regain. Worse than that, it was like he was mocking her by sitting in *that* spot, dressed in such a way, and with a book in his hands. If it weren't for the knowledge of how strongly her father despised Harold, she would've sworn the two had somehow conspired together to create a brand-new kind of post-mortem torture.

The pink clouds above her turned an angry grey and blanketed the horizon. Lightning cracked the sky, and Nancy's voice filled the atmosphere around her, echoing off the bricks of the dugouts on either side of her.

"*How dare you sit in that spot!*"

Thunder growled all around, and the twilight dimmed toward darkness.

"*He never showed up to watch me succeed!*"

The wind picked up, and a funnel of infield dust took form.

"*He only ever came to watch me fail.*"

It grew in size and tore at the bases, ripping them from the ground.

"*It's how he measured everything.*"

Dirt whipped through the air and coated the pitching machine in a layer of filth.

"*Nothing satisfied him.*"

Hard drops of water fell from the sky, burning as they pelted Nancy's skin.

"*I hated him,*" she heard herself yell. "*I hate you, too!*"

She rushed toward him, driven by the same rage she'd felt when she grabbed the wheel of the SUV. It was all-encompassing and consumed her entirely. Harold blinked in and out of existence, quick flashes with changing expressions, but always seated on the bleacher and with the paperback book in his hands. She crossed the foul line, ran past the dugout, and hopped over the fence enclosing the field in a single leap. Hands outstretched and ready to attack, she ran up the bleachers but they started to stretch and elongate in front of her, carrying Harold away into the sky on an endless set of metal stairs. Undeterred, she continued on, sprinting so fast that her braids snapped against her neck to the rhythm of her stride. She was gaining on him, and as she got closer, she could see the look on Harold's face change into one of shock. He fell back onto his elbows, like he was trying to scoot away from her, and the look of fear on his face only enticed her more. When she leapt toward him, pouncing as if she was going to strike him with a killing blow, she'd effectively jumped out of the angry storm of her afterlife and back into Harold's world.

A cheap motel room materialized before her eyes, and the scene unfolding before her explained the truth of why Harold was recoiling. It wasn't in fear of *her*, but of something else altogether. The woman she'd last seen in the diner was now wearing a different dress, one that suggested she had certain *goals* with Harold, and she was trying to achieve them right at that very moment. Harold, now on his back, was being straddled by this woman, and her hands were all over the place, one working at the zipper of his pants, and one... Was she *choking* him?

It could've been the idea that Harold was moving on with another woman, or it could've been that he was being sexually adventurous in a way that she'd never known him to be. Whatever the case was, the result was the same. The energy radiating from her slipped briefly beyond her control, as if the electricity in the room fed off of it. The light closest to her suddenly grew very bright, and exploded with a loud popping noise, charring the wall it was mounted to.

Nancy couldn't see anymore. She felt hurt and couldn't explain why. If she really didn't love Harold, then why couldn't she stand to see him with someone else? Hadn't she moved on from him with Damon? Why was it wrong for Harold to do the same? Did she secretly admire the way he was willing to kill himself to be with her? Why did she alternate between hating and craving the attention he lavished her memory with? Was she worried if she moved on without him that she'd be alone forever? What did *forever* mean for her now?

These questions were dizzying, forming rapidly one after the other, disrupting the remaining grip she had on her reality. The darkness threatened to close in on her permanently, she feared, and now there was this new emotion she never thought she'd experience with Harold, one that would alter the imagination of her environment. She was jealous.

***

Nancy didn't want to believe Harold could make her feel jealousy, and she lashed out, angry with herself more than anything else. She raged about the field wildly, as if the darkest and worst qualities of her personality had taken complete control. She set the grass in the outfield on fire, and the flames burned so hot that the sky above was no longer any color except for the dark char of the rising smoke. The bleachers where Harold (and her father) once sat were now twisted and deformed, orange with rust and decay. The foundations of the dugouts were cracked and loose, and the brick structures surrounding them crumbled into oblivion.

Lastly, she turned her attention to the pitching machine that she had so lovingly crafted not once, but twice from the depths of her most perfect memories. Slowly, the machine started to degrade before her eyes, like a flower wilting in tremendous heat, and just like the time before she jumped into Harold's world, she could hear her voice split the air around her and shake the ground beneath her feet.

The words came as the red paint cracked and curled away, revealing the steel frame beneath.

I hate the way you talked to me.

They continued as the metal legs of the tripod folded in on themselves, and the machine dropped to the mound with a dull thud.

I hate the way you thought you could fix me.

They drowned out the sound of the motor's creaks and whines, as sprockets became brittle, and operating belts snapped and flailed like angry snakes cut in two.

Everything I did, and all the things I didn't want to do, was because of you, and you never once said you were sorry.

The pitching machine continued to degrade into a twisted version of itself, decaying until there was nothing left but a pile of metallic fragments, and still Nancy was not satisfied. A reservoir of sorrow was unleashed now, and torrents of pent up frustrations had to be dealt with. With the grass burnt to nothing, the dugouts crumbled to dust, and the pitching machine reduced to a heap of lifeless scraps, there was nothing left to do but look out at the ruins and wonder why she'd built anything in the first place.

She laid down next to the pitcher's mound and stared at the black smoke overhead. If the darkness came, so be it. She needed time to think about all of the things she'd just done, and as she did so, uncomfortable thoughts started to surface, and they made her cringe when she considered them.

She hadn't been talking to her father when she spoke, and she wasn't talking to Harold, either. She realized she'd been talking to herself while she destroyed the pitching machine, and that was a thought she could no longer keep buried deep within her subconscious. It had escaped and manifested itself in the form of her destructive outburst. Who did she really need to hear any apology from? Was it Harold, her father, or herself? She could've laughed, and she could've cried; she felt like one of Harold's pathetic clients.

She wasn't going to apologize to herself, because what good would that do? As for her father, well... it was hard to get an apology from someone who seemed like they never wanted to see you. That left Harold. Unwelcome as he was, he was the only one making any kind of appearance, and every time he did, nothing good came from it. Nancy thought if she never saw him again, it would probably be for the best. She could keep it unresolved and let bygones be bygones, because the alternative seemed too exhausting. Naturally, as she came to that conclusion, Harold chose to appear again. It was as if she was subconsciously willing him into her reality.

He was back in the same spot on the bleachers, in spite of their condition, and this time, he looked happy. Moreover, he'd brought with him the sounds of new music.

A soft, melodious rock ballad filled the air, one she'd never heard before. Damon Alton was singing with low, melancholy notes, but the words, so clear and familiar, were in the style of Harold's voice. As she listened to them, she caught the meaning of every word, and knew the song was about her. She knew because Harold knew, and it was taunting in a way, as they seemed to address her directly:

Seems now the only things we'll ever say out loud are lies,
Like when I ask you if you'll love me tomorrow,
But the promise isn't there in your eyes...

These were lyrics written by the husband she'd cheated on, sung by the man she'd cheated with, and whatever moment of reflection she'd been experiencing was officially done. The song was an indictment, and it was as though the words were designed to make her feel more than low. She was reminded of her jealousy, anger, and the general bitterness she had toward the life she'd led. It poured out of her restless spirit and made her come up off the ground, like she was taking flight. Weightless in the air, she rushed toward Harold, meaning to stop him once and for all, riding on the misery stored within her broken heart. Her energy was being spread forward in a wave of disruption, and as she came closer to Harold, she could hear a burst of static, like white noise emanating from a loud radio.

Harold's world took shape before her eyes, and what she saw provided clarity. She'd been thinking about things all wrong, and she suddenly understood the root of all her problems.

Harold was idling in the parking lot, listening to the music on his car stereo, and sitting next to *her*: the woman sitting across from Harold at the diner; the one on top of Harold in the motel, doing those *things* to him; the new lover now sitting with him in a car, listening to new *Damon Alton* songs. She was the common denominator, and the reason for Nancy's jealousy. She could put it all on her and felt justified in doing so.

Her feelings shifted, and her ire no longer belonged solely to Harold. It now belonged to the woman sitting next to him, too.

Chapter Thirteen

Run, Harold, Run (A Story About Now)

"That green light," Harold stammered, turning his head in every direction, "was what I was talking about from that night I tried to hang myself."

"I thought you said you saw the ghost of your dead wife?" Shawnee asked, and the panic in her voice was a measure of the tension inside the car. Harold looked from side to side and front to back, inspecting every window and windshield. He even checked the rearview mirror, hoping for another glimpse of the green light that had washed over his car.

"That's how I saw her!" Harold answered, and rattled off a comparison as his eyes darted about the car frantically. "I saw her inside that green light, like some kind of aura. It was like when a camera flash catches your eyes, in the way that it burns an image of everything you were just looking at into your sight, and you can see it even when you try to blink." He turned his attention to Shawnee, and his voice dropped to a tone of utter certainty. "That's the way Nancy looked then, and I swear to you we just saw the same thing now."

Shawnee shook her head in disbelief, and her desire to rationalize what they'd seen took hold. "That's ridiculous," she said. "What we just saw now was a trick of the light and couldn't be what you say it is. You make it sound like we're living in some kind of *Poltergeist* movie..."

A second wave of green light broke over the hood of Harold's car, and the rush of energy shook its frame. For a second time, the stereo crackled loudly with unpleasant white noise, and songs from the demo cycled in two second interludes, one after the other, like someone skipping tracks, searching for a particular beat. Shawnee lost her composure and gasped in terror. Harold pressed the knob of the stereo to kill the music, but it wouldn't respond, and the noise continued on. He should've told Shawnee to get out of the car and run, following just behind her, but he didn't. It felt safer to stay inside and lock the doors, so he did, while throwing the car into reverse to peel out of the parking spot they'd been idling in.

In seconds, they were out of the lot and onto the adjoining street, skipping over unforgiving potholes that jostled them in their seats. Harold sped toward the main highway, and the traffic lights were mercifully cooperative. They travelled quickly through the varying intersections, unsure of where to go, and Harold's mind turned several thoughts over in his head while he drove. It was like having all the pieces of a puzzle, without any clue as to how they fit.

It made no sense. If Nancy's spirit had rescued him from suicide, why did it feel like she was attacking him now? Suddenly, he made the horrific connection. Every time he'd had an intimate moment with Shawnee, there was that feeling, like a cold chill, and then something happened. A coffee cup shattered, the motel light exploded, and now his stereo was malfunctioning...

The demo stopped skipping and settled on one of its faster tracks. If Nancy was controlling the music, then she'd just picked the song that best represented the intense movements of the car. A rolling drum beat was punctuated by crashing hi-hats, and Damon Alton's voice called out from the speakers, *"Let's go!"* A screaming electric guitar and thumping bass line followed their dizzying rhythm and changed chords at a galloping pace. Shawnee pressed, turned, and then punched the stereo dial, but could do nothing. She looked up at Harold and pleaded with him.

"Stop the car!"

"I can't," Harold said, as he emphatically stomped on the brakes, showing that they were unresponsive. "My foot's not even on the gas pedal!"

It was true. Cruise control had kicked on by itself, and there was no button Harold could hit to disable it. Without brakes and the car maintaining speed, Harold had little in the way of options. Even the steering was difficult to control, as if he were struggling with someone else's grip. With effort, he merged into the right lane and caught the on-ramp toward the highway. Once there, he forced the car into the fast lane, thankful that traffic was light enough so they didn't have to worry about other cars.

They went wildly along the highway, matching the speed of the demo, and Damon's voice began to sing to them, strangely in sync to the madness:

You're in my brain stem, terrorizing my head.
I keep on pushing, to try and make a stand.

"I officially hate this song," Shawnee yelled.

"Agreed," Harold said, and he gripped the steering wheel tightly, still stomping on the brake pedal, hoping to disengage the cruise control, while Damon continued to serenade them.

I'm paralyzed when you walk on by.
I can't let you go for peace of mind.
I'm drowning now in pools of time.
I'm falling down, I'm falling down.

"I'm calling the police," Shawnee yelled over the song on the stereo. "Maybe they can do something to stop your car!"

Harold hadn't caught what she said, though. An epiphany was forming, and he recalled the image of himself sitting on a set of bleachers, roaring at a ghostly Nancy. Had he known then that this confrontation was coming? Was this the end game of all that he'd experienced before? It was too much to be coincidence, and he now fully understood where he was and what he was doing. His conclusion was chilling.

"I'm in a car, travelling in the fast lane on the highway," he said to himself. "It's just the same as when..."

He glanced over at Shawnee, who was busy with her phone in her hands, dialing 9-1-1. As his eyes flashed up at her, meaning to ask her what she planned to say to the operator, he caught full view of Nancy's green light, keeping pace with the car, charging toward Shawnee's passenger side window.

If it's not about me, Harold realized, *then it's got to be about Shawnee.*

A faint clicking noise caught his attention, and he looked down to see Shawnee's seatbelt begin to slide away from its buckle. He looked up again, and now Nancy was right outside the car door, gliding toward them. What he did next was done with little thought for his own safety, but for Shawnee's.

Giving up his struggle to control the steering wheel, Harold took off his seatbelt, and threw himself over Shawnee's lap, right as he felt Nancy's presence pass through his own. A cold, disorienting chill ran through him, and he vaguely heard Shawnee call out to him.

"Harold, what are you doing?"

He glanced back over toward the steering wheel, and watched it pull slowly toward the left. The car drifted, and the concrete barrier came ever closer to the driver side door. Harold knew what was coming next, and in a move of desperation, he grabbed the emergency hand brake and yanked up on it as hard as he could.

The impact was immediate. Rubber burned and the engine bucked angrily as the car's speed was cut drastically. It fishtailed and scraped the barrier, narrowly avoiding a head on collision, but nothing could stop Harold from being thrown from the car. His body rolled over the dashboard and took out the entire windshield, just as Nancy's had only a year and a half before. Shawnee, having been braced by Harold's body, was able to catch herself and stay inside the car. She saw his body pass over the hood, and scared that it might fall under the tires, she instinctively grabbed the steering wheel and jerked it to the right. Harold fell over the side, hit the asphalt, his body rolling on the pavement, his flesh smacking the ground with every turn, until his left shoulder collided into the concrete barrier, where he fell forward, face down and motionless in a bloody heap.

The car drifted into a long arc across all three lanes and stalled out just as Shawnee managed to steer it onto the side of the highway. By the time it came to a complete stop, smoke was pouring from the engine. The car behind them that had been a half mile away, saw what happened, and slowed down to help and report the accident. Within minutes, traffic was backed up, flares were on the highway, and an ambulance was weaving its way between the lanes of cars. The EMTs rushed to Harold's aide, and as Shawnee was being attended to, she overheard them discussing his conditions. Harold's body had no pulse.

Chapter Fourteen

Harold and Nancy (A Story About Death)

Nancy's anger, which had carried her so forcefully into Harold's world, spent itself with a violence that was both blinding and exhausting. In the final moments of it, she'd lost herself completely, hardly aware of the destruction she was causing. When the wreck was done, she was burnt out, and the darkness came for her again. This time, however, she was not alone, and she felt someone guide her through the initial haze, until a room began to materialize around her, placing her in a state of tranquility.

They were lying in bed together, Nancy next to Harold, on their backs and atop the covers, staring up at the ceiling. Light poured in from a set of windows, and the white stucco above looked completely foreign to Nancy. She had no idea where she was.

"It's my childhood bedroom," Harold said, as if able to read her thoughts. "This is where I used to go when I heard my parents fighting with each other."

Nancy looked over at him and saw that he looked exactly as he had the moment he'd died. He hadn't transformed the way that she had and didn't appear to be some younger or stronger version of himself. He was the Harold he had always been, as though he had no reason to go back to a previous version of himself.

"Where did you go when your parents fought?" he asked her, not looking over, but continuing his study of the ceiling.

"You've met my parents," she answered, dully. "They didn't have time to fight. Mom was too busy refereeing the fights between me and Dad."

"Have you figured out why you were so angry with him since you've been here?" Harold asked, and there was no contempt in his voice. In life, Nancy would've chafed at a question like that, treating it as some kind of accusation, but in this place, she felt so relaxed being on top of Harold's bed while meditating on the grooves of the ceiling above her, that the question hadn't bothered her in the slightest.

"Kind of," she answered honestly, "but not really. I don't know if I'll ever really understand the root of the problem."

They continued to lay together in their thoughtful stillness, softly existing next to each other, and a total sense of ease took hold of Nancy. The old layers of resentment that she'd held onto for far too long were peeling away now, and she could feel some new aspect of herself gradually being uncovered. She just needed time to breathe, and it finally felt like it was safe to do so.

"You know, I don't think I ever saw your bedroom when we started dating in high school," she said to Harold, breaking the lengthy period of silence. She looked around at the setup he'd constructed in his mind. "Is this really how it looked when you were younger?"

"I think so," he said, taking the time to look around himself. "It looks plain enough, anyway. It's the same desk by the wall, and I bet if you looked inside the drawers, you'd find the same doodles from when I was a kid. Do you remember Jack Edwards?"

"Vaguely," Nancy replied.

"He used to come over after school, and we'd listen to ska music and work on this comic book we thought was going to be the next big thing," Harold said, smiling at his reminiscence.

"Those were really good times." Then, as an afterthought, he looked over to Nancy and added, "I'm sorry you never got to see my bedroom when we were in high school, if that's something you ever thought about. You probably understood you weren't dating the wildest guy in your class, though." He went back to his study of the ceiling, and they continued to lay next to each other in silence, until Nancy felt compelled to speak again.

"So, why did you bring me here?" she asked, unsure of what he might say. It was strange to be so close to him, and not have it feel adversarial. He seemed content, lying next to her, and she couldn't remember the last time they'd been so close to each other without there being some kind of tension.

"This is how I used to find peace," Harold answered. "I'd clean up my room, make my bed, and lie down on top of the covers, so as to not make anything messy. If my parents came up to check on me, they'd always see everything neat and clean, and it was like one less thing they had to worry about. When I think about it now, I took pride in that. I knew what they wanted, and so I did it. I created order through compliance."

Nancy listened to him speak, and it made her think about their marriage. She suspected that might be where the conversation was going, but abruptly, Harold changed subjects.

"You tried to kill Shawnee."

He didn't say it with any anger or sadness, but stated it as a neutral fact, and it was such a naked truth that Nancy could do nothing to wriggle away from it. Notions of guilt mingled into her state of being, and they complicated her thoughts.

"I did," she admitted.

"Why?" Harold asked.

"The same reason you cleaned your room and made your bed," she answered. "I wanted order."

"Is that why you tried to kill me last year?"

"I wasn't trying to kill you," Nancy explained, and it was the first time that she'd really considered what she had done to him on the highway that night of the first accident. Consciously or unconsciously, she never put any thought into the circumstances of her own death. Now, lying on the bed next to Harold and staring up at the ceiling with him, it seemed like the natural thing to do.

"I was just angry," she continued, "and I think I was only trying to hurt you.   I never really thought about the consequences."

"So if you wanted to hurt me, then why couldn't you let me kill myself?" Harold pressed. "Why did you stop me all of those times?"

"Because after I died, I wanted to be alone, and I thought if you died, too, then you'd be with me in my afterlife," she explained, and looked around Harold's room again. "Judging by where we are now, it doesn't seem like I was too far off, does it?"

Harold rolled onto his side and propped himself up on his elbow to look at Nancy directly. "That's just it," he said to her. "Now that I'm in this place, it's like I have access to all this new insight that I didn't have before, and that's what I was thinking about when I was staring up at the ceiling just now. I feel like every time I was ready to do something to end my life, you only showed up because I was the one pulling you toward me. I wasn't moving on, and I couldn't let go of you." He paused to concentrate on what he was going to say next, and his eyes drifted away in thought, as if he was still considering everything that had happened between them. When he looked up at her again, he spoke with such certainty, it was as if it couldn't be questioned. "These last couple of times were different, Nancy. I wasn't the one doing the pulling. I was the one being pulled."

"What do you mean?" she asked, rolling over to meet his gaze. They were in the same positions that they used to take at night when they would talk to each other in bed, back when they were younger and believed that their love was genuine. They would lay like this and talk until one of them was too tired to talk anymore, and Harold would always be the one to end things by kissing her on the forehead before rolling over to go to sleep. After her father died, they stopped talking like this, and occasionally Harold would try to goad her into it by asking her if she'd love him tomorrow, but she'd never felt like playing along. To think about it now, she wondered what about him had made it so hard to just humor him with a response.

"I felt myself moving on with Shawnee," Harold explained, still in contemplation. "Or at the very least, I was moving away from you, and I'd stopped bringing you into my world. After my last suicide attempt, you were the one pulling me into yours."

"I was not!" Nancy replied defensively. Her older self was trying to break through the peace of their mediation, but the look that Harold gave her in response was so confident that it made her feel like it was a childish thing to say, and he continued on, unperturbed.

"You're doing it right now," he said, as though it were a plain truth. "I can feel other people bringing me back to their world, and I know I won't be with you much longer, but that isn't stopping you from trying to keep me here. I'm being pulled in two different directions. You've been pulling me closer to you, but the others are so much stronger than you are on your own. That's what I don't get. Why are you trying to keep me here?"

It was a difficult thing to be confronted with, but when Harold said all of these things to her, she knew it was true. When she'd come out of the darkness after Harold's final suicide attempt, she hadn't fully understood what that feeling of isolation had done to her. Nancy had come to enjoy her interactions with Harold's suicidal tendencies, and she was lying to herself when she said she was fine to be alone on a softball field. It was her secret joy to see Harold, whose presence always disrupted the monotony of her new existence. Still, even now she could not come right out and admit these things. Her sense of pride was the last layer that had yet to peel away from her spiritual body. She'd carried it for so long in life that it felt like it was always with her, moving the needle that guided her moral compass. Harold's question was simple enough to demand a simple truth, but she could not deny the need to lie anyway. Her lifelong pride stuck fast to her, and it would not let her become suddenly vulnerable.

"I'm not trying to keep you with me," Nancy answered. "You're here because we're bonded to each other. We're married, Harold."

"But I don't think we've ever really been married," Harold replied. "Not if you consider what a marriage is supposed to be."

It was something she hadn't expected Harold Dancy, of all people, to ever say aloud. It put her at a loss for words, and Harold continued on for her, filling the void created by her silence.

"Married people are supposed to make vows to each other," he explained, "but you have to be *honest* when you make that kind of vow. I meant it when I said I loved you, but I know now that you never really felt the same way."

"So you think our marriage was a *sham*?" Nancy asked, meaning to sound offended, the way that she could when she wanted the upper hand in a fight, but Harold could not be bated. He meant to get to the root of the things that had festered between them, and there would be no stopping him.

"If it wasn't, why couldn't you answer me when I asked you if you'll love me tomorrow?"

Nancy was silent, and she could feel something begin to tear away at the layer of pride that made her want to be evasive, even in this place of peace. Harold's questions were eliciting from her a measure of humility that demanded she finally be honest, not just with Harold, but with herself as well.

"Because I didn't really love you," she answered. It was surprising how much it pained her to say it out loud, not as a weaponized phrase that could win some bitter grudge, but as a weighty truth that she'd had to avoid every time Harold had asked her that question.

"It's okay," Harold said, and his voice was docile. "That's the part I already knew. All I want for you to do now is just explain it to me. If that was the case, then why marry me at all?"

"My father said it wouldn't work between us," Nancy said quietly, "and I wanted to prove him wrong."

"Did you?"

"No."

"So have you finally figured out the root of why you were so angry with him since you've been here?"

A moment of quiet anticipation passed between them.

"Yes," she answered.

"I figured," Harold said. "Tell me."

"He was the first man in my life to tell me what I couldn't do, when he was supposed to be the one to tell me I could do anything."

He stared intently at her after she said this, like he was studying her features for some additional truth that would help him make sense of her reasoning. When Harold spoke again, he thoughtfully reiterated Nancy's position:

"You only married me because your Dad didn't think we were a good fit. You didn't love me, you just felt like you had something to prove."

"Yes," Nancy replied, and now she waited for the worst of it. Surely this admission would be enough to send him over the edge, and she braced herself for the weight of his emotions to come bearing down onto her. None of that happened, though. Instead, Harold looked her over once more, and then kissed her on the forehead, just as he had when they were newlyweds.

"Okay," he said. "I can make peace with that. Let's allow him to be right about just this one thing, and then there'll be nothing left to prove. You'll be able to let go."

In that instance, he had pried himself away from her. It struck her so hard that the deepest fears of what may come without him began to overwhelm her, finally making themselves known.

"But I can't let you go," Nancy said, and fear had crept into her voice. "I almost killed you once, and then I actually did kill you when I was trying to kill *her.*"

"True," Harold said, and his voice maintained its calm tenor, as if he'd already considered these things and found them to be of little consequence. "However, I think you got lucky on both counts. Shawnee's not dead, and I'm pretty sure

I'm not going to stay dead, either. This place feels temporary to me..."

Nancy sat up in the bed and looked down at Harold, stormily. "Why aren't you angry with me?" she demanded. "Why won't you get mad?"

Harold grinned up at her and answered in good humor. "You make it very tempting, Nance, but I just don't have it in me to feel that way. It was never in my nature to get mad. It doesn't suit me, and the few times I've felt that way, it's always been easier for me to let go."

"But *I* could never let go of things!" Nancy moaned. "What if it takes me to Hell?" She laid back down next to Harold and looked imploringly into his eyes. "If you'll stay with me," she said, "we can make this our own paradise."

"I might if I could," Harold said, "but in the first place, this other thing's pulling me back, and it feels like it's only getting stronger. Secondly, I think we'd end up making our own Hell, and I can't even help you out of the one you've already made for yourself. I never could in the time we were alive together, anyhow. Why would anything be different in death?" He stopped to regard the anguished look on her face, and when he spoke again, it was softly, and with finality.

"I've never thought you were a bad person, Nancy. I think we both just made bad decisions or made decisions for bad reasons. Either way, we both know now that staying together was a bad decision we made for bad reasons. My reasons might've been different than yours, but they weren't any better. In that sense, we both wronged each other. I forgive you for the wrong you did to me. Now you don't need to be angry anymore. If I ask you to, will you forgive me as well?"

"Forgive you for what?" Nancy asked, appalled by the suggestion. He had the upper hand. What need was there to ingratiate himself to her?

"Forgive me for letting things go on longer than they should have," he answered. "I held onto you long after it stopped feeling like the right thing to do, and I realize now that I was holding you back. I'm sorry."

She hadn't known that she'd needed to hear him say that, but when he did, it was a revelation, and the same words poured out from her and onto him. "I'm so sorry, Harold," she said. "I'm so very sorry."

"And now you can let go," Harold said, and his voice was soothing and encouraging. "There's something greater beyond this place. I know you can sense it, because I can, too. You just have to let go of the old things that are holding you back. Confronting your issues is the first step, but you also have to be willing to let them go. They won't weigh on you like they did when you were living."

Nancy turned over and looked up at the ceiling. "Okay," she said, and then repeated it in the way that only someone preparing for the unknown can. "Okay, okay, okay..." She focused on the irregular bumps of the white stucco and took in a deep breath. The air felt like it was stabbing her, and a look of panic spread across her face.

Harold, still lying next to her in the bed, whispered in a low, encouraging voice. "Let go, Nance."

She closed her eyes and took another deep breath, this time with greater ease, and felt herself become lighter. It was like being carried away on a breeze, and gradually, she felt herself fade from Harold until there was nothing left of him to hold onto.

Chapter Fifteen

The Common Miscreants Take the Stage (An Epilogue)

Although Shawnee considered herself lucky to be able to walk away from the accident with relatively minor injuries, it was nothing compared to the luck that Harold had cashed in on to be able to survive what he'd gone through.

When the first responders arrived, he'd gone into cardiac arrest from the way he'd been ejected through the windshield and thrown onto the highway. He'd been clinically dead for almost three minutes, but the EMTs that had arrived on the scene were able to resuscitate him and get him to a nearby hospital. In addition to that, he suffered a skull fracture, compression of the cervical spine area, multiple rib fractures, a shattered eye socket, a broken hip and collar bone, lacerations from the glass and rocks on the road, and one dislocated thumb. A partial recovery would've been impressive, and the fact that he'd eventually recover in full was considered by some a miracle. Father Ackley, the chaplain who remembered talking with Harold in the hospital once before, summed it up best: "God must really be close with this one."

The skull fracture had put Harold in a coma for eleven days, and when he finally came to, he was deeply disoriented, having no idea where he was. His only thought was that he'd just been in his bedroom, lying on top of his covers the way that he used to, and that he'd fallen asleep after saying goodbye to someone important, though he couldn't remember who it was. Now he'd woken up somewhere else entirely, and strangers were looking at him. When they saw that he'd opened his eyes, they'd made it seem like it was a very big deal, and he couldn't understand why. He only knew that he was still exhausted, and as people came over to examine his condition, he decided it would be easier if he went back to sleep and let them do whatever they needed to.

* * *

When Harold woke again, he felt much more aware, but couldn't do a lot in the way of movement. A splint was capped over his right thumb, and he felt a hand holding his own. When his eyes opened more, it gave him a gentle squeeze. He wanted to see who was near him, but his sight wouldn't come into focus. He'd remembered feeling a squeeze like that before, though, and knew who it was. Shawnee was sitting at his bedside.

He wanted to talk to her, but found it wasn't so easy. The most he could manage to do was squeeze her hand in return, and Shawnee was elated by even that much.

"You're going to be okay," he heard her say, over and over again, and she stroked his forearm gently, "Everything's going to be okay."

Harold concentrated, and gradually, Shawnee's figure became clearer to him. The touch of her hand, the sound of her voice, and the sight of her at his bedside made it feel like a million synapses were firing off in his brain. It was like coming back to life. Slowly, a smile spread over his face, and with the greatest of efforts, he pushed the words from between his parted lips, just loud enough for her to hear him:

"You stayed."

"Yes, Harold," Shawnee said, squeezing his hand once more, and returning the smile. "I stayed."

***

Recovery was not limited to his physical being, and while he did have to focus on regaining strength and mobility, including his ability to walk, he also had to focus on his mental and emotional well-being. For this aspect of his healing, Dr. Calm had become a trusted friend and advisor, and Harold relished his twice-weekly sessions. On his most recent visit, Harold came in with only the use of his cane, and when he sat down to begin the session, he was able to take off his shoes without any visible signs of struggle.

"Well, well!" Dr. Calm exclaimed, "It seems like there's a new surprise with you every visit! Physical therapy is progressing nicely, I take it?"

"I've always done well with goal-oriented tasks," Harold replied, and he leaned back in his chair to stretch out his legs. They were much stronger than they had been, but the soreness hadn't fully vanished.

"That's excellent to hear," Dr. Calm said. "You're adjusting remarkably well, I think."

"That's been the biggest goal of all," Harold replied, rubbing his hip. "Figure out what normal is and work my way toward there. So far, I think my progress has been consistent."

Dr. Calm nodded his head in agreement and glanced over at his notes. "That's what we were discussing last time," he said. "You'd said you were going to try and give your parents another call. Were you able to get through to them?"

"I was, actually," Harold answered. "Well, my father, anyway. We kept things casual. Mom's still pretty upset that she didn't find out about the accident until after the fact, but Dad tells me that hasn't stopped her from finding out about my recovery through him. We're working on building a bridge. I don't think either one of us realized how remote we'd become to each other, but now it's kind of nice to take the time to talk. I even told him about Shawnee."

"Was he receptive to the idea that you were dating again?"

"Well, I haven't told him the full context of how we met or anything. I've been taking baby steps with him, but he sounded excited. He even mentioned flying home to meet her, which is more than he offered when I was with Nancy. I think it's a good start."

"Any progress is good progress, Harold. You know that better than most of my clients. Have you put more thought into going back to work?"

"I have. It's one of the things Shawnee and I discuss a fair bit. We've done some research into programs where I can get an additional accreditation to add to my counseling practice."

"Grief counseling?" Dr. Calm asked, and Harold nodded his head in confirmation. They'd discussed the idea a little more than a week ago, when Dr. Calm had brought up the notion that Harold's unique experiences with death and loss might make him effective in that particular field, as he was equipped to provide a special insight. They discussed it further now, and Dr. Calm shared his own experiences with helping the bereaved, and the conversation took up the majority of their session. When time was nearly up, Harold began to put his shoes back on, and Dr. Calm wrapped up with a final question.

"Have you had any more dreams about Nancy?" he asked, and Harold looked up at him thoughtfully.

"Only the one I told you about from when I was under the coma," Harold answered. "It's still pretty vivid in my head though, like every day I can remember it a little more clearly than I could the day before."

"Well you certainly describe it in vivid terms," Dr. Calm agreed. "It's been an intriguing aspect of our discussions, and I find that your story occupies a lot of my thoughts. The implications are fascinating..." He trailed off as he said this, and in the moment, returned to the questions he'd been considering since Harold had told him what he recollected from his experience of being in a coma: How much of it was the truth, and how much of it was a distortion of his memory? Had Harold really experienced something beyond the plane of existence, or was it all the brain's effort to finally process his feelings toward Nancy and the guilt of experiencing love after loss? He only knew what Harold had told him, but it was recounted in such a way that made Dr. Calm pause to consider the possibility of something beyond this life. He found it fascinating.

"Have you shared the details of your dream with Shawnee?" he asked, continuing to pursue the subject. "If you have, I'd be interested to know her reaction."

"I did," Harold said. "We talk about Nancy a lot, actually."

"Really?" Dr. Calm remarked, impressed. "And that doesn't create any tension for either of you?"

"No, it doesn't," Harold said, and the expression on his face was proof enough that he was telling the truth. He was serene, and continued on, unprompted. "Sometimes, it's like we're reviewing the facts of a case. We go over all of the things that happened when we were together, and we can both agree that we experienced something. What that something was, we differ on. You already know what *I* think."

"Yes," Dr. Calm mused, "but what does she think happened?"

"She says we experienced a 'shared hallucination brought on from the stress of being in a malfunctioning car.' Honestly, I'm okay with her version of the events, and she's okay with mine, as long as we're open to each other's viewpoints. Shawnee says that the biggest takeaway from my marriage to Nancy has been my willingness for transparency. We don't tip-toe around our emotions. When someone's feelings get hurt and we need to hash something out, I always try to lead the charge."

Dr. Calm nodded his head in approval. "I think that's a very good policy, Harold."

"Well, it's like you've said before," Harold replied. "If you don't want any emotional baggage, you have to be willing to unpack your issues."

"I'm glad that one stuck with you," Dr. Calm said, and Harold stood up to end the session.

"Me, too," he replied. "It's been very sound advice."

When Harold left the office, Shawnee was sitting out in the waiting room, looking through one of the magazines that had been left on a table. The Common Miscreants were on the cover, with Erin front and center, wearing one of her tuxedos from the later era, while Jenna sat behind her, smiling coyly, and Damon stood in the very back, with his hand obscuring most of his face, as if he were in hiding. It was one of many magazines that they'd done photo shoots for to promote their reunion tour, which was getting a lot of positive buzz, especially on the strength of a few of the new tracks that Damon Alton had brought with him to the band. It was the opening night of their tour, and naturally, Harold and Shawnee had backstage passes.

"Good session?" Shawnee asked, peering over the page she'd been reading.

"As always," Harold replied, slowly walking toward her.

She put the magazine down, stood up, and threaded her arm through his, helping him to walk out of the office. Harold smiled at her. "Dinner before or after the show?" he asked.

"After," she said. "Damon wanted to catch up with you after the set, and I believe Jenna and Erin wanted to join us as well."

"That should be fun!" Harold said, and the thought of sharing a meal with his friend put a little extra strength in his step.

***

When they arrived in the green room of the sound stage, Shawnee rushed ahead and gave Jenna and Erin each a hug before making her way over to Damon.

"Last, but not least, I see," Damon said, wrapping his arms around her for a quick embrace. When she pulled away from him, he looked her once over and pointed at Harold.

"She looks more and more beautiful every time I see her," he told him. "If you're not careful, I might try to steal her away from you."

"Yeah, right," Shawnee said, and she playfully slapped him on the arm before walking out with Jenna and Erin to the holding spot backstage where they'd go over their typical pre-show ritual.

Harold grinned and rolled his eyes at the line Damon said, and made his way over to the couch. Damon could see that his friend needed to take some weight off of his hip, and the sight of him in pain made him immediately relent.

"Only joking, Harold," he said in mock-seriousness. "You know I'd never do that to you." He paused briefly, then added, "Not again."

"Ha ha," Harold said dryly. "That line gets funnier every time you deliver it." Whereas other friendships might've thrived on avoiding the ugliest moments of a relationship, Damon took to confronting the worst of his old behavior with a strong sense of humor, and he had enough charm to make it work. Jokes about his past exploits were used to great effect when he first got back in touch with Jenna and Erin, breaking a lot of ice that allowed him to segue into sincerer expressions of apology. Since Harold's recovery, Damon had given his friend the same treatment. Nothing was off limits, including suicide and adultery, and odd as it may seem, Harold appreciated him for it. The crass quips helped him to feel normal again, removing an aspect of the frailty he'd felt early on, and it deepened the already well-established bond between them.

When they were alone in the green room, Damon walked over to Harold and took the empty seat next to him on the couch. "Did you have a good day today?" he asked, and his voice was quieter now, absent of any rock and roll schtick.

"Every day I'm getting better," Harold answered.

Damon threw an arm around his friend's shoulders, squeezing him closer. "Good," he replied, "because there's a lot more music to write, you know? You keep writing the lyrics, and I'll keep making them songs. Even if they don't end up as Miscreant tunes, it'll still be worth doing."

"I know," Harold said. "You don't have to worry about me, man."

"Who's worried about you?" Damon asked, and he hopped up to his feet, getting worked up into his Common Miscreant persona. "Looks like the ladies are already out there for the pre-show huddle. I'll see you in the crowd, okay?"

"I'll be the guy waving a cane in the air," Harold answered, and Damon laughed at the quip before exiting the room, leaving Harold on the couch by himself.

Moments of solitude felt different to Harold now, having come back from the car accident. Whereas before he could relax in the comfort of silence, he found it now sometimes stimulated him, causing him to slip into deep thought. He was doing just that, staring blankly at the floor, reflecting on how surreal it was to be backstage at a Common Miscreants show, when Shawnee opened the door and poked her head into the room. "Are we listening from here tonight, or did you want to watch with the crowd?" she asked.

"The crowd, I think," Harold answered, thoughtfully.

"Well, let's go!" Shawnee replied, and patiently waited for him to come along.

Harold looked up at her and smiled. "I'm right behind you," he said, and he got up slowly and followed her out of the room, into the crowd of strangers, all chanting and cheering loudly, waiting for the show to begin.
